Lay Down Your Heart

Lay Down Your Heart

Lesley Caves

Text layout by Tim C. Taylor
ISBN: 978-0-9879677-1-8

A place belongs forever to whoever claims it hardest, remembers it most obsessively, wrenches it from itself, shapes it, loves it so radically that he remakes it in his image.

Joan Didion

This book is for Liam

Prologue

November 1971

Lilanda Township, Lusaka

The white Peugeot station wagon careened along the rutted township road. It was badly in need of new shocks and every pothole was a bone-crunching thud to the four men inside. It was October and there had been no rain for months. The car sent up a shower of fine red dust, covering the children who waved and called out from the roadside, covering the four men inside.

"Stop here," said the old one. He spoke English. He reached forward from the back seat and tapped the shoulder of the driver. The driver stopped at the bottle store. The old man in the back reached in his jacket pocket — a dirty tweed jacket, imagine in that heat! — and pulled out some kwacha. "Get us some drinks," he said to the man sitting next to him. He spoke his own language, which the driver understood.

That one, next to the old man, was young and skinny. He wore jeans and a t-shirt, none too clean. He took the money and waited. With a start the driver remembered that the door could only open from the outside and he jumped out and ran around to the other side of the car, pulling down hard on the door handle. The three men inside laughed. "It's good we have a chauffeur for our Mercedes Benz". This was the tall man who was in front beside the driver. He had a big laugh.

The bottle store was a low cement building, whitewashed with a strip of black paint running around the bottom. Several patrons, all

1

men except for one old woman, sat on the dirt in the compound, drinking from cartons. The only chair was reserved for the ghetto blaster, which was asking, "Is this love?" The driver leaned back against the hot metal.

It was stifling in the car, even with the windows rolled down. The old man in the back appeared to have gone to sleep. Anyway, his eyes were closed. The tall one beside in the front had taken out a book.

The skinny one came back with two Castle beers and a bottle of Bols brandy. Behind him was a boy, carrying four sweating Cokes. The driver shut the door after the skinny one and took the Cokes from the boy. He got back behind the wheel and handed them around. Downing his in four gulps, he started the engine. The others handled their bottles with practiced timing, knowing just when to raise the drink to their lips before the car shuddered and sank into another rut.

They had now come to a better part of the township. The houses were no longer shacks; they had two or three rooms and small, walled compounds with a mango tree or a papaya tree. The road was no better. The sun was beginning its incredible plummet towards the horizon. One minute it would be there, a brilliant red ball, then the earth would be dark, only a few trails of blood left smearing the sky.

The driver stopped the car in front of a dirty white bungalow with a red tiled roof. The yard was dry and overgrown, but the poinsettias and bougainvillea were flourishing. They ran along the brick walkway and up beside the cracked cement steps.

This time the driver remembered. He jumped out of the Peugeot and ran around to let out the skinny man, who in turn put down his bottles so he could help the old man, who walked with a limp. The tall one got out of the front and closed the door gently. Then the three men left the driver and walked up to the front door of the house. It opened and swallowed them.

The driver knew the routine. He had driven these men, and others like them, to this house, and others like it, many times in the past six months. These meetings usually lasted late into the night, sometimes all night. He got into the back seat of the Peugeot, locked the doors and lay back, with his head against one window and his flip-flops pressed up against the other. He closed his eyes.

It is November 1971.

Is this where this story begins?

Some of what I will tell you I saw, as they say, with my own two eyes.

But not everything. Obviously.

I, of course, was not present at these meetings, did not hear these conversations. Some of the people I will write about are people I have never met, and will never meet. Some of what I will write has been told to me. Some of the details, most of the details, are my own.

I was never told, for example, that the driver was thin or that the car was a white Peugeot station wagon with bad shocks, or that the old man walked with a limp. I am fairly sure that a stop was made at a bottle store. When I tell this story to myself, I always put in the joke about the Mercedes Benz, even though I never heard the tall man make that particular joke. Anyway, that's how I feel it could have been.

But this I do know. The sun did drop out of the sky like a brilliant red ball, leaving a bloody trail behind it.

And the tall man had a great laugh.

1

October 1999

Macheke, Zimbabwe

I had a farm in Africa. Okay, I know that line is already taken. And that my using it will lead you to think this is a certain kind of story. White colonist comes to Africa and falls in love with it. She is completely entranced by the exotic flora and fauna, including the people. Perhaps you are already picturing me in a pith helmet and riding skirt, being helped onto my horse by my faithful African groom. She falls in love with a rich, rugged white hunter. One or two safari chapters follow, with descriptions of campfires, stalking lions and the ubiquitous sunset behind the acacias. But then tragedy strikes. The human lover is struck down, either by the claws of a wounded lion or by a spear during a tribal skirmish, thus symbolizing the cruelty and violence lurking behind the beauty of Africa. The last chapter sees me standing by a steam train, the open veldt stretched out behind me. With quiet dignity, I bid farewell to my servants, who are begging me not to leave. The groom is weeping openly.

Now, it may surprise you to know that I happen to love that story. It is a story that is so "old-fashioned", so fraught with nostalgia, so simplistic and wrong in its depictions of, among others, the relations between invader and invaded, the loss of cultures and the degradation of the environment that sustained them, that it is difficult to read without rolling one's eyes.

So you'll be glad to hear that story is not my story. Any romantic notions about Africa I had floating around in my head in the beginning have long since disappeared. But I still like the line.

To be more precise, my husband and I lived on a maize and tobacco farm near Macheke, in the Mashonaland district of Zimbabwe. In addition to the 2,000 acres under cultivation, we had about 200 cattle, which were sold each year for slaughter to the Cold Storage Commission. We also grew enough vegetables to feed ourselves. This should not be taken literally. I hate gardening and, except when the tobacco was being cured, had very little to do with the day-to-day running of the farm. My husband and the sixty farm-workers we employed did almost all the work. So, while loving the red earth of Zimbabwe, I didn't actually have to stick my hands into it.

I heard the hoopoes before I saw them. I was standing at the pitted chalkboard, writing notes, and I could hear the rustle of paper and the shifting of the pupils in their seats as they copied. When I turned to explain a point, I saw the rows of desks and the children sitting in pairs — the boys in khaki shirts of varying states of cleanliness and repair, the girls in light blue blouses which were crisp and clean, though some were too tight. The girls' hair was neatly and often elaborately braided, making beautiful patterns. It was very hot, just before morning tea break; I didn't stop to reflect on the scene, or pause to take in the moment. I wanted to finish this chapter of the history text, so I could assign the questions for prep.

Then I heard the call. "Hoop-hoop, hoop-hoop-hoop". I went to the open door and stepped out on the stoep, polished red every morning with Cobra wax. I could hear Knowledge, lecturing from the next classroom. He often used a "call and response" style while teaching — he would call out a question and the students would chorus a memorized answer. Between answers, I listened for the hoopoe.

When I heard the lively call, repeated quickly, I realized there were two birds. After another couple of calls, I located them. They were hopping along the ground under the hibiscus bush in the centre of the yard, probing the ground with their long, pointed bills. I stood watching for a few moments. I would have liked to stay until they raised their comical black-tipped brown crests, but I didn't want the headmaster, Mr. Muzenda catching me outside again. I went back into the classroom and resumed writing notes on the board. The students didn't question or comment on my absence.

The headboy, Emmerson, came out of the Form 4 classroom, ringing the bell. I hastily gave out the homework questions over the shuffling of bodies and the scraping of desks. The children streamed towards the thatched-covered bhundu shelter, where their tea and bread would be served. I looked for the undulating, butterfly-like flight of the hoopoes, but they had already gone.

I lit up a cigarette and took a deep pull while I waited for Knowledge to join me. It was a local brand called Berkley, and came in a flat, blue box. In fact, I had originally started smoking them because I liked the look of the box. Now, of course, I was addicted to the sweet, strong taste.

Mr. Muzenda came out of his office. He nodded to me. "Good morning, Madam." He strode across the yard towards the staff room, shoulders back, swinging a stick. Students scattered out of his path. Teachers climbing the steps to the staffroom, moved aside to let him pass.

In the staffroom, I poured Knowledge a cup of tea, then watched as he put in four heaping teaspoons of sugar and a generous splash of milk. He looked happy and relaxed, in spite of his dark suit and tie. Knowledge was small and plump, with a wide smile.

"All that sugar will rot your teeth."

His smile appeared. "Those cigarettes will surely kill you."

We talked about the growing heat and the tobacco harvest, which would be starting soon. We talked about our families. He had a wife, Praxedis, and a baby daughter. Praxedis had been ill with some kind of cold or flu when last I saw her. I asked how she was doing.

"She is better. I think in a few more days she will be completely fine."

"I hope so."

We talked a little about the school and some of the pupils — the ones we felt were the most promising and the ones who we thought were too stupid to pass the Form Four exams.

"That Kazana, he is too playful!" Knowledge laughed softly and shook his head. This was a typical Shona way of describing a boy who wasn't studious. A girl would be called lazy.

"Yes, but he's clever." I loved Kazana. His grandmother, Miriam, was an old friend of mine and I had known him since he was a newborn. His father had died, of tuberculosis probably resulting from AIDS, and his mother always looked as if she was on her last leg.

"The examiners won't care if he's clever, if he's unable to answer the questions properly. He spends too much time playing about in the bush." I nodded, even though I didn't entirely agree. On the one hand, I believed that no time spent in the bush could really be called wasted, but on the other, Knowledge's point was well taken. The Cambridge exams tested a limited range of a student's understanding and were mainly based on the recall of facts. Knowing how to follow a honeyguide bird to a nest, or the Shona names for the trees and birds counted for nothing.

The rest of the morning passed as so many over the years. The day steadily grew warmer and warmer, so that by the last class, it was an effort to raise my arm to write on the board. The children, most of whom had been up at dawn to carry water or fetch wood before trekking to the school, slept with their heads on their desks, or leaning on one another's shoulders. Some of the girls undid the buttons on their blouses and not many of them were wearing bras, but this went unnoticed and unremarked upon. I slid off my old sandals. Lately, I found my feet swelled in the heat, as they had when I was pregnant in years gone by.

There was a dirt track that led away from the school, crossed the valley and climbed the hill to my house. At the bottom of the hill the path branched off and curved along the hill to the village, a collection of pole and dagga rondavels surrounded by maize patches.

This is where the farm workers lived with their families. It was also where Miriam lived, in the small cement house with a tin roof.

I walked up the hill, past the stone barn we called the Python Barn, where in a few weeks the women from the village would be singing and gossiping as they shelled the mieles. The dust from the maize cobs would hang in the air and my boys would raise more, jumping on the stacks of meile sacks. I walked past the small brick building which housed the crèche, empty now for the weekend. Samora and all the other pre-schoolers would have come bursting out when the noon bell rang. The grass was long and almost white in the heat. In the evening it would turn gold. In the early morning the dew and spiders webs would make it sparkle, but now the grass, the hills, the sky was an over-exposed photograph. The sun pressed down on my head, the cicadas vibrated all around. I could see myself, a woman in a faded cotton dress, walking along a path in Zimbabwe, to my rambling house filled with dogs, lumpy, overstuffed chesterfields and haphazard vases of flowers set on scratched mahogany tables.

Scotty's truck was parked in the drive. He was just getting out as I came near. His back was to me as he held the door open while his new dog, some kind of terrier, jumped out of the cab. He let down the tailgate so one of his farm workers could climb down. He took off his hat and wiped his face, like someone wiping a plate.

"Gosh, it's hot, eh?"

"Man, isn't she? You're going to have to invite me in for a beer, ja?"

I turned to the worker. "*Masikati.*" As we shook hands, a flash. When I first saw him getting out of the truck, I thought he was a young man, but now I could see his face. "I'm sure I know you."

Another flash, this time white teeth, one tooth missing, and a chuckle. "Of course you know me. I am Boniface."

"Yes," I said. "From Mutamba. You were the one who fixed things."

"Yes. I was the carpenter." He was still holding my hand. "And you are the lady who ran too much."

I nodded. I could see myself, white shorts and yellow shirt, running along the road that led out of the mission. "It was a long time ago. I haven't been back there."

He nodded and withdrew his hand.

I thought of something. "Your daughter was at the school. I taught her. What was her name?"

"Nyasha. You remember her?"

"Yes, she was a good student." And a beautiful girl. A fine-boned girl with large eyes, hair neatly braided. Quiet. Sweet. "She must be all grown up now. How is she doing?"

"Very well. She has got a job. She is a teacher in Harare!" Boniface chuckled "Yes, and she has got three piccanin."

I asked him about his grandchildren and he asked me about Miguel. We talked about the weather.

"We are remembering you there, Amai Miguel. Mrs. Zabedi and Mr. Msika are talking about you and Miguel and Miss Julia and Mr. Alex and Moses." He chuckled. "Moses showed me how to stop the ants from crawling up the table. You put the table legs in tins of water! Now that was a trick and a half!"

I nodded and smiled stupidly and managed to say, "He showed me that one, too. Very useful."

Scotty kept stroking his dog and said, without looking up, "Boniface is here to visit some family he has here in your compound."

"Ah, then you must say hello to Amai Mushana. She is living here. She is the crèche teacher."

I didn't offer to show him the way.

Lunch was called dinner and it was our big meal of the day, served at one o'clock. Roast lamb or beef or chicken, potatoes, sadza and relish, spinach followed by desert. No matter how hot it was, we always ate this kind of food. Washed down with gallons of tea. But today was Friday so we could anticipate the weekend with a beer or two.

Or three. Scotty was well into his third Castle before the melktart arrived.

I was twisted in my chair, my feet up on James' lap. He absent-mindedly stroked them, as we smoked between courses. The table was littered with plates and dishes the maid would eventually clear off. The dogs had stopped circling the table and were lying on the stoep. Samora was lying on his stomach in the lounge, looking at a picture book. Evan had wandered down to the compound, probably to play football. I felt light-headed and a little far away, yet I could feel my husband's hand on my foot and hear him bantering with his brother. I idly watched the smoke curl up from Scotty's cigarette. He had the same blue eyes, the same red hair, faded and thinning as my husband's. But where James' face was open and easily smiling, Scotty's was sharper, the mouth thinner, lines starting to run down alongside his nose. He was one of the first "White Rhodies" I met when I came to Zimbabwe. I remembered something I hadn't thought about in years — our first meeting at Mutamba. He had made a joke — something about one white man and one million black men — that was so racist I could only stare at him. He quickly backtracked ("We're not that bad, really") but I had still been left standing there, my mouth open and a stunned look on my face.

Over the years, this meeting had become family lore, a story I trotted out at Sunday braiis.

"No, I didn't think he was an ass," (pause for effect) "I thought he was an asshole!"

Guaranteed to get a laugh. I could get away with that kind of language; I was even admired for it. It went with my clothes, my friends, the books I read, my "communistic" ideas. This was in the mid 80's and let's face it, it wasn't just the fact that I was young and pretty and exotic. It really looked at that time as if history was on my side.

Tatenda put the tea on the table and began clearing the plates. I sat up to pour.

"How long have you had Boniface working for you?"

"Just a couple of months. I thought you'd know."

"Know what? That you had hired a new labourer?"

"No, I thought you knew about Mutamba. Didn't James tell you?"

James shifted in his chair. I saw the too-familiar look.

"No. What about it?"

"It's closing. Lock, stock and barrel."

I had never been back to Mutamba Mission. I had lived there for three years when I first came to Zimbabwe. Sometimes it would cross my mind; when the signpost caught my eye on the way to Harare, or when I got a postcard from Julia, or meeting someone like Boniface, but honestly, I didn't really think of it all that often.

"What's the story?" I fiddled with my wire bracelets.

"It's this bloody Land Act. Looks like the Brothers are set to lose most of their lands. They say they can't run the school without the land."

"Expropriation without compensation. Christ. Didn't I always say this was coming?" James spoke evenly, but I knew that righteous vindication.

"How do we know there's no compensation?" I could hear my voice rising defensively and stubbornly.

Scotty took a deep breath. Probably it was only his deeply ingrained ideas about the way a man should speak to a white woman that stopped him from yelling, "You stupid bitch!" Instead I got, "Look, there's no way Mugabe is going to hand over any cash to us. He's just announced he's going to take thousands of farms and he's demanding the Brits pay for any compensation. As if anyone will give more money to this lot to just throw away."

"You may be right," I countered. Over top of Scotty's spluttered "Of course, I'm right!" I raised my voice. "But you have to agree this issue has never been properly dealt with. Maybe Mugabe isn't going about it in exactly the right way, but something should have been done long before this."

My husband and my brother-in-law stared at me. James said heavily "We're the people keeping this country afloat. If it weren't for us farmers, this bloody government would be bankrupt. Taking away our land and giving it to a load of Afs isn't going to do a bloody thing. Not that the blacks are going to see much of this land, anyway. It's all going to people in the government."

"By farmers, you mean white farmers! There are thousands and thousands of black farmers in this country. They were here long before you. And don't give me any of your bullshit that this land was empty when your grandparents got here. Why should they be all crowded together on the communal lands? Surely you can see that they need more land?

"Is it our fault they breed like bloody rabbits?" Scotty looked at me defiantly as he delivered this salvo.

"Don't give me that bullshit!" I lifted my cup to my shoulder. Both he and James ducked, with good reason. There had been a time when I wouldn't have thought twice about chucking it and telling them both to fuck off. But what good had it ever done? I put my cup back down on the table and lifted the teapot.

"More tea?" I asked. But inside I was churning. What if Tatenda had heard him? Goddamn Rhodie. What an asshole!

A soft knock on our bedroom door. Tatenda's hand expertly opening the door with the tea balanced in her other hand. I sat up and pulled the mosquito net up and away as she placed it on the table.

"Mangwanani," she said.

"Mangwanani. Maswera sei?" (How have you slept?)

"Maswera, taswera wo." (I've slept well. How have you slept?)

She turned and left, closing the door behind her.

Weekdays, I pushed my hair out of my face and reached over to prod James awake. I poured him his tea, added a cascade of milk and sugar, de rigueur throughout Africa, and accepted his kiss in exchange. On colder winter mornings I would huddle next to my husband with the blankets wrapped around our shoulders. But this October morning the sun was already streaming through the French doors to the veranda, the dawn chorus had already subsided and James was already out of bed. He and the boys would have eaten and left the house before I had finished my second cup. I was free to rise late, wander into the kitchen and have a cup of coffee — real Vumba coffee, none of that instant shit most people served up — while I chatted with Tatenda. Then off for a bath before I got dressed and either read the newspaper or did some marking. Usually the newspaper won out.

Mugabe eats supper with spirit of dead rival

There was an unflattering photo of the president; fists raised, the shadow Hitler mustache, eyes glinting behind the large glasses. The face under the trucker's hat looked swollen, maybe the result of the cancer treatments he was rumoured to be taking.

According to the article, Mugabe's paranoia had now reached such a level that he believed he was being haunted by an *ngozi*, in this case the spirit of the long-dead Josiah Tongogara.

I skimmed over the first part of the story, which was rehash of the speculation surrounding the "mysterious" car accident, which had taken Tongogara's life on the eve of independence. Tongogara was the populist guerrilla leader, the "Che Guevara" of the Zimbabwean liberation struggle. Everyone I had ever spoken to in Zimbabwe, and this included government supporters, "knew" that Mugabe had murdered his rival.

But what was new and sort of interesting was that Tongogara's ghost was said to be "tormenting Mugabe with accusations that his mismanagement was destroying the revolution".

The Guardian has learned that staff at the presidential palace are seriously alarmed at the state to which Mugabe has been reduced by Tongogara's ngozi. An extra place is set at dinner for Tongogara and food is served for him.

The report gleefully went on to say that the Rain Goddess at Sengwa, an Ndebele, and the Oracle of Mlimo at Njelele, a Tonga, had both refused to come to Mugabe's aid, presumably because both *nyangas* were members of persecuted minority groups. The government psychiatrist, an ominous-sounding Dr. Vlad Rankovic, had diagnosed an anxiety disorder and had prescribed anti-depressants.

Moving away from this Shakespearian theme, there was some speculation that perhaps Mugabe's "anxiety" had more to do with present political realities. Namely the rise of the Movement for Democratic Change and its leader, Morgan Tsvangarai. This after all, was the first serious challenge Mugabe would face since becoming president. There was talk that Mugabe was considering a campaign "strategy" of putting the whole MDC leadership in prison and then dispensing with the presidential election.

Asked to comment, Tsvangarai said, "He could lock us all up, but he'd have to be crazy to do it." Which pretty much summed up the state of politics in Zimbabwe at that moment.

Passing by the lounge on my way to the kitchen, I picked up a battered red photo album. It was kept casually along with the others in the bottom of the bookshelf: Miguel; Wedding 1987; Nico and Hannah visit 1988; Evan 1988-89; Around The Farm 1990-92; Samora and Mauritius Christmas 1995 (the third baby doesn't even warrant his own album, I thought). The red album wasn't labeled. I hadn't looked at it in years.

But I knew every picture. Miguel and me in front of the Hotel Krasnapolsky in Amsterdam, was that Julia in the background? A group of young Canadian teachers on the veranda of the Bronte Hotel. Did anyone ever look so young and so eager? My little house at Mutamba. A field of sunflowers. Miguel standing in front of a banana tree. Our trip to the Zimbabwe Ruins. The tree in the back that was hit by lightning. Miguel on his new bike — it must be his fourth birthday. A Saturday night party, was that my 25th birthday? Julia sitting with Sampson and Mary Karambira at a table littered with beer bottles. Alex and me dancing. Alex and me at the bottle store, I look exhausted. It was probably taken around the time I took up smoking and stared eating meat. Photos of the school, different classes. Ah, here I am with Moses. Moses with Miguel, the three of us at the Inyanga Falls. Moses playing football. My favourite photo — Moses dancing with a group of men, laughing.

That's it. A few photos and four copper wire bracelets. Not much to show for three years.

2

August 1982

Harare

The organization, officially called the Fund for African Learning and Leadership was known by its acronym FALL and, colloquially by some of the "co-operants" who had been shipped from Canada to all parts of Africa to teach in rural schools, as Fuck-All. Constance Marinatos was recruited by FALL in the early spring. This meant that she answered an ad run in the Vancouver Sun for teachers in Zimbabwe, a new country in southern Africa. She applied because she had just graduated from university with a degree in History, a four-year-old son, very little money and, not surprisingly, given that her degree was in History, no job prospects. Of course, she was smart enough not mention all that at her interview. Instead, she stretched the single course she had taken in the African Studies department at the University of British Columbia into a deep and long-term interest in southern Africa. She was also able to steer her part-time job as an "activities co-ordinator" at an after-school program into some kind of teaching experience. At the end of the hour-long interview, when the FALL Programme Director, a friendly, pretty woman, offered her a contract to teach History for three years at a secondary school in Zimbabwe, Constance felt a surge of triumph. She was going to Africa. She was going to be a teacher in Africa. She felt incredibly special.

§

"Of course, that was before you realized that they were taking anybody and his dog," said her new friend, Julia. It was late at night, at least by Harare standards. They rolled up the sidewalks every night at six o'clock and by nine everyone in the hotel was in bed, except for Julia, Constance and a few other jet-lagged Fallers, who liked to sit out on the veranda, drinking their duty-free whiskey, entranced by the romance of the African night and the stars of the southern hemisphere.

"The question is, is there anybody they didn't take?" asked Ted.

Even after only a few days in Harare, the volunteers had divided into several sub-clans who heartily disliked each other. The veranda attracted the people who thought of themselves as socially progressive. They stayed up late, smoked and drank copiously, some had even smuggled cannabis from Canada, not realizing that *dagga* was readily and cheaply available in Zimbabwe. They believed they were completely without prejudice or "hang-ups". They were careful not to patronize the Africans they met and were eager to learn Shona. Constance was attracted to them for all these reasons, but also because they were self-aware and able to make fun of their own pretensions. Smart enough not to take themselves too seriously.

There were a few people who seemed to find fault with absolutely everything. Constance's friends dubbed them "The Whingers". You could hear them at breakfast, exclaiming incredulously at the stone cold toast, or complaining that their chloroquine tablets were making them nauseous. They fretted constantly about the dangers of malaria and bad water. They were obsessed with their bowel movements. They were constantly trying to phone home and constantly and loudly surprised at how erratic the phone system was.

The "God-Botherers" were sincerely and relentlessly cheerful. They did not complain about anything, but patiently bore all discomforts. God had brought them to Africa as part of His plan. They made it clear they were praying for you, whether you liked it or not. It was generally understood among the veranda crowd that a belief in a higher being, with the possible exception of Buddha, made you somehow less intelligent.

Constance was secretly fond of "The Old Hands". They tended to be older and had all worked in places like Malawi and Tanzania. The men wore khaki shorts that showed their knobby knees and their wives wore muumuus they had made from cloth purchased, one was meant to assume, from their last posting. They cheerfully predicted incompetence and corruption. They said things like "Africa Wins Again" and "he's just looking for a little baksheesh" without any rancour. They seemed unaware that they were no longer in East Africa, greeting each other in Swahili. *"Assante sana,"* they said to the bemused waiters in the hotel dining room.

But worst of all was a quartet of three women and a man who were so very earnest and well-informed about what they termed "development issues". While everyone else struggled to stay awake during the "orientation" classes, these four were dropping "neo-colonialism" and "Franz Fanon" into the sessions. Not that anyone would have minded them showing off, but it made the sessions longer. In the afternoons while everyone else lolled around the pool, they could be seen studiously writing in their journals or reading *The New Internationalist*.

Constance and Julia made the mistake of sitting with them at breakfast one morning. One of the women, Gina, smiled approvingly at Constance's copy of *Fanshen*.

"Isn't that a wonderful use of a microcosm to show the sweeping changes that the communist revolution brought to China?"

Constance wasn't sleeping well. "It's okay." She loved the book and had been devouring it avidly.

"When I was in China," said Laurie, "I visited the very village where Hinton did his research." She looked as if she had been waiting a long time to say this.

Not to be outdone, Margaret was reminded of some study she had recently read as part of her doctoral research, about land reform in China. This led to a discussion of whether or not China could serve as a model for developing nations like Zimbabwe.

The three women felt it could, but Jean-Pierre, citing his extensive experience in Latin America, disagreed.

"God, what a nightmare," said Julia that night. "I'm sorry Ted, but I'm just so glad that I'm not posted with any of them."

Ted shrugged and continued to strum his guitar.

Sheena, originally from northern England said, "Nobody came here for a lecture on Communism."

Laughter. Sheena and her husband, Ron, were posted with Jean-Pierre and Gina.

"And did you get a load of that shirt he was wearing? Some peasant in Guatemala probably went blind embroidering that thing."

"Did you hear that woman from Newfoundland complaining at supper that she didn't like the way the sun goes down so suddenly in the evening?"

"I found that a surprise when we first got here," said Ted. "I guess because the days are so long at home right now."

"Honestly, Ted!" said Julia, impatiently. "That Whinger is from Newfoundland. How do they even know when the sun goes down through all the fog? They've only had three days of decent weather since they joined Confederation."

"What did she expect?" asked Sheena.

What did I expect? thought Constance. The rush of adrenalin she had felt at her FALL interview had carried her through packing up her small apartment in Vancouver, saying goodbye to friends and family — her parents were already planning to visit during the long school holiday in December — the week-long orientation in Ottawa, and the horrendous flight to Harare via Amsterdam, Nairobi, Johannesburg.

"We have to stay here for three years," she had told Ted. He was holding a sleeping Miguel over his shoulder. They were standing in the aisle of the plane, waiting to get off. The pilot had recently told them it was 2:30 in the afternoon. "I won't be able to force myself back on a plane for at least that long."

One of the Old Hands, Constance thought her name was Dodie, turned and said, "The trip's not over yet! We could be waiting on this plane for ages. And we still have customs and immigration. And they've probably lost our luggage." She said this as if she was announcing Constance was eligible to win a prize.

Right on cue, a voice requested that all passengers return to their seats. There was a lot of grumbling as everyone shuffled back. They sat with their carry-on luggage on their laps. The stale air in the cabin got staler and warmer. There was no further announcement. A rivulet of sweat rolled from Miguel's damp curls across his cheek. After a while, people began getting up and leaving the plane, so Constance, Ted and Miguel followed. As they stepped down onto the tarmac, Ted looked around and said "Where's Dottie?"

"Isn't she called Dodie?" She's still on the plane. Probably still thinks she's in Zaire and she's going to get shot if she gets off without permission."

Later, Constance could only vaguely remember clearing customs, claiming her luggage, being bundled into an impossibly small taxi ("Look, Mummy, it's a baby car") and driven to a lovely old hotel in a quiet neighbourhood. Her next clear memory was of sitting on the grass in the garden behind the hotel, watching Miguel poke around in the garden. He had woken, bright and bushytailed and was now harassing his first lizard.

The sun was shining through the branches of what she would later learn were jacaranda trees. The air was rapidly cooling. August was the tail-end of winter. Yet the garden was gorgeous with colours: purple and red bougainvillea, pink hibiscus and so many others Constance could not identify. She watched, entranced as a bird with a crest flew down onto the lawn. It ignored her as it methodically probed the ground with its curved bill.

"It's a hoopoe." She started and saw a big man standing behind her.

He smiled at her.

A hoopoo? What on earth? Constance nodded and smiled back.

"That one is the male. The female is not that colour. See? She is just there." He pointed to another bird under the hedge. It was a duller brown. No match for the other. "Where there is one, you will see the other. They are always together."

Miguel ran up. He was still very excited about the lizard. "That lizard was playing hide-and-seek with me. It ran into the bushes, so I waited very, very quietly. Then I could hear it moving, so I chased it. It kept hiding on me." He turned his attention. "Hello. My name's Miguel. Are you staying at this hotel?"

Constance stood up and held out her hand. "I'm Constance Marinatos. This is my little boy. We just arrived this afternoon."

"Yes, you're one of the Canadian teachers." He pronounced it *teachaas*. "Welcome to Zimbabwe." He held onto her hand, with his other hand he touched Miguel's hair. "My name is Moses."

"Are you staying here?" insisted Miguel.

"No, no. I have my own flat here in Harare." He pronounced it *flet*.

"Do you have any boys and girls there? Can I come to your house?"

Moses laughed, a great, rolling laugh. He let go of Constance's hand. "Of course!" He looked directly at her. She could see a scar running from his cheekbone down to his chin. She lowered her eyes. She didn't want him to think he was staring at her because he was black.

A voice called from the veranda. They turned to see another African man waving to them.

"I must go. I have a meeting and he's telling me that we're going to be late."

"Thank you for telling me the name of that bird."

"It is my pleasure, Madam. The hoopoe is my favourite bird. Goodbye, Miguel. I hope to see you again before you leave."

He bent down and took Miguel's hands between his, shaking them solemnly, but when he straightened, he flashed a smile as he turned to leave.

Constance did not tell anyone about meeting a handsome man in the garden on her first day in Zimbabwe. Miguel mentioned Moses a few times, then seemed to forget the encounter.

Constance forgot too. She was busy during the day taking Shona lessons, going to workshops on topics such as "Combating Culture Shock", "Staying Healthy", and "The Struggle for Zimbabwe", and battling her jet-lag. But she remembered the hoopoe. The day before she was to leave the capital to go to her posting, she and Miguel walked into the town, along the wide, tree-lined sidewalks. They were the only white people on foot. Constance loved the sun, the warm breeze and the way her body felt in a light cotton dress, holding Miguel's little hand.

They came to a street of stores, with their roofs overhanging the sidewalk. She stopped and asked a woman for directions to a bookstore. There was some confusion, partly because of the woman's Shona accent, and partly due to the word "store". Once this was sorted out, the woman showed them the way to Kingston's bookshop.

The proprietress was large and over-weight. She had a red lip-stick crease for her mouth, pale blue eyes and a badly cut 1960's style bob. She wore a shapeless short-sleeved dress, and what Constance thought might be support hose ballooning out of high heels. She was ever so helpful and spoke in a high-pitched accent, with flat vowels.

"I know a supah book. It's just come out from down south." She turned to a small man who was dusting the books displayed in the window. He was wearing what looked like a blue lab coat. "Simon, get the new bird book. *Iwe!*"

She showed Constance a thick, yellow paperback with bright birds decorating the cover. *Newman's Birds of Southern Africa.* It cost 15 Zim dollars.

They found their way to the Harare Gardens in the centre of the city. People were sitting or lying here and there. They bought ice cream from a Lyonsmaid cart and sat, turning the pages of the bird book, exclaiming over the beautiful illustrations, until they came to the hoopoe. "Here it is," said Constance. "Look, the map shows it all over Zimbabwe. The African Hoopoe."

Miguel looked at it, while he solemnly took a lick of his ice cream. "That's Moses' favourite bird. It's my favourite bird too."

"Mine too," said Constance.

There are several official accounts of the armed struggle; sometimes called the Chimurenga. They all cover the same events and dates; give virtually the same thumbnail sketches of the main players. The ones which were published in the immediate aftermath of Independence are my favourite. They remind me of old-fashioned accounts of journeys written by colonial explorers to places like Persia and Siam, places that no longer exist. They were written with warmth and goodwill towards the new government of Robert Mugabe. Some of them even have forewords written by him, the ultimate stamp of approval. These are not dry histories of a guerilla war, but evocative portraits of a time and a place. Was the 1980's the last decade that words like "freedom fighter", "liberation" and "comrade" could be used without irony?

These accounts always begin with a chronology, which is supposed to neatly line up years with important events, introduce the reader to the important characters in the story and provide a list of handy acronyms; ZANLA, FRELIMO, UDI and so on. I have actually written such a chronology for my Form Two History classes, to use as study guide. Rest assured I have no intention of reproducing it here.

This is what you need to know at this point in the story.

In November 1971 in Lilanda, a township in Lusaka, Zambia, there was a meeting at the house of Mariano Matsinha, the FRELIMO representative to Zambia. FRELIMO means the Front for the Liberation of Mozambique. At this time, Mozambique was still under Portuguese colonial rule.

Sebastao Mabote was at this meeting. He was member of FRELIMO's high command and later became a Minister of Defence in independent Mozambique.

Samora Machel was at this meeting. He would become the President of independent Mozambique. Later he would be killed when the South African government shot down his airplane, but that is another story.

The Dare re Chimurenga (war council) of the Zimbabwe African National Union (ZANU) had sent a delegation to Lilanda in November 1971 to meet with FRELIMO and formally request that

ZANU be allowed to set up training camps in Tete, Mozambique and use the Tete corridor to move guerillas and weapons into north-eastern Rhodesia.

For reasons too complicated to go into here, the request was granted. I like to think the pact was sealed with a toast of Bols brandy.

The ZANU representatives at the meeting were Noel Mukono, William Ndananga, the legendary Josiah Tongogara, Cletus Chigowe and Moses Masekesa.

3

October 1999

Macheke

The Macheke Country Club is an unpretentious whitewashed
building, with red cement floors, a bar and lounge with a billiards
table. Outside are two clay tennis courts. There is a rondavel at the
back, surrounded by maize, where Undi, the custodian, lives with his
family.

Most of the white families in the district belong to the club, but
only about 6 or 7 couples regularly turn out for Wednesday and
Saturday afternoon social tennis. A few more show up at the club
on Saturday night when the bar is open. Undi puts on an apron and
chef's hat and cooks sausages and steakrolls in the little kitchen
behind the bar. He passes the dishes through to the couple whose
turn it is to tend the bar that Saturday night.

Then there is the annual Christmas party for the kids. Father
Christmas arrives in the back of a red Model-T Ford, driven by Steve
Potgieter wearing a green elf hat.

There is the annual tennis tournament, which is followed by a
braai and dancing to "Hits of the 50's and 60's."

That's it.

The Club has three black members. They are: Chief Inspector
Matanda, the chief of police; Mr. Muzenda, the headmaster of the
secondary school and my boss; and Mr. Situmba, a businessman who
owns the Macheke hotel. As far as I know, none of them plays
tennis.

The Club is near the African township, which after independence everyone is supposed to call a "High Density Suburb". In fact, the Club sits right across the road from the Macheke Beerhall. This large establishment has a tin roof, open on three sides, rickety tables and benches. A few tattered posters are tacked on the wall behind the bar: *AIDS — End The Silence*, exhorts one. *Listen, Learn, Live!* Another asks *DO YOU HAVE A DEATH WISH?* over a skeletal figure standing in a graveyard.

Apart from a few hard-core drinkers, most of the time the Beerhall is as quiet as the Club. On Wednesday and Friday nights however, it is filled to capacity. Virtually all the black adult males from the township will be at the beerhall, including Chief Inspector Matanda, Mr. Muzenda and Mr. Situmba. The only women are a few bedraggled prostitutes. The sound system blasts out the impossibly quick polyrhythms of Thomas Mapfumo or the sweet, infectious tunes of Oliver Mutukudzi. Men are talking and laughing loudly, some get up and dance with the prostitutes or with each other.

None of the white people from The Club has ever gone to the beerhall for a drink. The beerhall is run by the Macheke Town Council, with proceeds from sales of Chibuku, Lions and Castle beer, and Willards chips supposedly helping to fund services to the town, though of course everyone knows that a lot of the money is siphoned off into the pockets of the town counselors. The council has just enquired, through Mr. Situmba, if they might buy up The Club to expand the Beerhall.

"That's too cheeky," exclaimed Trish, over her shandy. Like the other women, she was wearing a white tennis dress and smoking.

Jackie Maddox, who with her husband Jake, owned a grocer's shop in Macheke, nodded but then added mildly, "Might be that it would work out. How much are they offering? It's terribly noisy over there. Maybe we could move the club somewhere better."

I was on my second double gin. "You'd better act fast or you won't get any money. You must have heard Mugabe's announcement? He's going to seize over a thousand farms." I affected a cheesy German accent. "First ve take ze farms, zen ve take ze country clubs."

James was drinking at the bar with Scotty and Steve Potgieter. He shot me a look. "Where's the scoff book? I need to order some grub. Connie, do you want anything?"

"Another one of these, thanks." I waved my glass at him.

"They won't take our farms. They need the hard currency." Trish stubbed out her cigarette as emphasis.

I decided not to mention Mutamba

The three of us were quiet. Each was sure she knew what the others were thinking.

"I reckon the country is going to hell, anyway," said Trish suddenly. "All the Afs have AIDS, the government's rotten to the core." She spoke angrily, but there was also satisfaction in her voice as well.

For a second I wanted to reach across the table and grab her hand and say, "I know. Isn't it awful?" But of course I did no such thing. Because when it came right down to it, Trish and I had never shared much. A terrible twist of fate had brought me here. Instead I said, "Maybe the MDC will win the next election." It was the polite thing to say in white company these days.

Later, as our car whined down the dirt track back to the farm, the two little boys asleep in the back, James spoke without taking his eyes off the patch of road caught in their headlights. "Scotty told me he's joined the MDC."

"When?"

"Tonight."

"No, I mean when did he join?"

"A couple of months ago, I think. He went to a meeting in Marondera."

"Was Tsvangirai there?"

"No. Some other chap. Young chap, a lawyer. Some other farmers have joined as well."

I could see flashes of light at the side of the track. Rabbits.

"Wow. I'm surprised. Scotty."

"Yeah, well."

"Did he tell you why he joined?"

"He reckons this lot have some sense. They understand how we're keeping the country from going to the dogs, that you can't just hand over the land without a decent plan."

"So in other words, you hope they pay lip service to land reform, but don't actually do anything! Where have we seen this movie before?"

James didn't respond, but I knew that I had made a cheap shot. He reached over and put his hand on my knee. I craned my head out the window, trying to see the Southern Cross.

"Are you going to join?"

"Maybe. They probably don't want too many white faces, but I'm sure our money's okay."

"Do you love me?"

"How does that feel?"

"I need you."

James was a silent lover. No whispered endearments, no grunts or moans of ecstasy. I knew he was close to orgasm when his breathing quickened and he moved more quickly. Sometimes, I wanted to hear him.

"Do you love me?" or "I love you."

My words, whispered into his ear, his mouth, my whimper of pleasure when he took my breast in his mouth, my cries and shudders when I came. After, he would hold me, stroking my hair. He would fall asleep quickly, his arm holding my middle-aged waist.

For James, sex was like everything else in his life — simple and not really worth dwelling on.

4

August 1982

Mutamba Mission

The white lorry tore up the rutted road and past the Mission sign. Constance and Miguel bounced around in the back, coated with dust. Her butt was sore, her back was killing her, and she was terrified that Miguel, who insisted on standing up and holding onto the sides of the box, was going to go flying over the sides every time Mr. Msika went flying around a corner. Julia, who had the seat of honour in the cab beside the driver, turned around and smiled and waved, pointing to the sign. In return, Constance gave her the one-figured salute. To her horror, at exactly that moment, Mr. Msika happened to be looking over his shoulder. He grinned broadly at her and then wrenched hard on the steering wheel.

They had turned onto another road. There were small cement houses on one side and a grove of gum trees on the other. Children scattered in the truck's wake and stood, laughing and waving. Miguel was delighted and waved and shouted back. Constance's heart lurched every time he took his hand off the box. Julia was leaning out her window, smiling and waving.

They came roaring up to an enormous tree and came to a dramatic stop beneath it. They were in front of a two-storey cement building with a glass door and a wide, cement porch. A man with thick glasses and dreadlocks was already helping Miguel out of the lorry. He hoisted Miguel onto his shoulders and paraded him around a small group of on-lookers. Mr. Msika lifted Constance down. The audience laughed and called out in Shona, and Mr. Msika, perhaps savouring his moment in the limelight, spun her around in the air. The crowd seemed to find this hilarious and called out louder. Constance, worried that he was going to flip her upside down and show everyone her underwear, gripped his shoulders and gave a loud squeal. Her hair, already loose from the jarring truck, had come down and was twirling with her.

Maybe Mr. Msika understood her discomfort, or maybe he became tired, because he immediately put her down. She staggered back and almost fell. . Someone, she never knew who, took her arm and steadied her. She heard a murmured "Sorry, sorry." Julia, looking collected and elegant in a long flowered dress and a straw hat — her hair was still tied back neatly — said, "I guess they'll be talking about you tonight in the beer hall." Two men stepped out of the crowd. One was tall, with thick grey hair. The short, chubby man was still chuckling as he held out his hand to Constance.

"You are welcome here at Mutamba." She remembered to shake his hand the African way. He turned to Julia. "I am Brother Julius, the head of the Mission. This is the headmaster Mr. Mhanda."

When Brother Julius met Miguel he said to Constance "But we must call you Amai Miguel!" He said something to the crowd in Shona, which made everyone hoot.

"And now we will show you to your house and the school and then we will have something to eat. Yes, you are most welcome here."

Mr. Msika had finished taking their duffle bags and backpacks down from the truck. Five women stepped forward. Each of them hoisted a bag onto her head and began walking away. Mr. Msika smiled and nodded at Constance and Julia. The he jumped back into the truck. They watched as he drove past them and, in a cloud of dust, circled several times around the huge tree. It was an old game. The children dodged as he swung around, horn honking, arm waving. After a few swipes, the lorry roared off down the road. The crowd dissolved.

The priest and the headmaster led the way and the two women followed, the child between them. They played a game where Miguel stopped and ran forward, while they swung him up between them. They walked across a field of patchy, burnt grass and turned onto a narrow road with houses on either side. It was quiet, except for one house where a man was washing a car in the driveway. He called "Welcome!" and they smiled and waved back. Mr. Mhanda shouted something to him in Shona. The man stood staring curiously after them, the water gushing out of the hosepipe.

"Everyone is still enjoying the holiday," explained Mr. Mhanda. "Most of the teachers are seeing their families in the rural areas."

"What about the other Canadian teacher here?" Julia asked.

"Ah, he is always off sight-seeing. He sleeps in the bush and looks at the flora and fauna."

They turned onto a path leading to a house set back from the road, dwarfed between two trees.

"This is your house," Brother Julius said. "What do you think?"

Constance smiled and nodded.

They walked up the path to the veranda. "You will want to *ban* the grass," said Mr. Mhanda, looking with disapproval at the patchy brown stalks. Constance nodded and smiled, looking over at Julia who raised her eyes and shrugged.

They waited in the shade of the veranda while Brother Julius carefully unlocked the door and handed the key to Constance. The house smelt of floor wax. There was a lounge, a small kitchen with a sink, a small fridge ("Look, Mommy, a baby fridge") and an appliance with two burners called a "cooker". Constance smiled and nodded. There were two small bedrooms with two small beds, a bathroom with a huge tub and a sink, and, the piece de resistance, a separate room for the toilet, which was reached through a door off the veranda. Brother Julius opened the door and ushered them into the tiny room. They crowded around the toilet. It was old-fashioned, with the tank high up on the wall. Miguel was given the honour of pulling the long chain that hung down. Julia and Constance smiled and nodded as the water gurgled and swirled in the toilet bowl.

The next few hours were an ordeal. Constance's face hurt from smiling. She smiled as Brother Julius explained that she needed to make a fire outside "in order to obtain hot wootah" and she smiled as he said again that she must *ban* the grass to keep away snakes and she smiled as they toured Julia's house, exactly the same except it had only one bedroom. Julia was also advised to *ban* the grass. Constance smiled as they were given a tour of the clinic, where a woman in a nurse's uniform curtsied and presented them with bouquets of flowers. She smiled as they were taken to the Brothers' house.

An old white priest was standing in the archway, waiting. He was old and grey and much taller than Brother Julius. He gripped their hands vigorously.

"Good day, Good day. You are most welcome here." He had a soft Irish accent. "It's hot, yes? We need some beer." The old man kept chattering as he led them through the passageway to a grassy courtyard. Julia asked his name. "Brother Joseph." Brother Julius chuckled and added, "But everyone is calling him Brother Joe. I have known him for many, many years." He turned to include Constance. "I was educated here at Mutamba. I have been here since I was a small child."

They sat and ate a huge lunch — sadza and relish, cabbage, huge beef short ribs, beer, and a chocolate cake, served by a man wearing khaki shorts and shirt. Constance was beginning to see that this was the uniform of the African servant or schoolboy. Labourers wore blue or red overalls and gumboots.

Brother Joe lit a cigarette and asked Julia about the journey out to the mission. The conversation drifted here and there, lightly resting on their histories, the mission, the weather. Constance slouched back in her chair, sandals off, beer resting on her stomach. Miguel was over at the fishpond, trying to catch something. Lazily she remembered something from the "Staying Healthy!" workshop about bilharzia: couldn't you catch it from messing about in water like that? But no one else seemed concerned. She smiled and nodded every so often, aware that she was drunk and sleepy. The afternoon sun felt so good, she could hear birds and the clatter of dishes coming from the kitchen, and Miguel singing to himself ("I'm a little green frog, I'm a little green frog") and Julia's voice and the voices of the men.

A few flies buzzed around, but that was okay because they kept her from drifting off to sleep.

August 1971

North-East border

"Almost all the popular movements undertaken against dictators in recent time have suffered from the same fundamental fault of inadequate preparation."

Guerilla Warfare
Che Guevara

The crossing was difficult. They crossed at night and the place was not well chosen. It was very rocky and the current of the Zambezi was swift. Also, the men couldn't swim, so they were very nervous and awkward. They didn't speak as they waded across, single-file, their packs on their heads, but they splashed and grunted involuntarily as they slipped and flailed.

Later, they would say they were "elated" and "joyful" after crossing into Rhodesia. In fact, they were only relieved to have made it across without having lost any men to drowning or hippos.

They had planned to camp, living off the land, but as they moved away from the river, they realized that, even a few kilometres from the Zambezi, the land was dry and barren. They began to run out of food and water. They were forced to go into the villages and ask the people for help.

The accounts of the Second Chimurenga written just after Independence, say that the demands of the comrades were met with enthusiasm. The peasants willingly gave them food and shelter. Of course, this is possible. Given the brutal nature of the Rhodesian regime and the novelty of an armed and uniformed guerilla "unit", it seems likely that the locals may have been eager to help their liberators.

Or maybe the guns the soldiers carried persuaded the villagers. Nowadays, we look at history through grey-coloured glasses.

In any event, the guerillas were given food and water.

Days of tedium and tension. They moved through the bush at night. During the day they took cover, dug foxholes and trenches in case of attack. The unit was aware that they were being "tracked" by the Rhodesian Security Forces. Planes flew overhead and the moon was waxing. The unit did not have radios, so it wasn't able to contact Military High Command in Mozambique. The guerillas shot the odd antelope or bushbuck, but shooting and killing game was risky because this could signal their position to the enemy. The men were often hungry and thirsty.

The first battle was in the afternoon. The guerillas had seen the tanks of the RSF and also helicopters flying overhead. They didn't try to shoot them down, because they had been taught that it was best to fight at night. But it seemed the enemy had gone to a different training camp. The RSF attacked in the afternoon, firing at random. Between rounds and explosions, they called upon the guerillas to surrender.

The comrades had orders not to fire back unless they had a clear view of the enemy. They only had the ammunition they were carrying, with no hope of being resupplied. The government forces grew tired of firing into the bush with no response. The Rhodesians stood up and asked, "Where are the terrorists?"

The reply was a "fusillade of furious fire". This caused the enemy to retreat. Meaning, they ran for their lives. They were in such a hurry they left behind rations, communications equipment and most importantly, ammunition and weapons. That night, the unit feasted on baked beans, biltong and cheese. They had captured some machine guns, uniforms and boots as well as a brand new LMG.

Three comrades were killed. They were Charles Seshoba, Sparks Chinodya and Castro Mutikiti.

The guerrillas were not able to stop and rest because they knew the government forces would regroup and attack them again. So they *pushed on into the bush. After a few days, they were once again running out of food. Their uniforms were tattered and the land was dry and dusty. The planes and helicopters of the enemy seemed to be constantly buzzing overhead.*

The commander of the unit decided that a raid was called for. The guerillas crept on their bellies until they were on the edge of the enemy's camp. They threw grenades into the tents and followed this up with fire from their Ak-47's and LMGs. The government soldiers fought back, but after a few minutes, the comrades called up reinforcements from the rear and soon after the camp was overrun. In that battle, the commander was killed. He was named Thomas — "a huge chunk of a man wearing size 10 boots." Some enemy soldiers were also killed.

Once again, the Rhodesians left behind supplies, weapons, grenades, uniforms and radios.

The guerilla unit had moved into a barren part of Rhodesia. As their supplies again ran low, the regime was sending in more reinforcements. It was decided to retreat back to the training camp in Tete, Mozambique.

I am repeating a story I heard many years ago, a story that was told to me, on a night so hot we lay spread-eagled out on the mattress, the sheet tangled at our feet, only our fingertips touching. So I might have the year wrong and some of the names. In those years people were still using their "Chimurenga" names and this was confusing. And truth be told, I let the murmured words drift across me and out the torn window screen. I didn't ask questions, probe for details, clarify disparities. I thought I knew the story. I believed in it, the essence of it. I was laying beside an African freedom fighter, a man who had been prepared to give his life in the struggle to free his people and create a new world.

Even now, twenty years later, I believe it still.

5

October 1982

Mutamba Mission

Constance had never been much of a morning person. Among the last to leave any party, she liked to rise well after sunrise and reenter the world gradually over many cups of coffee. At university, she had never taken an eight o'clock class. She liked to type out papers late at night, fueled by a glass of red wine.

Of course, when Miguel was a tiny baby, she had her share of pre-dawn feedings; walking up and down the living room of the basement suite with Miguel in her arms, rain muffling the cry of police sirens and ambulances one block over on Cambie Street.

Luckily, Miguel was an exceptionally "good" baby, and by six weeks he was sleeping through the night. When she had to be at the university for classes or to study, she carried him upstairs, into the care of her landlady, Mrs. Dangelo. At night, when she hit a roadblock while writing an essay, she would lift Miguel out of his crib and dance around the room with him, with Abba or Van Morrison turned up high on the stereo. Often she would read in bed until the early hours of the morning, shifting from elbow to elbow.

Here, she was woken before dawn by the crowing of roosters. She would lie in bed, until the pale light washed over the room and the birds' songs grew louder. After supper she tried to read or mark essays, but found her head nodding and her eyes refusing to stay open. More than once she fell asleep at the little kitchen table that doubled as her desk. She would wake, startled and disoriented, to the chimes of Big Ben on the short-wave and drag herself into bed, barely able to summon enough energy to untie and drop the mosquito net.

If Constance was mildly surprised by her nightly lethargy, she was completely amazed at the way she was able to spring out of bed at the whisper of dawn and get herself and Miguel washed and dressed while she boiled up a cup of tea and some sadza porridge. By 7:15 she was standing under a jacaranda tree at the school's assembly area, having dropped Miguel off at crèche. She had heard that water in the southern hemisphere swirls down the drain in the opposite direction than it does in the north. She thought maybe she was a human example of the phenomenon, her sleep habits having almost completely reversed themselves south of the equator.

The agenda for morning assembly was simple. The students, in blue jumpers and khaki trousers or blue cardigans and skirts stood massed in front of the headmaster, Mr. Mhanda. He was a tall, powerful-looking man in a green safari suit. Beside him stood the deputy headmaster, Mr. Murerwa who for some reason insisted on wearing the black robes of an Oxford don. Everyone bowed their heads while Brother Julius led the school in The Lord's Prayer, followed by a rousing Shona hymn. Then one of the teaching staff, usually someone from the Religious Education department, would give what was supposed to be an inspirational talk on a moral subject.

"You gels, you must stop having sexual relations with these boys. They are only playing with you. They will leave you with a big belly and you will be the one to suffer. You will be chased from school. You will have no future!"

"You gels, don't let these men from the towns have sex with you. These scum of the earth will try to convince you that it's okay because they're wearing a condom. A condom! Don't forget it's a sin to use one of these condoms."

Unlike Canadian students, the Zimbabwean kids didn't appear to be the least bit embarrassed by the strange juxtaposition of frank sex talk coupled with a "Just Say No" message. If anything, they seemed bored. They certainly weren't taking the message to heart, judging by the number of girls who had already been "chased" from the school for getting knocked up. Constance looked over at Benjamin Mwira, the carpentry teacher. It was an open secret that he was sleeping with one of the Form One girls.

The best part of the assembly, apart from the hymns, was the skits presented by the Drama Club. No false modesty or that depressing "coolness" that infected teenagers in Canada. The students were natural hams and the plays were lively and funny. They were almost always entirely in Shona, but even when they were put on in English, Constance found the accents too hard to follow. But it was still a joy to watch the students and staff, many of them doubled over with laughter.

She glanced over at Alex Shaw, laughing easily at one of the punch lines being delivered. She envied him his fluency in Shona and the relaxed, familiar way he related to everyone. He spoke easily and naturally, whereas she was still speaking rather carefully, afraid of being misunderstood. He was wildly popular with the female staff, flirting and joking with all of them, even the outrageously fat matron, Amai Tendai. The house he shared with Friend Tirivavi, the Physics teacher, was known to be party central for the male teachers.

The skit ended, to raucous applause and ululating. Brother Julius stepped forward to make the final prayer and the crowd quieted.

"Heavenly Father," he intoned. Constance looked around. Julia's head was bowed devoutly, though Constance knew she was most likely thinking about how to finagle a lift into town after school today. The call of a bird, "coo-coo, coo-koo-cuk-coo" drifted over the assembly. Constance shifted and craned her neck to look up into the jacaranda tree.

The bird called again and she located it. Was it a dove?

Brother Julius was just hitting his stride. Constance surreptitiously reached into the bag slung across her shoulders and extracted Newman's Birds. She turned to the index, and found the page she was looking for. Five doves were listed with corresponding illustrations on the facing page. She glanced from book to tree.

"That doesn't look like a hymn book to me." Alex reached across her to point to the second picture. "Redeyed Dove. You'll get to know it by its call. Listen."

On cue the dove called twice. "Coo-coo, coo-koo-cuk-coo." Constance stood quietly. She wanted to touch the golden hair on Alex's forearm resting on her book.

"Did you hear it?"

She looked up. "My son thinks it's saying 'Listen, you're such a dweeb'."

Alex laughed. The teachers and some of the students on the edge of the crowd had turned to look at them. He dropped his arm, but did not move away.

By noon the bloom was off the day. The Angelus bell finally rang, signaling the end of the week. The students suddenly revived. They jostled out of the classroom, anxious to get to their lunch. There were not enough chairs or tables in the dining hall, so they collected their sadza and relish and mugs of tea and sat under the trees or ate their meal back in their dormitories. Their week was not over. There were sports and clubs in the afternoons (optional) and two hours of supervised prep in the classrooms (compulsory).

Constance walked past the classrooms, and turned onto a path that wound toward a fenced yard and the school crèche. The yard was full of children running, their bell-like voices sweet in the air. Some of the kids had already liberated themselves by climbing the fence and were playing football in the field next to the crèche. One of the teachers was whacking a cow with her hand, trying to stop it from eating the leaves off a lemon tree. She stopped and shook hands with Constance. "These fences. They don't keep the animals out or the kids in." She pointed to Miguel, who was part of the soccer melee, all small boys in dirty worn shorts and shirts, no shoes.

Constance offered to help the teacher get the cow out of the yard, and together they pushed and prodded it out through the gate. The teacher slapped its hindquarters and the cow moved reluctantly off down the road in search of another gate to crash.

"It's the drought." The teacher spoke almost apologetically. "It's really terrible. We had almost no rain the past couple of years, so there's really nothing for the animals."

"When will the rains come?"

"They used to always come around this time. It gets hotter and hotter, until you feel it just has to rain. Every afternoon the clouds come, and you will hear thunder. The clouds get bigger and darker as they days go by and the rumblings louder and louder, and then one day, ah! the rains come."

"Well, let's hope the drought is over soon. It must be hard on the farmers."

"It's hard on everyone," said the teacher with a rush of feeling. "Without rain we can't live."

Constance held out her hand to say goodbye. "I know I've met you before, but I'm sorry, I've forgotten you name. I've met so many people since I got here."

The teacher held her hand and laughed softly. "My name is Miriam. But you will also hear others call me Amai Mushana." She nodded towards the footballers. "That's my son. That one there." She gestured toward a stocky, fierce looking boy who was standing on the near side of the field.

"Ah, so that's Mushana. I've heard about him. What does his name mean?"

"Sunrise. He was born at just that time. I'm so glad he is playing with Miguel. I hope he'll learn some English."

"But I want Miguel to learn Shona!"

Miriam laughed again. "Maybe they can teach each other."

"And your English is so good," Constance persisted. "I really envy you, speaking two languages."

"Three actually. I also speak Ndebele."

"So you must have taught some English to Mushana?"

"Unfortunately, he was with my mother the past two years, in Gweru. So he didn't know any Europeans."

Constance wanted to ask her about this, but stopped herself. She had already committed several faux pas with her curiosity. Just the other day she had asked the boarding master if he was married, and this had sent him into a fit of embarrassed laughter.

"Honestly," she said later to Julia. "You would have thought I was asking him on a date."

43

"Well, he probably thought you were flirting with him. Think about the way white women have spoken to him in the past. Maybe he doesn't know quite know how to respond to you. Cut the poor guy some slack."

Unspoken between them was the knowledge that Julia wasn't having any trouble communicating with the local males. Blond and curvaceous, exotic and erotic, her desk in the staff room was often surrounded by a group of male teachers trying to impress her. Boys offered to carry her books between classes and the girls watched her with open admiration. Was there some coolness from the women teachers? Constance couldn't tell.

She and Miguel left the track that led down to the crèche and turned onto the main road that would take them back home. They greeted a group of students returning their empty plates to the dining hall. As they turned onto the road leading to the staff houses they could see Alex Shaw and Friend Tirivavi sitting on old wooden chairs under a mango tree, sharing a bowl of sadza. They stopped talking and looked at her as she and Miguel came closer.

Constance felt awkward. She wanted to act naturally, but her smile felt stiff. "Manheru". She hoped they wouldn't laugh at her pronunciation.

"Manheru, Amai Miguel" said Friend. A flash of white teeth. "Mamuka sei?" Alex took a swig from his beer. He held the bottle out to Constance.

There was a moment, not of silence, since they could hear students talking and laughing, the whine of cicadas, but of waiting. Constance took a deep swig. The beer was not very cold, but it tasted good. When she tilted the bottle back down, her mouth couldn't catch all the liquid, and some beer ran down her chin and neck. Embarrassed, she quickly tried to wipe it away with the back of her hand. Both men stood looking at her. She had no idea what they were thinking.

"Well," she addressed Miguel. "It's time I got you home for some lunch, my boy."

"But I want to stay and eat with Alex and Friend," Miguel protested. "Look, their lunch is right here." He pointed to the yellow enamel bowl left on one of the chairs.

Constance hesitated. A woman with a child and no man, she knew there would probably come a time when she would be at this door, asking for help. She didn't want to squander a favour on something as trivial as a bowl of sadza.

"Join us," said Friend. "Sorry for saying this, but you look as though you need it. The first time I saw you I said to this one here", he shrugged towards Alex, "I said, 'Look, a little stick has come to Zimbabwe'. "

She was surprised. She had supposed that Friend had never taken any particular notice of her. She looked over at Alex, wondering what his response had been. He was smiling, but she couldn't read his eyes.

She ended up staying for most of the afternoon. They finished the sadza and shared several large bottles of beer. Miguel and Alex wandered off into the bush at the end of the road to look for insects. Friend lay down under the mango tree and fell asleep. He had turned down Miguel's request to go along. "I'm a physics teacher, not a biologist. You two biologists go and mess around in the bush. The physicist must have a siesta!"

Constance went into the house to use the toilet. Their house was bigger than hers, though a bit oddly designed. A long, deep veranda ran along the front, covered by a torn screen. Stepping inside she was in a huge lounge/dining room, with a brick fireplace. There wasn't much furniture — a table and only one chair, a sagging red chesterfield and two bookshelves on each side of the fireplace, crammed with books. She could see a bit of the kitchen through an open door at the far end of the lounge. On the other side was a door leading to a hallway. She went through and passed by two bedrooms on her way to the toilet. She wondered which room was Alex's.

She took a long pee, then realized that her period had started. "Shit". She knew she had some hoarded tampons in her bag, but she had left it out in the yard. She would have to go out and get it. She pulled up her skirt, but left her panties lying on the floor. She collected her bag, careful not to wake Friend, rummaging in it as she ran back up the steps into the house. She was thirsty and felt the familiar throbbing in her head.

When Constance emerged from the toilet a second time, she wanted to stay in the house, where it was marginally cooler. She went into the kitchen. There was plenty of beer in the fridge but no water. She was still several months away from risking tap water, but she found a kettle on the stove with water in it. She reasoned that there was a good possibility that it had been boiled to make tea that morning and she rapidly drank two full glasses.

The bookshelves disappointed her. Mostly animal and plant identification guides. Physics and Biology texts. A biography of Che Guevara. Several of those ghastly Flashman novels. Then she saw a couple of books by a writer she had been wanting to read. She pulled out *Waiting For The Rains* and read the first page, standing by the bookshelf. It looked promising, so she dropped onto the battered chesterfield, kicking off her sandals. The sofa was surprisingly comfortable.

It must have been an hour later when she looked up to see Alex standing in the doorway. He had his terrycloth hat in his hand. For a moment they looked directly at one another. Then his eyes flicked along the chesterfield and Constance realized that her skirt had ridden up around her and that she had let one of her legs fall off the couch.

"Good book?"

She nodded as she failed to nonchalantly sit up. She was trying to remember if she had shaved her legs that morning. Probably not. She had found it harder and harder to keep up the myriad of ablutions that had seemed so vital back in Vancouver. Plucking her eyebrows had been the first thing to go.

She sat up, digging into the pocket of her skirt for some hairpins.

"What is it?"

"Charles Mungoshi. It's good. Can I borrow it?"

Alex shrugged. "I guess so. It's Friend's, but I'm sure he won't mind." He crossed the room and sat with his back to the table, watching her as she wound and pinned her hair.

"Where's Miguel?"

46

"He's out in the front frightening Friend with his new pet."

Constance almost swallowed a pin. "What is it, a snake?"

"No, a chameleon. A big one." He smiled at her wary look. "They're completely harmless and make good pets. Eat up all the mosquitoes. Miguel can keep it on that vine growing up the wall of your house."

"If it's so harmless, why is Friend afraid of it?"

"He's not, really. Well, maybe a bit. He's just having some fun with Miguel. But lots of Africans don't like chameleons. They think they're bad luck."

Constance wanted to see the chameleon, so they went out into the yard. My first chameleon, she was thinking. Definitely something to write about to the folks back home.

The chameleon was perched on a long stick Miguel was proudly holding out to Friend. It looked comical, not a hint of danger in its long curled tail, precise toes gripping the stick, its bulging eyes.

"Is it a male or female? Or can you tell?"

"Ah," said Alex, picking up the creature. "Flap-necked chameleon. *Chamaelo dilepis*. You'll find lots of them here in Zimbabwe." The chameleon was turning from dark brown to tan. "Chameleons are loners but a female can be courted by several males. Supposedly, they can really get it on. Female lays eggs in the spring, about twenty eggs and it can take up to a year for them to hatch." He gave the lizard back to Miguel. "The locals don't like them."

Constance was impressed, not just with the knowledge Alex had about this chameleon — he was famous on the campus for his interest in all wild things and the students were always bringing him snakes and spiders to identify — but with the casual way he imparted it. As if he had just told them something they already knew but were maybe not sure of, like the correct spelling of a word.

She knew it was time to go. She collected her bag and asked Friend about borrowing his book. *Now I have a good excuse to visit again.* Miguel carefully put the chameleon back on the stick. Alex walked with them over to the gate.

"Have you heard, we often have a braai here on Saturday?"

"Really?" She said. Then she winked at him. "Blaring music, raucous laughter, general carousing – that's not you, is it? I can't imagine where that pile of empties over there came from." She pointed to a rather large heap of bottles at the side of the house.

"All for a good cause. We donate all those to the Wildlife Club. They're fund-raising for a trip to Hwange and Friend and I just want to do our bit."

She held out her hand to say goodbye. He shook it gently, his left hand under his elbow. "Why don't you and Miguel come over tomorrow? We throw the meat on the braai at around seven."

"I'm a vegetarian. I could bring a salad. Anything else?"

Alex shrugged. "Beer, if you've got it. If not, don't worry. I can make a run over to the bottle store tomorrow." He let go of her hand and tousled Miguel's hair. "Take care of our chameleon." He turned back to Charlotte. "By the way, if you see Julia could you tell her that I'll swing by her house in the morning in case she still wants a lift into town." Did his voice sound deliberately casual?

Constance had to wait until well into the afternoon before she could bathe and wash her hair. Saturday was laundry day for the students and the water pressure at Mutamba, low at the best of times, was a trickle by eight in the morning and had dried up by noon. In the afternoon, when the hundreds of jerseys, skirts, blouses, shorts, shirts and socks were pegged up on the lines behind the girls' and boys' dormitories, the pressure gradually increased until it only took thirty minutes or so to half fill a tub.

She could have hot water if she lit a fire in the donkey boiler outside. This was a kind of outdoor chimney with a large metal water tank set on a shelf above the fire. But this involved arranging to hire a donkey cart to bring a load of wood and then lighting a fire an hour or two ahead of when she and Miguel wanted to bathe. In these early days of her new life, she was still having trouble organizing decent meals for the two of them. She still hadn't opened a bank account and was cashing her pay cheque at the bottle store, and keeping the cash in an old Milo tin. The tin was getting pretty full and she thought she might have to open an account at Barclays in Marondera. Either that or get a bigger tin. Her sunglasses had broken and getting them either fixed or replaced seemed daunting.

"I can take them into town with me next time I go," Julia had offered. "Better yet, why don't you come along. You haven't been off campus since school started. We can stay over at the hotel, get a decent meal and a shower. Maybe catch a movie." She leaned closer. "And you haven't lived till you've been to the Studio 54 nightclub."

It might be fun, though she'd have to find someone who was willing to look after Miguel overnight. They could most likely bum a drive to Marondera, but then how would they get home? And she loved being at the mission on the weekends. She could go for a long run before the day got hot, catch up on some marking, write letters, walk in the bush with Miguel and laze on the veranda, reading, switching from coffee to gin as the sun went down.

Well, no need for hot water at this time of year. A cold bath was actually quite refreshing, though she couldn't luxuriate in it. She quickly washed and shaved her legs and armpits, then lay back and dunked her head under.

When she stepped out, the breeze blowing through the open window made goosebumps on her skin, but the air was so dry and hot, that by the time she had wrapped a towel around her hair, she was beginning to feel warm again. She found her stash of tampons, idly wondering why women didn't bleed in the bath, maybe Alex would know, he was a biologist, after all.

The only mirror in the house was a small one over the bathroom sink. Constance never bothered to weigh herself, but judging by her hipbones, she was sure she was even skinnier than usual. She combed out her hair and, standing on tiptoe, stared at herself. Small face, one slightly crooked tooth, blue eyes, heavy black eyebrows, she would have to watch she didn't develop a Frieda Khalo unibrow, maybe it was time to pull out the tweezers again, long poker-straight hair, too dark to be called brown but not black. Her bangs could use a trimming, but she had learned to leave well enough alone.

In the bedroom, she looked at the pile of dirty laundry in the corner. Something else she needed to organize or else just get off her butt and do. Or at least get one of those big woven baskets so she didn't have to keep looking at it. Underwear was easy, she just washed it out at night and it dried in no time, so she and Miguel were okay in that department, but she was aware that they both had been wearing clothes lately that were none too clean.

She remembered she had some cloth folded in the bottom of the wardrobe, the kind African women wrapped around themselves and used to carry their babies. She and Julia had bought several pieces each at Mbare Musika in a last-minute impulse before leaving Harare. Constance had saved hers to use as a tablecloth, or make curtains or give to her mother when she came to stay at Christmas. She and Julia had agreed they'd rather be caught dead than wearing one. Of course, they were both picturing Dodie, her squat figure wrapped like a loaf, with the image of yet another discredited African tin-pot dictator emblazoned across her bum.

But this one, blue with a pink hibiscus pattern was rather nice and would probably look okay with a black camisole.

It had been quite a while since she had cared this much about what she wore.

She finally found Miguel over at the football pitch, where he and some other ragged little boys were hanging around, watching the older boys play. Then he had to bathe while she found him some relatively clean shorts to wear. Then she had to make some kind of salad — not coleslaw! Looking in the fridge, she found some spinach that didn't look too bad and couple of oranges and half an onion. She loaded a basket with some beer and a bottle of South African wine – she had scrupulously avoided South African products at home, but here the shops were full of them — and she and Miguel set off in the dark, guided by the voices and music.

By the time they arrived, the party was well on its way. They made their way around the house to the back and came upon a group of men sitting around a large fire, talking loudly to each other. They looked up at her blankly, but seemed happy to see Miguel. As the only paleface child on campus, he was treated as a sort of pet by many of the male teachers, who had nicknamed him "Peanuts".

50

They greeted her politely, then went back to arguing, in Shona. She knew, having heard the same conversation ad nausea in the staff room every day for the past six weeks, that they were discussing the latest football match.

She looked around and was surprised to see Mr. Murerwa over at the braai, talking with Friend. Mr. Murewa had left Oxford and was wearing a shirt so loud that even in the dark it practically glowed. Both men greeted her and Friend waved a fork, but then they both turned back to each other.

Alex was nowhere to be seen. If she stayed, she would feel like an idiot, with her pathetic salad, which no one would eat. But there was no way to leave gracefully or even unnoticed. Miguel was perched on the Agriculture teacher's knee, listening to the men. She would have to call him over, and draw attention to their departure. Maybe she could pretend to take him into the house on some pretext, then leave by the front door.

"Miguel, you have a very dirty face, my boy. Come with me and we can wash you."

Miguel protested that he had just had a bath, but he was gently pushed off Mr. Chirombo's knee.

Constance dropped the wine and beer onto the table in the kitchen. She took Miguel's hand and began leading him out of the house.

"Aren't we washing my face? I don't want to go home."

"Shh!" she hissed. It was awkward trying to steer Miguel and hold onto the dammed salad bowl. "Stay with me, okay?"

Out on the veranda they found their way blocked by someone sitting on the stairs. The dark shape turned.

"Leaving so soon?" It was Alex.

She didn't know what to say. It was hard to think of a pressing excuse to rush home from a party at Mutamba Mission in Zimbabwe on a Saturday night.

"We're not leaving. Mummy just wants to take me home to wash my face. Right, Mummy?"

Constance managed a forced laugh. "Yes." She began to maneuver down the stairs. "I left some booze in the kitchen." She almost stumbled as her foot hit something. She realized she had kicked over a beer. "Oh! Sorry!"

Alex reached down and picked it up. "Don't worry, it was empty. Listen, do you want a beer? Miguel can go back to the braai." He dropped his cigarette butt into the bottle. Then she felt his hand circle her ankle.

"Come on, sit down on the stoep. I'll be back in a minute. Lets go, Miguel"

Something surged within her. She sat, resting the salad bowl in her lap. She slapped at a mosquito on her shoulder. The music thumped in the back yard. *When you see the Southern Cross for the first time.* She leaned back to look up at the sky, strewn with stars.

Alex came back and handed her a beer. "I managed to find a couple of forks. They might even be clean."

They took turns stabbing at the salad.

"Why are you here?"

For a moment Constance thought he was asking why she had come to the party. Then, relieved, she told him her story. Graduating from university with a useless degree. Seeing an ad in the paper. Applying to teach in Zimbabwe.

"What about Miguel's father?"

"What about him?"

"Doesn't he miss Miguel?

"I don't know and I don't much care. He was someone I met when I was really young and he was not very nice to me." She felt her voice tighten. "He was a drummer!"

Alex chuckled. "I thought you were going to say he was a drug dealer. But I take your point." He pulled out a cigarette and offered one to Constance. She shook her head, no.

"What about you, eh? What's your story?"

"Ah, me. Well, I wanted to come to Africa since I was a kid and read my first Tarzan book."

"Were you always interested in bugs?"

"All animals, really. I had a pet owl and a crow. And a raccoon. Studied spiders at university."

"Farley Mowatt in Africa."

"I guess you could say that. But I also like geology and plants. I guess you could say I'm a bit of a dilettante. The only part of science I could never really get into was physics."

"What about astronomy? Can you show me how to find the Southern Cross?"

He leaned over and took the salad bowl out of her lap. He put his arm on her shoulder and gently pulled her back. For a moment she thought he was going to kiss her, but then he was lifting her arm, pointing it to the sky. She could see a swathe of milky sky stretching above them, packed with stars. "First you find the Pointers. See those two really bright stars just there, close to the horizon? Alpha Centauri and Beta Centauri. Okay, now you draw a line with your eyes, through the Pointers up just a little," he raised her arm, "and there it is, lying on its side."

She saw it, pulsing like a heartbeat in the perfectly black sky.

Every night after, Constance would look for those stars. She didn't always find them. But she always looked for them.

6

February, 2000

Macheke

There was an aura of urgency around the farm these days. We grew flue-cured tobacco, which meant that the leaves had to be harvested in sequence as they ripened from the bottom of the plant to the top. As the sun scorched the leaves, they became thick and rough and yellow. For over six weeks now, the farm workers had been out in the fields, taking a few leaves from each plant as they ripened. James was spending long days in the fields, organizing the passes over the fields, when one or two leaves would be cut from the stalks. And there were more people around the farm these days. Most of these were extra workers, hired to help with the harvest. Many would be related to our steady labourers, but this year there seemed to be an unusually high number of what Scotty called "lay-abouts", people who could be seen hanging around the workers compound without much purpose. One day after school I had to pass by a group of five men I didn't know sitting in the shade.

They stopped talking and watched me as I came closer. When I greeted them, they mumbled at me. When my back was to them, I could hear them laughing.

"Maybe they weren't laughing at me, but it sure felt like they were," I said to Miriam. "Cheeky devils."

I half-expected her to dismiss my complaint, or at explain it away, but instead she looked troubled.

"Most of these men are just those who can't work or maybe they want to sit and smoke" she meant dagga "but some of them are bad men. They are tsotsis. Why don't you get Baba Miguel to clear them off?"

We both knew it wasn't that simple. I didn't claim to know much about the economy, but it seemed that Zimbabwe's was in freefall. The cost of basic things like mealie-meal and cooking oil had skyrocketed, leaving the working poor in an untenable situation, unable to feed and clothe their children properly, let alone send them to school. Unemployment was like an epidemic and the real epidemic of Aids had left thousands of children orphaned. This meant that crime, which up to now had mostly been of the petty kind — muggings and break-ins of cars and houses — had become more violent as people became increasingly desperate. The government, led by a paranoid and thuggish Robert Mugabe, was unwilling or unable to attempt any solutions. It was common knowledge that it had set its' sight on the white farmers, who, as the only group which had remained relatively unscathed by the Aids crisis and the economic disasters, was a convenient and not altogether unworthy scapegoat.

It was in this context that the ruling party was holding a referendum which, if approved, would change the constitution and make Mugabe "President for Life." There was a kind of Orwellian ring to it, given the spike in mortality rates he had presided over.

"Why doesn't he just come clean and declare himself 'African Tin-Pot Dictator'?" I asked Knowledge bitterly one morning at tea break. I knew that all my colleagues were paying school fees for Aids orphans or kids whose parents had no work. But more and more students were forced to leave school so they could care for sick parents, or worse, their younger brothers and sisters after the death of their parents. It seemed there were funerals on the farm or in Macheke every week.

"Because that title is already owned by Mobuto Sese Seko," answered Knowledge, calmly. "And believe me, the people of Zaire paid dearly for it. But maybe now that he is dead, Mugabe can inherit the tin pot."

Knowledge was too polite to point out what we both knew. That even now, the miniscule white population (were we even one percent of the population?) controlled most of the farms and businesses in the country. The point being that the whites had thrived under ZANU-PF rule. The point being that they had tacitly and cynically supported Mugabe's scandal-ridden government. The point being, the white tribes of Africa, from Zaire to Zanzibar and from South Africa to Senegal have always appreciated the "stability" that the "Strong Man" gives them.

In my experience, both black and white Zimbabweans were guarded with each other. Though I had heard Zimbabweans of all backgrounds complain about food shortages, the corruption scandals, or Grace Mugabe's shopping sprees in London or Dubai, people seldom spoke openly against the government in mixed company. Blacks probably didn't want to hear "I told you so" from whites. Whites were hardly in a position to complain to blacks, who were so obviously baring the brunt of the regimes disastrous policies. Though the whining at the country clubs and on the verandas was the shrillest I'd heard since my early days in the country.

"It's ironic, really," I commented to Knowledge, stubbing out my cigarette. "The whites in South Africa absolutely despised people like Joe Slovo and Bram Fischer, but after the elections, they became symbols of non-racialism. Their struggles in the anti-apartheid movement give the whites there at least some credibility, keep them from being completely sidelined."

"Bram Fischer and Joe Slovo are dead."

"I know! But their example means that whites can at least speak out without seeming to be completely self-serving. They have Nadine Gordimer. We have that fool, Ian Smith!"

"What about Doris Lessing?"

"Don't get me started." I laughed. "Doris Lessing is even less of a Zimbabwean that am I. No, we white people need someone who was chucked into jail by Smithy, escaped to Mozambique and fought in the Chimurenga. Even better if he could have died in battle and been buried at Heroes Acre."

"The whites were tricked by their leaders. Today it is our turn."

I thought this was too magnanimous. "But many people oppose Mugabe. Look at the rise of the MDC." Was Knowledge a member? I wouldn't dare ask.

"Ehe. But everyone knows it is getting most of its money from the whites and from the British. The whites must understand something. Mugabe did not create this land problem we have. Even if he goes, the problem will still be here. The land must be redistributed."

"I agree! But there has to be some kind of plan. Don't you feel that we are on the verge of disaster here?"

Knowledge looked at me blandly. "We're always on the edge of disaster. As you say, Amai Miguel, what else is new?"

"But where has our hope gone? It seems like just yesterday we all felt so optimistic. We really thought Zimbabwe was going to be a new country."

Knowledge looked at me with the pitying eyes of a young man. My use of the phrase "just yesterday" to hearken back to a golden age — a time that would seem an age ago to him — made my opinion as relevant as the stories of the old men and women. I remembered when I first came to Macheke and heard the nostalgic country club moaning of "before the war" and how I had despised it. What was happening to me?

Emmerson was out in the quadrangle, ringing the bell. I stubbed out my cigarette. "Well, let's get back to work. Those pupils aren't going to educate themselves."

7

November 1982

Mutamba Mission

It was another month before Julia could persuade Constance to go into Marondera. Her lethargy continued and she still felt no real urge to leave the little world of the mission. The days grew steadily hotter and hotter. Often now in the afternoon clouds would form and the air would become heavy and oppressive. But the clouds never seemed to grow big enough to blot out the sun, which shone relentlessly, day after day. More and more cows, goats and donkeys from the village broke through the perimeter fence and made their way steadily through what was left of the gardens around the staff housing, the workers compound and the dormitories. The mission fields, which had not been over-grazed like the communal farms, were none-the-less reaching the end of their season and it was an open secret that the small boys who stood watch over the Brothers' flocks and herds were no longer bothering to drive out the village strays. The mission's borehole was drying up and water rationing had been imposed at the end of October. It didn't much affect Constance or Miguel. While Constance rather welcomed the excuse for her son's and her own unkempt appearance, Julia was complaining that she was having to get up at two o'clock in the morning to sneak enough water to wash her hair.

"You'd better watch yourself," said Constance to her. "You're starting to sound like one of The Whingers."

It was Friday night and she and Julia were sitting in the staff room. Constance was on the last night of prep supervision and Julia had dropped by to chat. Constance had her bare feet propped up her desk. Julia lay draped across the next desk. It belonged to Mr. Karambira, one of Constance's colleagues in the History department.

The sterile afternoon clouds had long left and the sky was pulsating with stars. The fluorescent lights hummed, casting ugly shadows in the long, dusty room. Moths swirled around the lights. Coughs and shuffles, the scrape of a chair or desk, drifted up from the First Form block below the staff room.

"I wonder how they're coping with the drought?" said Julia idly. "I heard that the Smiths and that nutter, Laurie, have already left."

This was really old news, having reached Mutamba a few days ago, but gossip was a huge source of entertainment in a world without television, movies or People magazine.

"The Smiths I can see," said Constance. "I knew they weren't long for this part of the world when I saw her washing a banana after she peeled it". They laughed, then quieted their voices as they heard the coughing and scraping below grow louder. "But what was Laurie's problem? I thought she was all set to be one with the people in a little hut out in the tribal trust lands somewhere?"

"Turns out her headmaster was hitting on her. Or so she claimed. I guess she only wanted to be one with the *povo* on a strictly theoretical basis. My guess, though," Julia paused to take a cigarette out of Mr. Karambira's desk. She offered one to Constance, who shook her head, no, and went on while rooting through the drawer, "my guess is she just couldn't stand to be stuck out there in the middle of nowhere, with a bunch of people who weren't interested in her self-righteous drivel. Hell, I can't find any matches in here. Which one's Alex's desk? He smokes."

"Down in the biology lab. It's probably locked."

"Well, you're on duty. Give me your keys."

Constance hesitated, then tossed over the keys that were lying by her feet. She wondered if the casual disregard Julia had for Alex's privacy implied a proprietary interest, but then she reminded herself that Julia had just ripped through Sampson Karambira's desk. A

60

slight, studious-looking man with grey hair and glasses, he taught A-level History and was an unlikely candidate for Julia's interest. Also, he had a very large and very formidable wife. Constance had once seen the two of them out in the yard beside their house. Mary vigorously chopped wood while several little children were wrestling in the dust. An older girl, hair beautifully braided, was polishing her school shoes on the stoep. Sampson was sitting in a kitchen chair, reading. He only looked up when Constance yelled out her greeting. Then his face was transformed by his smile.

Julia came back up the stairs into the staff room, carrying something. "Look! I found this in his desk."

"You were supposed to be looking for matches."

"Oh, right. And I found them, too." Julia tossed the keys back onto the desk, then fished into the pocket in her dress and pulled out the matches. She put the photograph down in front of Constance while she lit her cigarette.

It was a close-up of an extraordinarily beautiful woman. High cheekbones and dark, slightly slanted eyes. Delicate. Exotic. The woman was looking sideways into the camera. Her expression was unreadable.

"Who do you think she is?" Julia was adding to her sense of drama by whispering. "I bet you she's an old girlfriend."

"Not so very old, I think," said Constance. She showed Julia the writing on the back.

Like gold to aery thinness beat

"It's John Donne, The two souls are one and even if parted they stay —"

"I know its John Donne. *Forbidding Mourning*. I may be a Maths teacher, but there is more to me than quadrilateral equations. The question is," and Julia took the picture and turned it back over to show the beautiful face again "who was sadder about the parting, Mona Lisa here, or Alex?"

"What do you mean?"

"Who is the roaming compass point and who is the fix'd foot?"

"Isn't it obvious? Alex is the one who has left, and Mona sits in the centre, leaning and hearkening after him."

"Quit showing off. What about the next line 'And grows erect, as that comes home.' She chuckled. "That must refer to Alex, surely."

"Now look who's showing off."

They were startled to hear the bell ringing. Blessing, from the Form A1 class ran up and down the corridors, clanging joyously. In the same instant, the school erupted with banging of desks, laughter and chatter. Julia grabbed the keys off the desk.

"I'll hightail these back. Listen," she grabbed Constance's arm, "I know you have to get over to Amai Mushana's to pick up Miguel, but lets go to town together tomorrow. We'll hit the bank and then go to the Hotel for lunch. We can hitch a ride in the school bakkie and be back by four o'clock. Miguel can play with Mushana tomorrow."

Constance thought of the overflowing Milo tin. "Okay. What time do we leave?"

"At seven out by the magnolia tree. But I warn you, Brother Joseph is driving."

Brother Joseph leaned forward over the steering wheel and changed gears. The truck charged down a hill on the rutted road leading to Marondera. The goal seemed to be to drive as fast as possible, regardless of potholes, pedestrians, livestock or other vehicles. Approaching a herd of cows, Brother Joe leaned toward the dash, pushed insistently on the horn, yelling, "Get out of my way, you fecking mombes!" The bakkie swerved and thumped, just missing the back end of a cow too skinny and tired to care. Thankfully, the kids were faster to move out of the way. They scrambled to the side of the road, laughing and waving in the clouds of dust, as the old priest shook his fist and yelled, "Get off my road, you bloody baboons!" Constance was slightly shocked, but felt herself laughing nervously.

Beside her, Julia was holding her hat with one hand, with the other gripping the door handle, as she and Constance bounced and crunched into each other. No gracious waves to the povo today.

Constance was thankful that Miguel was safely back at the mission, herding cows with Mushana and not in the box, being thrown about with the mailbag and a broken generator.

The bakkie finally reached the tarred road, but, if anything, the journey became more frightening. There was more traffic and Brother Joe threw the engine into fifth gear, charging down the road, swerving left to right, overtaking other vehicles even on hills or corners, scattering both humans and animals in his wake. Constance kept her eyes on the fields whipping past at the side of the road. Msasa trees lined the road. Beyond, fields of maize and tobacco, undulating across the plateau, broken by the occasional kopje or dirt road winding down toward a large, white-washed farm house, clumps of huts. Some of the maize was being irrigated, other fields were waiting for the rains.

They were nearing Marondera. The msasa trees gave way to jacarandas in full bloom. The truck slowed with a lurch and turned left at the Marondera Hotel onto the main street of the town. Constance saw shops with tin roofs and wide, covered verandas and took in some of the signs as they rumbled by — Patels, Vandoro's, Barclays' Bank. She got Julia's attention and pointed.

"There are more white people here than I've seen in a long time."

Julia nodded, but Brother Joe spoke. "This is a very white town. Lots of prosperous tobacco farmers. Big country club, grand hotel, cinema." He charged through a traffic circle, cutting off another bakkie, filled with a load of farm workers, who laughed and gestured in response to his horn. "This was quite a troubled spot during the war. Known as "the terror triangle". Lots of farms from here to Rusape and up to Mrewa were hit and quite a number of whites killed."

They pulled up in front of the post office, braking at the last possible second. Shaken, Constance slid down off the seat after Julia and slung her pack across her shoulders. "I'll leave you two ladies so, and meet you back at the hotel when the shops have closed."

He strode off towards the post office, pausing to greet a group of young men lounging on the steps before disappearing inside. "Let's cut across The Green to the bank," Julia suggested. "I want to make sure I get my cheque cashed."

The park was empty except for a man they passed on the path and another who looked like a city employee — he was wearing a blue overall and was down on his hands and knees, cutting the grass with shears. More jacarandas, bougainvillea and frangipani.

They left the dappled shade of the park and were back in the glaring sunlight on the busy street. Marondera had a prosperous, though slightly shabby, old-fashioned look to it. There were many people on the sidewalk, some of them white, carrying large shopping baskets or sacks of mealie-meal on their heads. Constance looked longingly in the window of a craftshop, and was even able to stop for a few seconds and take in a display of baskets, drums, carvings and colourful batiks, before Julia hustled her off.

"Focus, Constance, focus. We can hit these stores on our way back to the post office."

"Okay, but I have to get those sandals."

"You won't get anything without some cash. Hopefully this won't take toooo long."

Constance's heart sank. The bank was packed, with long lines snaking back from the wickets to the doors. Many of the customers appeared to be employees of one sort or another, as they all wore the ubiquitous blue, red or green overall. Some had gumboots on, even though the temperature outside was probably now in the high 20's and the last puddle sighted in the country had been at least eight months ago. There were large canvas sacks in front of them on the floor, which they pushed along with their feet as the queue shuffled forward.

"I'm getting in line here," said Julia. "You're lucky. You get to go to that counter over there, " she pointed to New Accounts, "where you'll have to fill out reams of paperwork, but at least you get to sit down."

A handsome young man, well turned out from the top of his carefully cut hair to his polished black oxfords, introduced himself as Munorwe Simango. They exchanged greetings and Constance was offered a chair. She had heard horror stories about the bureaucracy in Zimbabwe, mostly from Dodie and the other Old Hands, and craning around to see the clock on the wall, she thought wistfully of the perfect little leather sandals in the window of the handicraft shop. She knew the stores closed early on Saturdays.

But Mr. Simango was the epitome of professionalism and efficiency. He filled out some forms, copying the numbers of her passport and residence permit neatly and quickly, had her sign them and then took her pay cheque over to one of the tellers — all men — and came back with some cash and a small red bankbook. Constance smiled as he came towards her and for the first time he broke into a smile — a wide smile with flashing white teeth that instantly transformed his face, like lifting the lid on a piano.

It was well after one o'clock when Constance and Julia made it over to the Marondera Hotel. Constance was lugging a huge laundry basket she had bought at the Jairos Jiri; inside were many bars of chocolate, a bag of nartjies, a loaf of crusty French bread, the Guardian newspaper and her old sandals. Julia was likewise burdened. She was carrying a toaster in one hand, in the other a bag of groceries from the Food Giant, which included several bottles of wine and a large pepperoni sausage.

They found the school truck in the parking area at the side of the hotel and deposited their loot. No need to lock up. Father Joseph was already parked on the veranda of the hotel. He was sharing a table with three young male teachers from the mission. It seemed they were already on their second round, as the table was littered with bottles. Chairs were shifted, another round of beer ordered and more cigarettes lit. Constance sat back in her chair, holding the chilled beer to her chest between gulps. Julia sat between Sydney Sekeramayi and David Mubvuma. They were also teachers in the Maths department and members of a larger group of male teachers known as "The Bachelors". They were both speaking very loudly, whether because of the music, the beer, or because they were vying for Julia's attention. Constance didn't know the other teacher, another one of The Bachelors, except by sight. He was chubby with a sleepy smile. He had a cross-shaped scar on his forehead.

The afternoon wore on, as afternoons in Africa often do. Lunch was brought to the table — steak, boerwoers rolls and chips — the ashtray was emptied several times and more drinks were brought. Chairs were shifted to follow the shade around the veranda. Constance, on a trip to the loo with Julia, wondered if Brother Joe would be able to drive.

"Don't worry. It actually improves under the influence. You'll see," said Julia.

It took a minute for Constance's eyes to adjust to the darker hallway inside the hotel. They were passing by what must be the pub. She paused for a moment, looking in at the white men sitting at the bar and the white men and a couple of white women sitting at the tables. There were two black people in the room — the bartender and a waiter in a white tunic and a red fez.

Constance turned to follow Julia. She collided with someone and jumped back in surprise, almost losing her balance. Two hands reached out and grabbed her waist and pulled her forward.

"Sorry about that. Are you alright, miss?"

"Yes, I'm fine. I didn't see you behind me. Sorry."

He smiled and thrust out his hand. "Name's James Fielding. I saw you sitting with Father Joe from Mutamba. Are you one of the new Canadian teachers?"

"Yes." My heavens, she thought. My first Rhodie! He has the khaki shorts, red face and those funny boots made out of some kind of endangered animal. "I'm Constance Marinatos." They shook hands.

"Hell of a hospitable country, isn't it, when you almost get knocked over on a trip to town, yah?"

She smiled. "It's been great. Everyone I've met so far has been very friendly."

"How long have you been here, then?"

"Three months. This is my first trip to town."

"You're a brave woman, riding in with Brother Joe. He once gave me lift when my bakkie broke down. A truly frightening experience."

"Get off my road, you bloody baboons!" Constance was a very good mimic and James Fielding threw back his head and laughed.

Everyone in the bar looked over at them. His laugh was loud and expressive.

"I'm here with my friend Julia" she paused and looked around fruitlessly, "and we thought we'd make a day of it."

Something passed across his face. "Yes, well. I saw you out on the stoep when I came in." He started to say something, then stopped. "I don't get into town much myself."

"So you don't live here in Marondera?"

"Hell, no. I've a farm near Macheke." James smiled again at her blank look. "Of course you wouldn't know it. About 40 kilometres from here, on the way to Mutare."

"What sort of farm?"

"Tobacco, mostly. But some maize. And we graze cattle."

Julia was coming down the hall towards them. She affected a look of girlish surprise as she came closer, but Constance had seen her toss her hair, a sure sign that she had spotted James.

Constance introduced them, then excused herself to go to the toilet. Returning a few minutes later, she was surprised to see James standing alone by the door to the bar. He stepped forward as she came closer.

"I wanted to make sure I saw you before you left. Can I see you next time you're in town?" He spoke quickly.

"I don't think so." She smiled to soften her rejection, but his face reddened and her own face was hot.

"I'm seeing somebody," she lied.

"Och, yes" he said, nodding. "Well, that's my bad luck." He thrust out his hand.

"Listen—"

"Cheers. I think you'd better hurry, your friend said she thought your lift was ready to leave."

Father Joe waved his cigarette at Constance, then took off in a roar of diesel fumes and dust. She began to lug her loot up the walk to her house. The sun was still strong, but a band of clouds was massing in the east. The air was still, the cicadas and birds silent.

Her head throbbed and she knew she had to have a cup of coffee before a migraine set in.

It was slightly cooler in her small, dark kitchen. Averting her eyes from the cockroach droppings littering the cupboard, she found the coffee and the only pot. Her hand shook as she turned on the tap. A gurgle and swish of air, then splat! A gush of brown water, which soon became a thin stream, but never mind. Constance put the pot down in the sink to fill while she lit the cooker.

She remembered her mail stashed in her pack. Here was a birthday card from her brother *"If you don't have a cake out there, I'll get one and eat your share"*, and a long letter from her father.

". . . so we hope to book our flights in the next couple of weeks. It's hard to believe it's only a few short weeks we'll be seeing you and Miguel again. We're bringing a bicycle for him. Let us know if there is anything else you need.

Your mother and I thought it would be worthwhile for you to buy a car. Not only will this make it easier for us to see the country on our safari, but it should be more convenient for you in general. So I'm enclosing a cheque (hope you can cash it) for this purchase.

I'm writing this while watching the hockey game and eating popcorn, so please excuse any butter smears on the page . . ."

The water was boiling. She took it off the stove and threw in some coffee.

Her mother had written in her large script at the bottom *"Constance, we're so excited about our trip. We're counting the days! Lots of love, Mom"*

Constance smiled to herself and picked up the cheque. Four thousand American dollars. She should be able to get a decent car, with lots left over. And it looked like her coffee was ready.

It turned out Julia had spilled the beans about her birthday. When she learned that Constance was turning 25, Miriam had gone around the mission inviting everyone to a party at her little house. The concept of "late notice" was foreign to Zimbabwe. Most people, blacks and whites, took life as it came. Any plans made were quickly and easily changed if something better came along. And what could better than a party, even if the birthday girl wasn't a close friend? So it was that later that night, Constance found herself sitting at a long table, borrowed from the dining hall, on Amai Mushana's veranda, surrounded by the teachers, workers and priests of the mission, watching as she tried to stop laughing long enough to blow out the candles on the lop-sided cake, covered in lurid green icing that Miriam had baked that afternoon in Mary Karambira's oven.

The party had started with Mr. Murerwa, in his Hawaiian party shirt, formally welcoming everyone, followed by a prayer, led by Lovemore Sibanda, a pretty young teacher from the religious education department.

"Dear God! We thank you for sending us Amai Miguel from Canada. Please bless her. Please bless her teaching. Give her strength and love to become a good teacher. Please bless this *mwana*, Miguel, and please bless her with many more children. In the name of the Father, Son and Holy Ghost, amen."

There was a brief moment of silence, broken by Miguel's clear, bell-like voice saying forcefully, "I'm not mwana, I'm mkomana!" (I'm not a baby. I'm a boy.)

Everyone laughed. Amai Mushana stood up, brandishing a bottle opener. "Please, everyone. Go and get some meat from the braai, which has been very generously donated by the Brothers," she pointed the opener at Brother Julius, "and I will now officially open the drinks!"

Constance found herself perched on the veranda wall between Mr. Musami, the owner of the Sunrise Bottle Store and Butchery, where she had cashed her cheques, and Mercy Dube, the school librarian. Preoccupied with trying to balance her plate of meat and sadza in one hand and her beer in the other, she missed something from Mr. Musami. He had a very strong accent and experience had taught her that she needed to give her full attention to him.

"I was asking if you were worried about coming here to Zimbabwe?"

"No, not at all." She picked up her meat and began gnawing at it.

"But what about the dissidents"

69

Constance looked blank, then turned to Mercy for help.

"He means the abductions, the kidnappings. There were six tourists taken from the road in August. They were on their way to Victoria Falls for sightseeing."

"Ah, yes, we heard about that before we left Canada. But isn't that an isolated case?"

"Not at all, not at all," said Mr. Musami. "These elements are many. They have deserted from the army and taken their weapons with them. Now they are moving around Matebeleland, killing and kidnapping the white farmers."

"Why?"

"They are dissidents!" said Mr. Musami forcefully. "They don't want to accept the election results. They have been plotting to overthrow Mugabe and hiding weapons on Nkomo's farms."

"So you're talking about the Ndebele."

"Yes, yes."

"No," said Mercy. "It's not that simple. They are former guerrillas – ZIPRA –and —"

"ZIPRA is the Zimbabwe Peoples Liberation Army. It is the military wing of ZAPU, the party of Joshua Nkomo," Constance murmured to herself.

"and they are angry because the government has arrested Dumiso Dabengwa and Lookout Masuku. These are two of their generals. So they are Ndebele, but not all Ndebele are running around kidnapping tourists."

"So what do you think will happen?" Constance turned her head from side to side to include both Mercy and Mr. Musami.

"Well, I hope that Nkomo and Mugabe could talk with each other, otherwise —"

"Otherwise, the government will have to act forcefully. We can not afford to have these elements causing problems."

Mr. Musami's raised voice caused several people on the other side of the steps to stop their own conversations and look over at them.

Mercy leaned towards Constance. "Let's not discuss this thing. This is a party, not a *pungwe* and we should not be lecturing you about politics."

Mr. Musami stood up. "Let me get you ladies another drink. Beer for you, Amai Miguel and do you want another Fanta, Amai Emmanuel?"

Constance posed for the camera. She pursed her lips exaggeratedly and waited, poised to blow out the candles. At the last second, just as Sampson Karambira went to snap the photo, she crossed her eyes and distorted her face into a grimace. The crowd laughed, then cheered and clapped as she blew out the candles.

Amai Mushana had exchanged her bottle opener for a knife, which she brandished happily as she shouted above the noise. "Before Amai Miguel cuts the cake, we will be having the Vote of Thanks from Alex. We have chosen him because he is not just her countryman, but because we can count on him to keep his words short and sweet." More laughter.

Smiling easily, Alex stepped out of the shadows. "I was warned about this." More laughter. "Now, if we could all make sure we have a bottle or glass of something in our hands." He waited while Friend, manning the beer and soft drink crates, handed round bottles.

"We want to thank Amai Mushana for organizing this wonderful party for Amai Miguel. We want to thank Miss Julia for telling us about Amai Miguel's birthday today. We want to thank the Brothers for the cow they donated for the braai. We want to thank Mr. Musani to helping out with the drinks. Mind you, we'll be passing the hat later to help reimburse him. So, those of you who have had lots to drink – not mentioning any names – " he pointed at The Bachelors – "must pay your fair share. But most of all," here he put his hand on Constance's shoulder "we want to thank Constance for coming to Mutamba School and bringing little Miguel with her. I, for one, don't know how we got along without them before this. So let's raise a glass to Amai Miguel and wish her Many Happy Returns".

"Many Happy Returns", everyone echoed. Some of the women began ululating. Alex raised his hand. "There's one individual I forgot. I suppose you'll want to thank Friend Tirivavi for offering to lend my stereo and cassettes for the dancing" (more laughter) "which will start NOW!"

At Bob Marley's urging everyone began to get up, stand up. Alex took Constance's hand and pulled her down the steps onto the packed red earth of Amai Mushana's yard. The clouds had vanished with the sunset and the stars shone down on the pulsating crowd. Men danced with men, women with women, children with children. Everyone left room for the matron, Amai Tendai, as she shimmied and waggled her large butt with extraordinary grace. Mary Karambira, her daughter Spiwe, and some other girls danced together in a line, feet moving in perfect split-second timing. Sampson and Mr. Okense, a refugee from Uganda, were pounding on drums and singing back-up with the Wailers. Alex pointed to Miguel, who was dancing in a circle with the little ones, a game where they each had a leg hooked around the straight leg of the child next to them. She smiled and grabbed his hands, wanting to hold him, to hold onto this perfect moment. He responded by pulling her against him.

They danced for a long time. Sometimes they moved apart. Alex was called over by some men and he joined their circle, their arms around each other, stamping, jumping and whirling. Constance danced with the women, trying, not very successfully, to copy their steps. Then the music changed again and she and Alex moved back towards each other.

As time wore on, the crowd on the veranda and down on the "dance floor" thinned. The Brothers had left first, along with the women with young children. Then, when the supply of drinks had been exhausted, there was a mass exodus of the men for The Sunset Bottle Store and Butchery. Most of the candles on the long table had burned down. Amai Mushana and a couple of young girls, nieces who stayed with her, began clearing the tables. Julia and David Mubvuma waltzed by. Julia tapped Constance on the shoulder and whispered "I'll take Miguel home with me tonight." Constance nodded, not wanting to say even to herself what this meant.

"Don't you want to go with the other men to the bottle store?" she said to Alex.

"Ssh," he murmured into her ear. He pulled her closer and hummed along with the music, *"oh, let the moon come shining in, into our life again"*. So their affair began on the night of her 25th birthday.

After they made love, Constance felt such a sense of relief that, to her shame, she began to cry. Curling away from Alex and the tangle of sheets, she held her hands over her face as sobs racked through her.

"Ssh, ssh," he murmured into her ear. He folded her into him. He drew her hands away from her face and stroked her cheeks. "It's okay, don't cry." The moon shone through the curtainless window. He did not ask her why she was crying. He continued to caress her. "You're beautiful. Your hair is beautiful."

After a few minutes she stopped crying and sniffling. He kissed her and then shifted in the bed. A little later she could hear his soft, sighing breath. She reached up and untied the mosquito net, spreading it around them. Then she too lay down and found sleep.

8

February, 2000

Macheke

The banner strung across the side of the Macheke Hotel read: *"A New Constitution, A New Era".* I turned the corner and drove up the road to the grocer's shop. I parked my old Volkswagen beetle by a newish Toyota Hilux with a campaign poster in the back window declaring *"We are proud to be Zimbabweans on our land -Vote Yes".* I climbed out, and pushed the front seat forward so Amai Mushana and Praxedis could get out.

"Listen, I have to get some things in here. You must walk over to the rally and back. James will kill me if I drive around town, wasting petrol. He had to queue six hours last week. Shall I meet you over there?"

"Oh, yes," said Praxedis. Miriam looked none too happy, but I said, "I'm going to leave the car here and walk over myself."

"Oh, yes," said Praxedis again. She bent over and slung the baby around to her back, tying him securely with her chitenge. "Come, Amai Mushana. We can toyi-toyi over there. We will be just like all the agitators from Harare."

This small town dhukan was like many others strung across Africa. A small, white-washed cement building, with a black line running across the bottom, tin roof, and cracked cement steps leading up to the veranda, on which an old man, the village tailor, sat working at his pedal sewing machine. We exchanged greetings in Shona and I noticed he looked older and shabbier than ever.

Jackie was sitting behind the wooden counter that ran around three sides of the room. Behind the counter, everything that the shop sold was piled onto shelves — without any attempt to organize or group items. Socks, tinned peaches and Dandy chewing gum on one shelf, soap, pens and flashlights on another. When I first came to Macheke, the shelves had bulged with tins and boxes, but now many were empty. I no longer bothered to make a list. "What have you got?"

Some matches, Pronutro cereal, a sack of maggoty flour, groundnuts, tea and some bags of kapenta for the workers. No cooking oil or mealie meal, paraffin or sugar — the staple grocery list of the average Zimbabwean.

"How are you managing?"

Jackie shrugged and took a deep drag on her cigarette. She had the freckled, doughy arms, badly permed hair and yellow teeth common to many whites. "We hang on. Jack is working as a farm manager for the Vanderhouks. You know, they have Lekkerwater farm." She leaned forward and said confidentially "It's basically slave wages."

I nodded sympathetically. Old Hermanus was known to be a hard taskmaster and he would have been quick to take advantage of the Maddox's hard times.

"We'd sell the shop but there wouldn't be any buyers. No one's got any money now, except" leaning closer again "the big men in Harare".

She came around the counter and over my protests, helped me carry my stuff to the car. Ephraim, the man who used to carry boxes, run errands and deliver groceries on his bicycle, had been laid off many months ago. I locked my baskets in the trunk.

"Can you watch the car from the shop? I'm going to walk over to the rally."

"To the rally! You're not serious? It's not safe, Constance."

"I'll be fine. I have some friends there and we're going to stay at the edge. Tsvangarai himself is supposed to be there."

§

76

There were many people heading toward the empty lot near the edge of town, next to The Hollywood Beauty Saloon (sic). I fell in beside a man who introduced himself as Chris. He wore a ball cap, dreadlocks and an Iron Maiden t-shirt. He pointed to a middle-aged woman in front of us wearing an MDC shirt.

"To wear an MDC shirt in this area," he said, shaking his head. "That is a very brave woman."

"But you're going to the rally yourself," I pointed out.

"Yes, indeed. But I can't wear one of those shirts. Someone told me that if I support the "No" side, I will be sorted out after the vote. I am going there very carefully. Because I can't agree with what is happening. I don't want Mugabe to stay."

The crowd at the rally was large, noisy and cheerful. Several entrepreneurs had set up makeshift stalls selling soft drinks, cigarettes and biltong. Hawkers roamed brandishing t-shirts in the MDC colours. Someone handed me a paper entitled "15 reasons to vote no!" Over at the edge of the plot, someone was roasting goat meat and hawking it.

I caught sight of Amai Mushana and Praxedis at the far side of the crowd, with a group of other women, some with babies. They were watching a group of young men dancing and singing around three drummers. As I got closer I could make out some of the Shona words "Mugabe is hanging on by a thread".

I had a hard time getting over to them. The crowd began shouting and running towards the centre of the field and I thought Tsvangirai had arrived. But no, a party official was handing out free MDC headbands. We stayed put on the sidelines and didn't join the melee.

"Who are they?" I shouted over the din, nodding toward two men and a woman in orange vests who were taking notes.

"They are from the Electoral Commission," yelled Amai Mushana. Her next words were drowned out in cries of "We want change!" A white Toyota Landcruiser had pulled up and Morgan Tsvangirai was getting out. There was a stampede towards him, people shouting *Chinja, Chinja* which even I knew meant Change, Change. Even I was caught up in the moment, waving my hands in the air in the open-handed salute of the MDC.

Tsvangarai stopped as the crowd broke into a song. Praxedis translated "How can we help Tsvangarai? Can we put him on our backs?" He was wearing a wide-brimmed leather hat with crocodile teeth around the rim. He grinned broadly and responded with the open salute. The crowd went wild and began ululating.

A battered chesterfield had been brought out from The Hollywood Saloon and dropped down under a msasa tree. The other women and I edged closer to hear the speeches, which began with several locals (I recognized my boss, Mr. Muzenda) acting as the warm-up act. They spoke in Shona and my attention wandered. Tsvangarai also looked bored. He rubbed his eyes and looked at his watch.

Amai Mushana took a packet of biscuits out of her basket and began offering them to everyone around her. Praxedis had slung Tapera around to nurse him. I looked idly over the crowd. I almost choked on my cookie when I saw a familiar red face under a battered terrycloth hat. My brother-in-law Scotty was standing smack dab in the middle of the crowd, arms folded across his chest. I waded through the crowd.

"What the hell are you doing here?"

"Lovely to see you too," he said. "I'm here to see what's up and give any support I can to this lot. I reckon Zimbabwe needs a man like Tsvangarai."

Well, well. Times have really changed. Scotty actually admires a black politician.

"You don't think he's a communist agitator?"

"He probably is, but at this point he's the lesser of two evils, isn't he? With any luck it'll take him another twenty years to become as corrupt as that bugger Mugabe."

Well, well. Times have kind of changed. Scotty sort of admires a black politician.

It was Tsvangirai's turn now, and he perked up. He grabbed the loudspeaker and ranged it over the crowd. "The people have not lost their talent or resolve. — but the leaders have lost the people," he shouted to tumultuous approval. "We must stop the bleeding in this country. We must defeat this referendum and this so-called constitution." He paused dramatically. There were cries of *Chinja* and *Zvakwana* (Enough is Enough). "ZANU is still using violence and intimidation, but we are going to surprise them by defeating this referendum and then we are going to get a majority in parliament." Roars from the crowd. "It is time to stop the plundering of the rich resources and skills in Zimbabwe for those few rich and time to direct them to the talents of the many. It is time for us to deal with the poverty and degradation in our country. It is time for us to pull out of that crazy war in the Congo. Zimbabwe has no business there. It is time for Mugabe to go back to his own area and rest." Laughter, cheers and ululating from the crowd. People began chanting and singing, their hands raised in salute.

Scotty shifted uneasily. "Something's wrong."

"What do you mean? They're just happy."

"No, something's wrong. Listen."

I listened. Maybe he was right. People were still chanting and singing, but there was a crosscurrent coming closer. I could hear shouts of "Mugabe, Mugabe," and "ZANU-PF". Screams and shouts were coming from the edge of the crowd. Tsvangarai raised his bullhorn again.

"Mugabe's youth wing thugs are here. We will not be intimidated, but we don't want any violence. Please everyone; let us leave this place peacefully. We want you all well and able to get to the polling stations on February 12th. Thank you. Zvakwana!" He handed off the loudspeaker and was hustled away. I lost sight of him.

The crowd was getting rough, as people jostled those in front to move back out onto the road. The screaming and shouting were getting louder and closer. People began running by us. A couple of them were wearing orange vests.

Scotty grabbed my arm and began pulling me in the other direction.

"Wait. I have to find Miriam and Praxedis." Someone pushed me forward and I almost lost my footing.

"Don't be foolish, woman! Get out of here, before you get beat up."

"No, I can't leave without them. Scotty, Praxedis has her baby with her! We have to look for them."

He hesitated, his face set and angry. Then I saw his face go white. Or at least as white as a face can that has spent too many years under the African sun drinking whiskey.

A tall black man wearing aviator sunglasses — one of the essential fashion accessories of the African thug — had grabbed another man and knocked him to the ground with a knobkerrie. He continued to beat the man who was writhing on the ground, trying to shield his head with his hands.

Scotty grabbed my arm and pulled me. We followed the hysterical people. I was sure the thugs would catch up to us. We reached the edge of the field and stopped to jump over the drainage ditch. Some frantic person behind me couldn't stop in time and smacked into me, pushing me into the ditch. I slid down into it, my thigh scraping on the exposed roots of a gum tree. Scotty, already on the other side, turned and waited. When I was close enough, he reached down and pulled me up, grunting.

I looked around, hoping to see Miriam and Praxedis. People were still running by me, screaming, but the crowd was thinner now and I could see more clearly. ZANU-PF had driven an estate car across the narrow road leading onto the field and the only way out was over the ditch. The militia must have realized this and we could see a group of them running towards us, swinging their knobkerries above their heads. Some young men had picked up rocks and were chucking them at the militia. They were shouting in Shona.

The rest of the crowd turned away from the village and began back toward us. I looked around wildly.

I could see Scotty yelling something at me, his hands cupped around his mouth. He pointed to some women climbing over the barbed-wire fence on the other side of the road. We pushed our way across the current of the crowd. The women already there were holding the loose fence down so others could climb over. We took our turns and stayed there, pushing the fence down, until the militia broke through the line of stone-throwers and began heading up the road.

We turned and ran through the field, then cut back onto road and around the corner, past the hotel and over to the station. The crowd had thinned, but there were still people running by, wailing. Some had blood streaming down from gashed heads. A few people were milling around on the stoep of the hotel, watching curiously. I leaned against one of the pillars, shaking.

"Christ!" Scotty's face was as red as I'd ever seen it.

"Where are Amai Mushana and Praxedis?" I croaked. "God, I hope they made it back to the car okay. Knowledge will kill me if anything happens to Praxedis or the baby. They were near the edge of the crowd, so I think they must be okay. Let's go find them."

Scotty nodded, still gasping for breath. I thought about leaving him to look for my friends, but he was already straightening up a bit.

"Thanks for pulling me out of that ditch back there."

"Ach, well, that's the last time I'll ever tell James you're too skinny. Hauling you up took all my strength."

I smiled weakly. The banner across the street at the hotel caught my eye. Someone had got the last word. *"A New Constitution, A New Error"*.

9

"Welcome back, madam," the desk clerk smiled at Constance. Looking down at Miguel, "Hello, my friend."

"We're here to pick up my grandma and grandpa," announced Miguel. "We're going to take them on our holiday. Where are they?"

"Ah, yes, your grandparents." He winked over Miguel's head. "They are a bit excited to see you, too. I think they might be out in the garden by the pool, having some drinks." He winked again, this time at Miguel. "I believe they have something for you."

"Did they get my message? I wanted to meet them at the airport, but —"

"there was a problem with petrol. I don't know, madam. They came here yesterday evening in a taxi."

Miguel was pulling on her skirt. He ran ahead of her, through the French doors and out into the garden. The brick path led to a small swimming pool. Miguel still remembered it from last August.

Constance immediately spotted her parents, sitting at a small patio table, reading. Her mother, small, in a khaki skirt and t-shirt, heavy beaded necklace, a straw hat on her permed brown hair, sunglasses. Her father, in jeans and striped shirt, thick grey hair and eyebrows. No hat or sunglasses for him.

They were already up, embracing and crying hello to Miguel. Two white couples, sitting on the edge of the pool, watched curiously.

"And Connie!" said her mother, hugging her. "We knew you would find us eventually. Didn't I tell you, Nico? I told you Connie would find us?"

Her father put down Miguel to give her his bear hug. "I didn't doubt it for a moment, Hannah."

"Didn't you get my message? I hoped someone at the airport would let you know that I couldn't be there."

"We didn't hear a thing," said her father. "We sat around at the airport for a while, wondering what to do."

"It was a nightmare," interjected Hannah. "We didn't have a clue, we sat there like zombies. I was so exhausted I ended up taking a piece of cardboard I found behind the luggage carousel and sleeping on the floor."

"Oh, dear," said Constance weakly.

"Then a nice little girl came over and helped us out. Got us into a taxi and told the driver to bring us here to this hotel. Then I called the school, but one of the Brothers there said you'd already left."

"How did you find us?" cried her mother. "I thought we'd have to get on a bus and travel down to that god-forsaken place you're living."

"But the man at the front desk here is really on the ball. He recognized our names from when you stayed here in August. He remembered Miguel. He said you'd find us."

"Well, there are only two or three hotels that white people stay at, so it was just a matter of time before I tracked you down. It's this petrol shortage. The ANC blew up an oil storage tank in Mozambique, so the South Africans are restricting the supply to Zimbabwe."

"Well, sit down, sit down," said Hannah. "Nico, order us some more drinks. Miguel, did you bring your bathing suit? You can go for a swim in this beautiful pool. Isn't this place beautiful, Connie?"

Miguel said something in a thick Shona accent. Hannah stared at him.

"He's asking for his suit. It's okay, Mom. All the little white kids who hang out with Africans start talking like that." She turned to Miguel. "Get our bag out of the car. I'm going to have a drink with Grandma and Grandpa. Do you want a Fanta?"

Miguel dashed off. Nico looked around. "Oh, good, there's that nice little girl who brought us our drinks before. What'll you have, Connie? I'll have another beer, what was it called? Castle? Okay, I'll have another Castle. Connie? A gin and tonic? Ah, just like your mother. And a Fanta for my grandson. And have you got any peanuts?"

"We're so excited about seeing Zimbabwe!" Hannah handed the waitress the empty bottles. "Nico, move your chair over, the sun is in my eyes again."

"It's okay, Mom, just change places with me."

"No, no, you're photosensitive, just like me. Let your father face the sun. He's got brown eyes. Look, here comes Miguel. Nico, take a picture of Miguel by the swimming pool. Make sure you get that tree in the background."

"Connie, you get in the picture, too. What about you, Hannah?"

"No, no, not me. God, I look terrible. Yes, that's right, but make sure you're close enough."

"Get closer together. That's right, Miguel. Smile. Just a second. Oh, this is going to be good. Karsh, eat you heart out. Smile. Great."

"We're so excited about seeing your car!" greeted Hannah the next morning as Constance came in to breakfast. "We're all packed and ready to go. Nico, did you get them to leave our bags in the reception?"

"Those are your bags?" said Constance. "I thought they belonged to a tour group. Mom, there's no way we can get all those bags, plus you and Dad, plus a bicycle, into a Volkswagen Beetle!"

Hannah turned to her husband. "I told you to send her enough money to get a decent car. Honestly, Nico, we're not paupers."

"I have a decent car," said Constance. "We'll just have to leave the bike, that's all. No, it's okay," she said to Miguel. "The hotel will look after it and then we can fetch it when we bring Grandma and Grandpa back to Harare."

"What a smart idea! You wouldn't be able to ride your bike anyway while we're traveling. Nico, go and ask that nice man at the front desk to look after Miguel's bicycle. Look at that buffet! Unbelievable. Come on Miguel, what would you like to eat?"

"Nico, don't let me eat like that ever again. Why on earth would they be serving all that food at breakfast? Well, at least we won't have to have any lunch. In fact, I'm good for the rest of the day."

In the front seat, Constance and her father exchanged glances. They were heading south out of the city on Samora Machel Avenue. Constance, aware that she was not a good driver at the best of times, gripped the steering wheel and tried to keep pace with the rest of the traffic. In the back seat, Hannah had the map spread out on her lap. Miguel was perched in his favourite spot, between the back seat and rear window.

The road was good. Two-laned and tarred, it left the city, passing signs for the former white suburbs of Borrowdale and Newlands. Sometimes they caught glimpses of the large bungalows and gorgeous gardens — not just purple jacarandas, but also the wonderful pink, yellow and orange bougainvilleas, the creamy flowers of the frangipani, the shocking red of the tulip trees. Her mother was even now gushing over the flame trees along the sides of the road.

On the left they passed a former "African township" now renamed a "high density suburb." Impossibly small, tin-roofed houses laid out in neat lines, every house surrounded by small yards, planted with maize. The maize looked brown and dispirited in the hot sun.

"Look at those trees." Nico pointed to a grove curving from the road back towards the hills. "What are they, oranges?"

"Oranges, grapefruit, avocado, mango. All these farms we'll pass now are owned by whites."

"Can you stop? I want to get a picture of that. Hannah, can you hand me my camera?"

"And get Miguel and Constance in the picture. Miguel, climb out, that's a good boy. Nico, lift him over the fence. Here, Constance, I'll hold it down while you climb over. Careful, don't tear your dress. Nico, make sure you get close enough. Wait, I'm going to climb over. Nico, lift me over. Here, Miguel you hold this while Grandpa takes a picture."

"For heaven's sake, Mom, you can't just take an avocado off the tree like that!"

"Why not? It's just one. Isn't it gorgeous? I've never seen one this big or this smooth. Look at it. I love avocados. Hold it up a bit higher, Miguel. No, a bit lower, we want to see your face. Constance, kneel down. Get closer, Nico."

"Oh, that's a beauty. Karsh, eat your heart out. Smile."

"Mom! Stop picking those. Do you want to get me deported?"

"Don't worry. I just wanted a couple more for lunch. We should stop for beer in the next town."

It was dark when the little Volkswagen rumbled up in front of the hotel at the Great Zimbabwe Ruins. The five passengers couldn't wait to get out, but on the other hand, were so shattered they could hardly move. Though no one said anything; they were all good and fed up with each other.

The trip should only have taken about five hours, but Hannah had insisted they stop for lunch and a beer or two in Gweru. Then south of Gweru, Nico had wanted a photo of Miguel beside an enormous anthill Hannah had spotted by the side of the road. Hannah had insisted they stop for a break (more beer) in Masvingo. Outside of town, Nico had spotted someone by the side of the road selling drums.

"Dad, there's no way we're going to be able to fit that into the car," Constance protested feebly. "Look at it. And how on earth are you going to get it home?"

"I'll put it between my legs there in the front seat. I really want that drum for your brother, he'll love it."

Constance and Miguel wandered up the road a little way, while her father haggled with the drum maker. They were approaching the lowveld and it was much drier and hotter here. Two little ragged girls came out from behind a tree. They had some bananas for sale. They spoke in careful, singsong English. "Good morning, madam. How are you? I am fine." Miguel began talking to the kids in Shona. She walked back towards the car to find some water. Now Hannah was organizing a photo. She wanted Nico to take a picture of the drum maker with his wares. A lorry roared by on its way to Birchenough Bridge, covering them with dust. Constance found the water behind the front seat and took a few sips, saving the rest for Miguel. She wished her parents would hurry up. It was so hot. The shadows were beginning to stretch and soon it would be getting dark.

Her father finally paid for the drum. Good, they could go. But no, now Hannah wanted him to take a picture of Miguel and the little girls. Miguel was only too happy to translate for her.

"You, vasikana! My sekuru will take your photo. Stand here."

The girls came forward, tittering. They were both thin, with large eyes and braided hair. They had outgrown their dresses, which were the same colour as the hard dust blowing along the side of the road and across the scrubland. This area was part of the old TTL, the Tribal Trust Lands, renamed the Communal Areas. This was hardscrabble land, poor soil, poor rains, over-crowded, over-grazed. They easily and naturally put their arms around Miguel while the photo was taken.

"What are your names?" asked Constance.

They were called Nyarai and Dambudzo.

Did they go to school?

Yes. The smaller one, Dambudzo was in Standard Three, Nyarai was in Standard Five.

Were they sisters?

They laughed. Yes, sisters.

Constance bought some bananas. When she held out the coins they clapped their hands twice quickly, and then held out their cupped hands, bowing slightly.

Hannah worried about leaving two small children in such a god-forsaken place.

Did they need a lift?

They laughed and pointed through the thornveld. No, they lived just over there. They could walk to the place.

But they made no move to leave, watching as Constance and her family climbed back into the car. They waved and called "Good bye, good bye!" as they became smaller and smaller in the rearview mirror.

Constance climbed out of the bath, feeling like a new woman. Miguel had finished jumping on the bed and was now kicking his soccer ball out on the veranda. She wrapped a towel around herself, and lay spread-eagled on the bed.

The old wing of the hotel consisted of the reception, bar and several rooms, each with a door leading onto the L-shaped veranda. Peacocks roamed the grounds, shrieking and jumping up onto the thatched umbrellas and tables on the patio. The dining room was in a separate building and at seven o'clock each evening, one of the waiters would walk up and down the veranda, calling the guests to dinner on a xylophone. On Saturday nights there would be a braai down by the pool, followed by a movie.

She forced herself up. Her parents would not want to miss anything. They were probably already in the bar, having their sundowners. Her mother would be gushing about the hotel and her father would be trying talk to the waiter about politics in that slow, loud voice he used whenever he left Canada. Constance had heard him use that voice to order beer and chat up the locals in France, Russia and Ireland.

She had noticed some postcards for sale in the reception. She would buy one to send to Alex, though he wouldn't read it until he got back to the mission in January.

The postcards were displayed on a rack in the corner. Going closer, Constance could see that each slot held exactly one card and that there were only three choices — all views of the Ruins in rather odd, lurid colours. She chose one — it showed a sort of stone tower, half hidden by a large msasa tree — and then bought six more cards for her father.

Her parents had happily colonized the only overstuffed armchairs in the lounge. Their books, drinks, a dish of peanuts, Hannah's hat and sunglasses, Nico's camera and a deck of cards were strewn across the table in front of them. Miguel was sitting up at the bar, chattering to the barman.

"Connie, we've saved you a place. Sit down. You must be exhausted after all that driving. Isn't this place gorgeous? I love those peacocks. Nico, order Connie a drink. We're just hoping to get a few hands of bridge in before supper," Hannah leaned forward and lowered her voice "but we don't have a fourth. Do you think that man at the bar might play?"

Constance looked over, past Miguel. Large, stolid, khaki shorts and shirt, veldskoens. A bit like that farmer she had met in the hotel in Marondera. She turned urgently back to her mother.

"Mother! That man is a Rhodie. We don't want to get stuck with him all evening. I don't care how much you want to play bridge."

"I'm not thinking of me, I was thinking of you. I thought he looked sort of nice."

"Nice until he opens his mouth. He and Dad would get into a shouting match before the cards had even been dealt. Those people aren't very bright. I bet the only card game he knows is 'Go Fish'."

Just at that moment, the Rhodie, who had probably sensed them looking at him, turned and raised his glass. He caught Constance's eye and said, "Cheers."

She felt herself redden and dropped her gaze. Hannah was thirstily drinking this all in.

This would have been a good time to say "And anyway, I already have a boyfriend." But she didn't. The waiter was coming over with their drinks and anyway, she wasn't really sure of her claim on Alex. He had casually, and, she thought, coolly informed her that he would be canoeing in the Okavango over the long break. Of course, it made sense in one way. Her parents were coming and they would take up most of her time, but still, it would have been nice if there had been some note of longing or regret in his voice. Waking on their last night together, she had reached out for him and found his place empty.

He was in the lounge, lying on his stomach on the floor, books spread around him, making notes. His pack was propped up against the wall, already bulging.

"You're up early."

He raised his head and shifted onto his other elbow. "I need to leave by first light. I want to get to Maun by nightfall."

"I'm glad I woke then. Do you want some coffee?"

"Sure, that would be great." But it sounded to her as if he was going through the motions. He probably wished she had stayed soundly asleep until he made his escape. He could have closed the door quietly behind him, hoisted his pack over his shoulder and taken off down the road, whistling.

They had sat side by side on the sagging red velvet chesterfield, sipping coffee. Constance was flicking through *Trees of the Okavango Delta*, wanting to reach out and hold Alex's hand, but he had gone back to making notes. She glanced back down at the page, which showed a tall palm tree on the banks of a river, and two close-up drawings: a large, fan-like leaf and a branch clustered with round, brown nuts. She showed him the lovely black and white line drawing of a curled mopane leaf. "Oh, Alex, I wish I was going with you!"

He made a small laughing sound in his throat. "You'll get there some day. This is my second time and I can't wait to get back. Miguel would love it."

"Maybe we can plan to go together next time."

He made the same small laugh in his throat. "Maybe." He put down his notebook and pulled her down into him. *Trees of the Okavango Delta* fell out of her hand onto the floor. "I will miss you, you know." He began kissing her, sliding his hands down her back, lifting her t-shirt. She felt herself melting into him. It was a relief to not to feel sad or uneasy for these moments. She felt she was gliding in the Okavango in a mokoro, she imagined the palm trees, the sunset, the elephants reaching up to browse on the fruit. She remembered a song her mother hummed sometimes. *See the pyramids along the Nile; watch a sunset from a desert isle.*

Constance had always been disappointed with ancient ruins and monuments. Having seen the pyramids and sphinx depicted as lonely icons in the desert sands, with, at most, a Napoleonic soldier or a camel to show the scale, it was unnerving to see the real things, engulfed by the suburb of Gizeh, crawling with throngs of tourists, while men in tatty jebayas hawked souvenir papyrus scrolls, miniature replicas of King Tut's burial mask or rides on mangy camels. The Acropolis was not a glorious white marble wonder, but had been infested with so many tourists it was impossible to snap a photo of the Parthenon before some straw-hatted, chubby German or American stepped into the frame. This was not a problem at Stonehenge, where visitors were kept well away from the stones and herded like the members of some pagan cult around the perimeter of the site in counter-clockwise formation.

Apart from her postcards and a drawing in the From One history textbook, Constance had never seen any pictures or drawings of the ruins of Great Zimbabwe, though her professor in her African history course had described them, inaccurately, it would turn out. The hotel had on its walls some lovely watercolour prints of various views of the Ruins, but Constance was not about to be fooled again. She debated whether or not to take her camera. She didn't have much film and she wanted to make sure she saved some for Victoria Falls.

Because of the on-going petrol shortage, the hotel, which was within walking distance of the Ruins, was not full. The only other guests seemed to be the Rhodesian from the bar and a youngish South African couple with two small children. Hannah had struck up a conversation with the parents and Miguel had played with the children at breakfast, but Constance pointedly ignored the whole family, though only after making sure that they knew she was working at a "local" school. It was important to her to distinguish herself from the local whites.

"I don't think you've got much to worry about on that score," said her mother, as they wandered over to the Ruins after breakfast. "Look at that bee-hive! And those" she hesitated, searching for a word "those slacks. Don't these people know anything? Who wears polyester in this heat?"

"Shh, Mom." The South Africans were just ahead of them and Hannah had a voice that carried.

"But really," Hannah lowered her voice a tad, "don't you think it's interesting that their racial policies and their fashions are about twenty years out of style? There's a masters thesis here, Constance, just waiting to be written. *Bouffant Hair and the Broederbond: How White South Africans Maintain Their Ugly Separation.* I swear, that woman is wearing a girdle under those things."

The Ruins were not at all what Constance had expected, but everything she had hoped for. They were quiet, except for the whirr of the cicadas. They paid their entrance fees at the National Park office, a small thatched building and were directed toward the path that led up to the top of the hilltop ruin.

"You can take the new route to the top, but I think you will be wanting to go the old way," said the warden. He eyed Nico and Hannah. "It is more steep, but I think you are still quite vigorous."

It took Constance a few seconds to see what the warden was talking about. The hill was like thousands all across the country — maybe a bit larger — a red and green hill with granite jutting out all over it. She looked in the direction he pointed and could just make out that some of the granite was a series of narrow stone steps, winding up the kopje. The greyish-red granite, over-grown with grass, blended in beautifully with the hill itself. The steps were curved and worn like the hill, in no hurry to get to the top. Miguel was enchanted. He ran ahead and began clambering.

The adults followed more sedately, but they all felt the growing excitement the true explorer feels. The old trail was indeed steep and they stopped a couple of times at Hannah's request.

"Nico! Take a picture from here. The view is breathtaking. Connie, get in the picture. Where's Miguel?"

As they neared the top, they could see the walls of the Ruin, loping along the crest of the hill. Like the steps, they so marvelously

93

blended in with the rock and soil around them; a careless eye could have easily missed them.

They spent a wonderful morning exploring the kopje. The walls, about shoulder-height circled up and down and curved back upon themselves, making smaller enclosures. Low, narrow archways in the walls, dirt paths and rounded stone steps beckoned them on. In some places they were in one enclosure, looking down into another as if from a balcony. They came upon an iron smelter in a place where the granite floor was smoother and flatter. Looking up, they could see a high, crumbling wall. Behind it, was a massive boulder. It had been split and shaped by the searing sun and cold nights into a cubist sculpture. Miguel recognized it immediately.

"The Zimbabwe bird!" he shouted. "Look, Grandma, the Zimbabwe bird." And he began singing. *See the water in the river. See the big Zimbabwe bird. They are calling for a new life. In the new land of Africa.*

Miguel's perfect little voice drifted across the still air, mixing with the singing of the cicadas. Nico and Hannah clapped. Then they hoisted Miguel up onto an outcrop to immortalize the moment ("Eat your heart our, Karsh"). Constance looked out over the veldt. Off in the distance, part of the brown scrub and msasa trees, she could make out a round stone wall. Soon they would go down there and explore and Nico would take more photos.

10

April 2000

Macheke

I was in the kitchen, chopping onions, when I heard a soft knock on
the doorframe. It was Sunday afternoon and Tatenda's day off, so I
was responsible for getting supper. Amai Mushana's grandson,
Kazana was at the door. I stepped over Lady, the old border collie,
who opened one eye and looked without interest at Kazana.

"Evan isn't here, Kazana. I think he's over at the cattle dip with
his brother and Baba Miguel."

"I have not come to see Evan. I have been sent by Ambuya to
fetch you. My mother is very ill." Kazana stepped into the kitchen
and waited as I took off my apron. He sidled over to the table and
pocketed a rare apple. When I smiled and nodded, he took another
and began eating.

I had not seen Miriam since the day of the rally. I had kept busy
around the house and at school. At the school break, our family had
gone to stay at a cottage in Nyanga, where the boys and James had
gone fly-fishing. The days passed quickly and the nights were
becoming cooler now.

It would have been nothing for me to have walked over to Amai
Mushana's house after supper, to join her at her fire for a cup of tea
and a packet of biscuits. But, and this was a feeling I had not voiced
to anyone, the violence at the MDC rally had shaken me. Of course,
I wasn't stupid. I knew these things happened, had been happening
for years, but at a distance and easily dismissed as the usual moaning

95

by the whites. But to see the citizens of Macheke, people I had lived and worked among, being harassed and beat up by Mugabe's thugs was a shock. It was like one of those moments when one looks in the mirror and sees, not the young woman one has looked at for years, but an old hag, with wrinkles and grey hair. And even more galling was the fact that Scotty had rescued me from the chaos. I knew I was being petty, but I dreaded the moment I would have to face his "I told you so."

Once upon a time Kazana's mother had been called Agnes. The Agnes I remembered was chubby, dark-skinned, wearing purple plastic sandals and braids that looped and stuck out from her head. When she was still in her teens her first child was born. She became Amai Kazana and I never heard the name Agnes again.

It took a minute or two for my eyes to adjust to the dark of the hut. I groped my way to the back where I knew she would be lying on a metal cot. I could make out a small mound of blankets, then I realized the small mound was Amai Kazana. I knelt by the bed and touched her shoulder. It was like touching the bone directly, there was nothing between my fingers and her shoulder blades. She was shivering. Her eyes were open, but unseeing. She did not acknowledge my presence in any way.

Kazana placed a stool behind me. I sat and reached under the blanket for his mother's hand. "Where is the mwana?"

It turned out the baby had become the toddler I had almost tripped over when I first came into the hut. Miriam had swept it up, crying, and taken it outside. I reached under the blanket and took Amai Kazana's hand. My eyes adjusted to the dark. I could see two more small cots placed against the walls. On a shelf was a sack of mealie meal, bottle of cooking oil, tea, some yellow metal bowls and cups. Below was a small kerosene stove, but most meals were cooked outside over the fire. There was a table, covered in a spotless tablecloth, three chairs and a tall bureau with framed photos crowded on top. I remembered the neat little house at the mission, the long table on the veranda, my friend with her happy, healthy children. I remembered Miguel and Mushana playing football in the red dust, walking hand in hand to school. Now Miguel was at university in British Columbia. Mushana was dead. For the past 15 years I had been living a dream, eating my meals on a shady veranda, prepared and served by servants, the rose trellis shading me tended to by the gardener.

"How many people have to share those beds in there?" It was hard to keep track of the members of Amai Mushana's household. Sisters, daughters, grandchildren, nieces and nephews came and went, often leaving my friend with another mouth to feed. A grandniece, say, from Masvingo, would show up, pregnant. Her body would be thin, racked by tuberculosis. If she didn't miscarry, the baby would most likely be born early. Within a year, both the grandniece and baby would be dead, the older children left as orphans.

Miriam shrugged. "The picannins sleep where they can. I sometimes think I'm running a hospital here. As soon as one bed is empty, we fill it with another patient."

I didn't suggest the Marondera hospital. Everyone knew the wards were chaotic, jammed with Aids cases.

I could still feel Amai Kazana's hand in mine. "What can I do?"

She shrugged again. "We need too much," using the phrase too much in the Zimbabwean way, meaning a lot. "Medicines, food, money. Anyway, it's too late for her."

I tried to imagine saying that about one of my children. It's too late for him. I stood there awkwardly. "I'm so sorry, Miriam. You're an angel."

She waved that away. "Not at all. This is simply what it has come to. I do my best."

At that moment the baby ran up to us, chasing a chicken and I had an excuse not to meet Miriam's eyes.

"What about the baby? Has she been tested?"

"No. She is very healthy so far. And if she does have the disease, we would not be able to do anything for her. There are no treatments here."

"What is her name?"

"Nyarai."

"It's a fine name." We stood silent for a moment, watching the baby trundle around the yard. The chicken disappeared into the

97

maize patch and Nyarai ran back to her ambuya, throwing her arms around her legs. The eyes that peered up at me from around the corner of Amai Mushana's skirts were clear and bright.

Miriam leaned towards me and confided, "Sometimes I don't do my best. Sometimes I want to give up. I am just muddling through."

"I haven't been a good friend to you."

She waved that away too. "We could all be better angels."

11

December 1982

Constance, Miguel, Nico and Hannah took the overnight steam train from Bulawayo. Fifty Zim dollars bought a private berth. A serviceable relic, the taps that poured water into the mahogany sinks in the berths still bore the stylized monogram of the Rhodesian Railways. Though it was the height of the long holiday season and the road through Hwange to The Falls still considered dodgy after the August kidnappings, the first class section of the train was almost empty and they were the only customers in the dining car. After an unpretentious meal of steak and chips, they felt no compulsion to leave their table. Nico ordered another round of beer. Hannah and Miguel began a game of Crazy Eights. Constance wrote another card to Alex.

We're on the train to Victoria Falls — saving petrol. Enjoyed Bulawayo. Having lots of fun. My parents are born tourists — taking loads of photos and buying souvenirs like crazy. Miguel is great. He says hello.

It took her several minutes to write those few lines. The knowledge that Alec wouldn't get the card until after they both returned back to school after the break, and the possibility that he might even collect it out of his mail slot in the staff room and read it in front of her during morning tea break, made her choose her words carefully. She wanted to adopt the right tone — casual but with a hint of intimacy. She thought for a moment, then added

I wish I was lying beside you under the stars of the Okavango.

She had to cram this last bit in at the bottom. She hoped he would be able to read it.

The knock at the door woke her. It was one of the stewards, bringing tea. She pulled on shorts and a t-shirt, her Marondera sandals and stepped out into the corridor. She pulled down a window and leaned out, sucking in the fresh, bright African morning. The thornbrush swept along, patches of dry red earth, yellow grass, scrubby bushes. A troop of baboons jostling around a water tank, looked up at the train as it passed by. Miguel came out onto the corridor, followed by Hannah and Nico, both with cups of tea. Constance held Miguel up to the window and moved to make room for her parents. They stood watching for a few moments and she was about to put Miguel down when she felt him squirm. He pointed to a group of three giraffes loping along, red dust rising from their hooves. Constance knew she was seeing a cliché; that this was not the "real" Africa, but she felt herself responding whole-heartedly to the moment. Listening to Miguel and her parents chattering about the giraffes ("Nico, you should have had your camera!") she smiled, not cynically, but with pleasure. She knew that this moment would become part of family memory and would be reminisced about over and over. *"Remember the time we saw those giraffes from the window of the train. We were on our way to Victoria Falls, remember?"* And each of them would see the bushveld streaming by the train, the red earth and the thorn trees, the giraffes, just as it was at that moment. They would speak with regret and nostalgia about the passing of the steam train, with sadness about the "discovery" of The Falls as a tourist destination. What they would also be remembering and regretting was the loss of their younger selves.

Constance had written the truth to Alex. Her parents were born tourists. Every roadside craft stall was worth a look, every fellow traveler might be the source or recipient of an anecdote, every sunset was another photo. No bar was too dingy if it held the promise of a cold beer. Victoria Falls was heaven made for them. The long, winding path down to Zambezi gorge. The exotic rainforest. The huge expanse of The Falls, even in the drought. The dozens of viewpoints, great backdrops for yet another picture of Miguel. The giant baobab and the statue of Livingstone.

They spent the entire day walking the trail along the Zimbabwean side, bargaining with a young man selling a huge wooden giraffe at the foot of the hotel path ("Dad, how on earth are you going to get that thing on the plane?"), clambering up and down the steps to The Devil's Cataract, pausing to read every metal identification tag on the trees and bushes in the forest, chatting up another middle-aged couple wearing Tilley hats and socks with their sandals, discovering they were from Regina! And also visiting their daughter who was also a teacher! Yes, her name was Margaret. No, she hadn't come with them to The Falls; they had flown here from Harare yesterday. Margaret was spending the break teaching English to Mozambicans in the refugee camps on the border in Manicaland.

"A refugee camp!" said Hannah. "That sounds so interesting. What was it like?"

Margaret's parents hadn't been there, so had no idea, really. It sounded as if they were in no hurry to find out.

"Oh, but you should go!" cried Hannah. "What an experience. Your daughter surely wants to share it with you."

"Well, Hannah," said Nico jovially. "You're a nurse. You could probably volunteer yourself."

Constance had an image of her mother sweeping through a refugee camp, jabbing people left and right with a needle, while Nico took photos.

Well, Margaret had told them that the conditions in the camp were very difficult. She was one of the only ex-pats allowed in, because of her good connection with the local education officer. Of course, she was used to living simply. Did Constance know that Margaret had refused to live in teacher housing on the school compound, but had taken a hut in the village?

"I think I heard something about that." Margaret had mentioned to everyone at the orientation her intention to eschew the luxury of teacher housing so that she could "live authentically" and had written several glowing ("or crowing", said Julia dryly)) articles about her experiences, thus earning the moniker "Mother Theresa" from the other Canadian teachers.

They left Margaret's parents and headed back up the path to the hotel. They stopped on one of the bends, where the young woodcarver was waiting.

"Dad, it's gorgeous, but I still don't see how you're going to lug it all the way back up to The Hotel, let alone back to Vancouver."

"Don't worry, Connie," her mother assured her. "Remember, we brought all those wall hangings back from Guatemala, didn't we Nico?"

"Perhaps I can be of some help?"

They all turned, including the woodcarver, and stared at the tall man who was standing on the path just above them. Constance thought, *"Isn't that a line from some movie?"* Then Miguel spoke.

"I know you, you're the hoopoe man from the hotel!"

A great laugh from the man. He reached down and took both of Miguel's hands between his palms and shook them solemnly. "Hello, my friend."

"I'm Miguel! Do you know me?"

"Of course." The deep, rolling laugh. "And this is your mother." He turned and shook Constance's hand.

"I'm Constance!" She blushed as she realized how she sounded like Miguel.

"Of course. And these must be your parents. The daughter looks just the same as the mother."

Constance introduced her parents. "And this is Moses -," she paused.

"Masekesa. We met at the Bronte Hotel in Harare. So, you are seeing the wonders of Zimbabwe."

"Well, some of them, anyway," said Nico. Hannah began a detailed account of their safari up to that point, with Miguel and Nico putting in their two cents worth now and again. Constance was silent, looking up at the tall man, looking down on her family. Occasionally, he looked over at her, smiling broadly.

"And now we've spent the whole day seeing The Falls. They were simply gorgeous, weren't they Connie?

She agreed, then added "but my dad's bought this huge carving and we're not sure how we'll get it up to The Hotel."

"And that's where I came in. I think this problem is not a problem."

Moses turned and spoke to the woodcarver, who was leaning against the bank. The carver nodded and gesturing them to move aside, hoisted the giraffe over his shoulder as if it was a coat and began moving up the cliff path.

"That man will expect you to give him another five dollars for carrying the carving to reception, where I'm sure they'll store it for you until you leave."

"Are you staying at The Hotel? Can we buy you a drink?" asked Hannah.

"Unfortunately, I'm not at The Hotel this evening."

"What about tomorrow? We're here for another couple of days, aren't we, Connie?"

Why don't you just throw me into his arms right now, Mom? "Yes, we thought we'd laze around tomorrow, let Miguel swim in the pool."

"Perhaps I'll see you then." Moses ruffled Miguel's hair. "I shall look for you by the pool if I'm back this way tomorrow." He shook Nico's hand the African way, then gently touched Constance's arm. He moved easily past them down the path.

The next day she was careful not to go down to the pool too early. Though it was already stifling by the time they finished breakfast and Hannah casually mentioned she'd like to go for a swim, Constance persuaded them to go into town to visit the arts and craft cooperative before it got too hot. The intricate crocheted tablecloths, carved walking sticks, baskets and masks distracted Hannah and they did not get back to The Hotel until just before lunch. After lunch, not to be put off any longer, she hustled Miguel, Constance and Nico down to the pool below the terrace.

Sitting around a hotel swimming pool is an integral part of the ex-pat social scene in every part of Africa, from Cairo to Cape Town. Grubby Peace-Corps volunteers surreptitiously put on their bathing suits in the pool changing room and slip into the water as smoothly as seals; on lounge chairs UN personnel and other higher echelon bureaucrats order lunch and drinks, shaded by large hats and sunglasses; health workers and teachers with various NGO's lie on towels on the grass, smoking, drinking, reading or playing cards. Tourists were still a minority and easy to spot. Margaret's parents, for example. The Tilley hats were a dead give-away. Constance noted her own parents had managed to blend in a little better, though Hannah sported a huge necklace made out of some kind of animal bone that just about screamed "world traveler".

"Nico, get a chair for Connie. Do you want something to drink? We were waiting for you to come down before we ordered. Nico, we can order now. I'll have a —"

"Gin and tonic. I'll just see if that nice little girl is around. I could use a beer. What about you, Connie? A gin and tonic? Ah, here she is. You're just the person we wanted to see."

While Nico ordered the drinks ("And do you have any peanuts?"), Hannah leaned toward Constance and said, "He hasn't been here."

"Who?"

"You know. That nice man yesterday. With the giraffe."

"You mean the guy Dad bought the carving from?"

"Very funny."

Another good time to say "I already have a boyfriend," but again, she let the moment pass.

About an hour later, Constance felt the air cool slightly. A low rumbling came from the west and looking up, she saw a gathering of clouds moving from the west into the path of the sun. This weather pattern had been repeating almost every day since October. In the afternoon the air would become heavy. There would be the quick build up of clouds. Rumblings and the occasional flash of lightning, maybe even a drop or two of rain. The clouds helped make for a beautiful sunset, but that was about all. She went back to her book. The heroine was a thin, neurotic American living in South America and beginning an affair with the charismatic and ineffectual brother of the country's ruthless dictator, who, naturally, also had the hots for her.

A huge clap of thunder, strong and sharp, jerked Constance from her book. The clouds were thick and dark and the air carried the promise of rain. People began climbing out of the pool. She called to Miguel and Nico, who were playing in the shallow end and pointed to the sky. A waiter and waitress began quickly taking the cushions off of the loungers and lowering umbrellas. She stood up and wrapped a towel around herself.

"I guess we should go in if it's going to rain?" Hannah was clearing her stuff off the table and putting it into her bag. "Do you think it'll last long?"

"I don't know. This would be my first rain. If it does rain. It often threatens like this."

More thunder. Louder. "So there!" laughed Hannah.

Miguel ran up, covered in goose bumps, his teeth chattering. Hannah put a towel around him. They stood waiting for Nico, who had stopped to talk with one of the other guests. A gust of wind, followed by the first heavy drops. Nico was pointing up at the sky and moving towards them. "Come on," called Hannah.

A white flash of lightning hit the lawn on the other side of the pool, followed almost immediately by the loudest roll of thunder Constance had ever heard, and then the sky opened up.

The rain came down in a liquid wall. They ran towards the hotel, but within seconds they were completely soaked. They tore up the steps to the veranda, panting and laughing. They hesitated at the French doors, but the smiling waiters beckoned them in. Guests and staff were looking out, talking loudly above the constant rumbling and crashing of thunder, the rain hammering down onto the veranda. At first the water pouring down from the eaves was red from the accumulated dust of the drought, but it soon ran clear. Miguel was being held up to the window by one of the waiters, Hannah and Nico beside them. Constance stood, shivering, but not wanting to miss the moment.

"That's some rain, eh?" Margaret's father was beside her. He and his wife must have been inside when the deluge began. They were calm and dry, each had a cup of tea in hand.

"Yes, I've never seen anything like it, even in Vancouver."

"Ah, Vancouver." He didn't elaborate, just took another sip of tea.

"I just mean, it rains a lot in Vancouver."

"Well, we're from the Prairies", *where real weather happens*, his tone implied, "and we get some pretty wild thunderstorms in the summer." Another sip. "Though nothing like this."

Her wet towel was plastered to her body and her hair fell in long, dripping ropes down her back. She eyed Baba Margaret's cup of tea. She looked around the room, trying to catch the eye of someone on staff who wasn't engrossed by the rain, and found herself looking directly at Moses Masekesa. Something told her, maybe the way he smiled and raised his eyebrows, that he had been observing her. She moved across the room towards him, feeling slightly foolish as she clutched her towel around herself.

"Isn't the rain great?" She had to speak loudly, which added to her awkwardness.

"Ah, yes. We have been waiting for the rains. It is our national obsession." Then he laughed. "That and the beautiful game."

"The beautiful game?"

"Football. What you call soccer. I believe you Canadians prefer hockey."

"Well, I have seen a few games in my day, but I'm not really a fan. You could never call hockey 'the beautiful game.'"

"So you prefer football?"

"Not really. I've never seen a real game and I don't understand the rules. But Miguel plays every chance he gets."

"Ah, then he is becoming a true African. I see he is over there with your parents. I must go and greet them." Constance looked over her shoulder to catch her mother gaping at them like someone who has just seen water turn into wine. "You and I must meet later for a drink. Perhaps out on the terrace after dinner?" He laughed again at Constance's doubtful expression. "You can bring your mother along, if you want."

"God, no!" Another rolling laugh. "I'm just thinking about the rain."

"This rain will be gone in an hour. The sun will shine and by the time we meet again, all this" he waved his arm towards the terrace "will be completely dry. Trust me."

March, 1975

Lusaka, Zambia

The bomb that killed Herbert Chitepo, interim leader of ZANU, went off in the morning of March 18 at five minutes after eight. It was planted in his Volkswagen Beetle, the night before, in the compound where he was living in Lusaka. The force of the blast blew the roof off the car and uprooted a tree next door. Chitepo, along with his bodyguard Silas Shamiso, was killed instantly. Another bodyguard, Sadat Kufamadzuba, was injured, but survived. A child playing in the next compound was not so lucky and died from his injuries a few hours later.

These are the "facts" as stated in the Report of Zambia's Special International Commission on the Assassination of Herbert Wilshire Chitepo, which had investigated the assassination and published its findings in April 1976. Other details, claims, motives and means vary, as if the death of Chitepo was a lake, with many streams and rivers draining away from it. The bomb was made of plastic explosives and fixed with a magnet to the undercarriage of the car by agents hired by the Rhodesian government and detonated with a switch often used by the Rhodesian army. Or the pentolite bomb was lodged behind the car's right front wheel because it was too heavy for a magnet. Or the bomb was made from TNT. Or the bomb was not a bomb at all, but a landmine. Chitepo was killed by operatives of the Rhodesian security forces or by South African agents or by rival members of ZANU, including Robert Mugabe, or by the rival liberation movement, ZAPU. The report of the Special International Commission, pointed the finger at Josiah Tongogara, who was at that time commander of the Zimbabwe African National Liberation Army. President Kenneth Kaunda was either "greatly saddened" by the death of Chitepo, or he was behind the assassination.

Whatever Kaunda's role in the events of March 18, he used them as a pretext to close all the ZANLA camps in Zambia. Aaron Milner, the Zambian Home Affairs Minister, also announced the banning of ZAPU and FROLIZI. Did the Zambian government really believe that the three rival liberation movements were about to engage in a bloody civil? Or, as some journalists suggested at the time, was this a way to put pressure on them to join together under the ANC banner? One of the many streams draining away from the lake. In any case, by Monday, March 24 Radio Zambia had reported the arrest of "those responsible for the death of Chitepo." Hundreds of ZANU leaders, members and supporters were rounded up and detained.

Moses Masekesa, a ZANLA commander who had received military training in China, had just returned from the front in north-eastern Rhodesia when the news reached him that ZANLA military headquarters in Chifombo had been raided by Zambian soldiers. He also heard that Tongogara had slipped through the Zambian cordon and was making his way to Mozambique. At a FRELIMO camp near Cabora Basa, he caught up with Tongogara. Together, they journeyed to Tete and had a meeting with Sergio Viera, Samora Machel's private secretary. They were ordered to return to Zambia to appear before the commission of inquiry investigating the assassination. Machel felt he had to respect the request of the commission, which was sanctioned by the Organization of African States. Or he believed Tongogara had killed Chitepo and sent him back to Zambia to face justice.

As soon as they reached Zambian soil, Masekesa and Tongogara were both arrested and taken in chains to Central Prison in Lusaka. There they were beaten and tortured. Masekesa had his ribs and fingers broken. He was released a few weeks later, without explanation. Tongogara would remain in prison for another 18 months.

12

January 1983

Mutamba Mission

To everyone's relief, the rains continued. The ephemeral rivers of southern African filled; the water ran into dams and boreholes. The red dust turned to thick, greasy mud that stuck in layers to the soles of everyone's shoes. The maize grew and there was no longer talk of having to import mealie-meal.

"This is very good," said Miriam. They were sitting around the fire outside her little house, roasting mealie-cobs. "I was very worried that the government would be forced to buy that 'Kenya' mealie-meal. Imagine! That stuff is white! Imagine! I'm sure we would all be getting terrible stomachs from that stuff."

And this from a woman who thinks roasted termites are a delicacy. Constance had been amused, but also a little grossed out to see Miguel and Mushana crunching avidly on a cookie tin full of ishwa. After the afternoon rains the students ran out of the dormitories with jars and biscuit tins to catch the flying ants that rose in small clouds from the ground and tree stumps. Mushana's mother cheerfully roasted them for the boys.

Constance stretched out her legs. The air was still fresh from the afternoon rain. The sun was casting long shadows. A group of students walked by, singing a song, their arms linked. "Masikati", they called softly. "Where are the vakomana?" "Good evening, madams."

"Shall I put on some tunes, eh?" Constance suggested. "It is Saturday night, after all. We have to at least pretend we're making an effort."

Miriam giggled. "Please, none of that awful music you played last time. My neighbours thought an evil spirit was coming for them. Mr. Mazebedi ran out of the house so fast he forgot he was in his undergarments." She giggled again.

"Are you saying the Mazebedi's didn't appreciate the sweet music of Neil Young?"

"No, and what was really funny, Mr. Mazebedi was in such a hurry to escape from the demon, he left his wife and children to face it alone."

"Well, he told us his wife knows karate."

This set Miriam off again.

"Okay, we'll choose from your vast selection." Constance got up a walked over to the veranda and pulled down a basket sitting by the cassette player. "Let's see, we could listen to Bob Marley," she rummaged some more, "Bob Marley, and oh, let's see, Bob Marley. Oh, wait just a sec. What do we have here?" She held up a cassette with no case. "Wonders will never cease. Not Bob Marley." She squinted in the fading light. "Oliver Mutukudzi. Any good?"

Miriam looked almost shocked. "You don't know Tuku?" Her voice was scolding. "Put in that cassette. You will hear one of the great Zimbabwean musicians."

"Okay, but I hope this thing still plays. I think I'm going to have to a get a brio from the house and tighten it. You should be more careful with your national icon. This thing doesn't even have a case. I'll be right back."

It took Constance a few minutes to find a pen on the table in Miriam's kitchen. She came back out onto the veranda, tightening the tape as she walked.

"God, look at this thing. At least my Neil Young tape was in excellent condition. Granted, that's probably because I never play it."

"And all of Zimbabwe thanks you, I'm sure."

Constance looked up and smiled, surprised. Alex was supposed to be away for a few days at the Matopos Hills near Bulawayo.

"Nice to see you. Amai Mushana and I were just trying to liven this party up a little."

"Nice to see you." He came forward and kissed the top of her head. He pulled her close, sighing in and out deeply. "You always smell so good," he murmured.

They stood that way for a moment, arms wound tight, each one completely aware of the other, heart beat, breath in and out, tensing of muscle. Then Alex gave a small laugh and released her.

"Manheru, Amai Mushana." He looked around. "This party is missing a few things, I'd say. Music, beer and—"

"Men." Miriam giggled at her own boldness.

"Au contraire, Amai. I see we have music" he took the tape from Constance, "I have the beer" he pulled two bottles from his pack "and, not to brag, but I think I'm worth at least two or three men. Don't you agree, Amai?" He reached into his pack and came out with an opener. "So crank that thing up and let the dancing begin!"

The Bachelors were the first to answer the music's call. Sydney Sekeramyi and David Mubvuma showed up within minutes. "We were driving by on our way to the bottle store," they explained. "We were hoping to see Miss Julia here."

Then the Mazebedi's walked over from next door, bringing Mercy Dube with them.

The Boarding Master stopped for "just one" and stayed.

No one seemed to know where Julia was.

The sweet voice of Oliver Mutukudzi, even if slightly warped, seemed to satisfy the crowd. *I was born in the ghetto* ("born in the ghetto" the crowd sang loudly and not at all sweetly after him).

Alex grabbed Constance and drew her back from the dancers. He took her face in his hands and kissed her.

"Can you stay with me tonight?"

Her heart surged. "Yes." They kissed some more and his hands reached under her shirt to her back.

"Let's go now."

"Okay, I just have to tell Miriam. Miguel is sleeping here anyway."

She woke to the rain pounding on the tin roof. Alex was sitting up beside her, smoking a cigarette. "Hey." He didn't turn. Maybe he couldn't hear her over the rain.

She reached up and touched his back. "Hey".

He twisted to face her, then turned away.

"Are you okay?" He shrugged and took another drag. "Fine."

"Why did you come back today? I didn't expect you until Sunday." She knew she had to tread a bit carefully here. "What happened? Did you run out of bugs to study or something?"

"No. I came back early because I was sacred."

"Scared?" Constance sat up. "What do you mean?"

"The Fifth Brigade. They're all over Matabeleland. Rooting out the dissidents."

"That's good isn't it? They'll stop the kidnappings and find all the arms caches and then —"

"For Christ sake, Constance! I wasn't afraid of being kidnapped by the Ndebele. I was afraid of being killed by the army!"

"What?"

"Just what I said. The Fifth Brigade is all over the south, beating people, killing them. The people call them the *Gukurahundi*."

"What does that mean."

"The rains that wash away the chaff. I tell you, it's just unbelievable."

It was unbelievable.

"How do you know about this? You were only down there for a few days."

"I didn't even get out to Matopos. I stayed the first night in Makhokhobato with Friend's sister, Lebokhana." He reached over the side of the bed and stubbed his cigarette out in a saucer. "I'd been there before, with Friend, so they gave me a great welcome. Cooked up a huge pot of sadza, sent the little ones over to the bottle store for some libation, invited the neighbours over. You know, the usual African hail-fellow- well-met- routine." Constance leaned into him and he shifted so his back was against the wall. He wrapped his arms around and leaned his chin on her head. "I needed to take a leak, so I was heading outside, when I heard this screaming and wailing. I didn't think too much of it. I thought maybe someone had died — you know how the women carry on when anyone dies. But when I got back inside I could see something was wrong. The whole family, their friends, everyone was sitting in total silence. In the dark. Even the kids. I thought maybe they knew the person who had died, that there was like a minute of silence or something. I tell you, it was weird, sitting there in the dark, but I wasn't worried. I just thought, 'well, here's a new one.' I expected that at any minute someone would light a candle and we'd go back to drinking and eating and Lebokhana would explain the custom. But the lights didn't go on. The screams got louder and we could hear men shouting and dogs barking and guns firing."

The mosquitoes floated lazily around them, settling now and again. Constance brushed them away from her face.

"We were there for a while, then there was silence, except for the dogs."

"What happened?"

"We waited until we heard the soldiers leaving."

"The Fifth Brigade?"

"Yeah. They sure knew how to put a damper on that little shindig. Ever seen a scared shitless African? Their faces go a kind of ashy colour. And I must have looked truly white. Probably someone who was there that night is telling this story and saying 'Ever seen a scared shitless white guy?'"

"What did they tell you?"

"This has been going on for weeks now, all over the south. Not just in the townships but in the villages. The soldiers go in and round people up for interrogation, trying to find out about dissidents. People are beaten up and tortured, women are raped, people are shot. Lebokhana said she had heard that in Neshango, two pregnant girls were shot."

"Why haven't I heard about any of this?"

Alex snorted. "You and the rest of the world."

"But do the locals, I mean the locals up here in Mashonaland, do they know?"

"Probably. Maybe. On some level anyway. How could they not know? I mean, I knew the Fifth Brigade were down there. Everyone knows. I knew they were beating people up, but I thought it was the kind of rough justice that goes on all the time here. You know how it goes. Men beat their wives, mothers beat their children, big kids beat up little kids."

"Teachers beat their students."

"Yeah. But this isn't like that. This is pure fucking terror. I was scared, and I didn't even know what was going on until Lebokhana filled me in. She told me to hightail it back here. The soldiers wouldn't look too kindly on a scruffy white guy moving around in the bush, crashing with the locals."

The rain had stopped but small gusts of wind shook drops of water off the roof and trees. They sat there, watching the sky lighten through the burglar bars on the window. The world began to take shape again. The neglected lemon trees, the scraggly grass, the barbed wire fence and the thornveld beyond. The roosters had already begun to crow. The doves and francolins, the guinea fowl and louries began their competing chorus. The air was deliciously cool. Constance snuggled down against Alex and felt herself being pulled back down into sleep.

There was no more rain that year.

It would have been hard to gauge at what "level", if any, the people around her were affected by, or even knew about the massacres taking place in their name. Zimbabwe was under the same state of emergency that had been in effect since Ian Smith had declared UDI in 1965. Radio Zimbabwe was strictly a mouthpiece of the state, extolling the virtues of the ruling party when it wasn't reporting the latest football scores or playing the latest Michael Jackson hit or the latest "indigenous" hit song on the Gallo Record Hour. The Herald was also firmly non-critical in its news coverage, at least as it pertained to local matters. Foreign governments were fair game, especially Great Britain, the United States and "The Racist Pretoria Regime". However, buried in the section of the paper reserved for Question Period in the National Assembly, which under the Emergency Powers Regulations were exempt from the censors, Constance noted this exchange:

Edson Ndlovu (Matabeleland South) (ZAPU): *It has been reported to me that soldiers have gone into Kezi and shot six young men. They were accused of failing to report anti-government guerrillas. These young men were beaten and shot. They were buried in two shallow graves. I am calling on the Zimbabwe Government to make a full official investigation of this incident.*

Emmerson Munangagwa (Minister of Home Affairs) (ZANU-PF): *This is a ridiculous allegation. If any one has been harmed in Matabeleland, they have been harmed by Super ZAPU bandits. Cde. Speaker, it is sad to inform you that Super ZAPU is responsible for all assaults and murders and other crimes committed against Zimbabwean citizens.*

Edson Ndlovu: *Cde Speaker, it has been reported in the Herald newspaper that the government has "unleashed" the Fifth Brigade in the Midlands and Matabeleland to rout out the so-called bandits. What does the Minister think is happening there?*

Emmerson Munangagwa: *The will of the majority is prevailing.*

November 1975

Maputo

To move forward, it is sometimes necessary to go back. Back to the front, to the north-east bordering on Mozambique where, in mid-November, 1974, Raphael Chinyanganya, chimurenga name 'Nhari', led a group of about thirty rebels who ambushed and captured Chifombo, a ZANLA CAMP in Zambia. Their grievances: the high command was stealing funds meant for the war. They also complained that the leadership in Lusaka was living high off the hog and did not

115

spend any time at the front. The rebels traveled back and forth to Lusaka a couple of times, kidnapping, among others, Joseph Chimurenga, a member of the high command, Kumbirai Kangai and Mukudzei Muszi, both members of the Dare (the war council) and Tongogara's wife and three small children. Tongogara was furious and allegedly told the Zambian police, who were thought to be in collusion with the rebels, "You get my family before I cause trouble." (The police did find them two days later). On December 12, Tongogara ordered the high command to re-take Chifombo. Rex Nhongo, back from China, was sent to Mozambique to obtain Samora Machel's support, while Dzinashe Mashingura, Robson Manyika and Moses Masekesa traveled to Tanzania and brought back 250 fighters. On Christmas Day this force, called the Gukurahundi (the first rains of the season that sweep away the chaff), led by Tongogara, entered Chifombo.

Masekesa was disgusted by the Nhari Rebellion and its aftermath. He had some sympathy for the rebels. The high command was riddled with corruption. He knew that Dare members were living the good life in Lusaka, living in nice houses and sending their kids to good schools. He had personally delivered a case of whiskey and Cuban cigars from Tongogara to his cousin Josiah Tungamirai. But the timing of the revolt was all wrong. The pressures to unify with ZAPU had already weakened ZANU. Worse than that were the senseless kidnappings and killings. 'By all accounts' over 40 people had been murdered by the rebels and, in the weeks following the re-taking of Chifombo, between 60 and 250 rebels were 'executed' by ZANU.

It was almost a relief then, to be sent back to the front in January with the Gukurahundi, fresh from their 'victory' at Chifombo. This campaign however, turned out to be a disaster for the guerillas. There was a total lack of radio communication between the front and the bases in Mozambique. The sectional security officers had to rely on messengers and couriers, rendezvous points and pre-arranged meetings.

According to the Maoist ideology he and Tongogara had learned in China, the guerillas were to be the fish swimming busily in the sea. Unfortunately, the area they were operating in had only a few puddles, being mostly unpopulated. The people that did live there had not attended any pungwes and so were unaware of their role as supporters of the struggle. Many fighters were taken prisoner or killed or wounded in skirmishes with Rhodesian forces.

Somewhat ironically, the rains were good that year. What was left of the Gukurahundi, a company of about 60, was ambushed near a flooding river. Some of the guerillas scattered, but the only escape was by diving into the waters of the swift-flowing river. Some were killed or captured.

Masekesa managed to lead a small group back into the bush, where they walked for days and days, going in circles. Unable to shoot game for food, for fear of frightening the locals or giving away their location to the enemy, they existed on bush plants and water, which luckily were in good supply at that time of year. In March, with the help of some 'povo' they were able to cross the Angwa River into the relative safety of Mozambique. Finally able to re-establish communication with headquarters, Masekesa learned that Chitepo had been assassinated.

So, we now find Josiah Tongogara where we last left him, along with many other ZANLA cadres, languishing in Mpima prison. This was widely seen as Kaunda's way of 'persuading' the political and military leadership of ZANU to join up with Nkomo and ZAPU. Though 'languishing' may not be the right word to describe someone who was receiving visits from Jason Moyo, his ZAPU counterpart. By all accounts, these visits were 'talks', aimed at unifying the two liberation movements. For by now the writing was on the wall. Along with Kaunda, the OAU no longer recognized either ZAPU or ZANU and all money and arms were to be given to the ANC. It was well known that both Samora Machel and Julius Nyerere thought it was time for the formation of a united front and indeed, Machel had made it plain that he would only accept the use of Mozambique as a rear base by one army. The guerilla war was not going anywhere. There were only about 30 guerillas still active inside Rhodesia.

So, in November 1975, several ZANLA field commandeers, Rex Nhongo, Saul Sadza and Moses Masekesa, met Jason Moyo in the Zona Militar in Maputo to negotiate the creation of a joint guerrilla force. They had the blessing of the ZANLA leadership in the form of a 'ten-point memorandum' issued from Mpima Prison. Thus was born the Zimbabwe People's Army, which in the way of all things Zimbabwean, became ZIPA. Rex Nhongo (from ZANU) was made Army

Commander, with John Dube (from ZIPRA) as the Deputy Commander. Moses Masekesa was named Director of Operations.

ZIPA lasted all of one year, until the re-emergence of ZANU with the mysterious Robert Gabriel Mugabe at its head.

13

May 2000

Muraro Farm

The auction was late that year. Usually the tobacco has been cured by the beginning of April. The barns are opened to let the leaves reabsorb some moisture, so they are pliable enough to removed by hand, sorted, packed into bales weighing 100 kilos and loaded onto the lorry to be taken to the floor of the auction house in Harare — the largest tobacco auction in the world! — where it is bid on by a few multinational companies such as DIMON or by Chidziva, one of a handful of smaller, local players.

I don't know what happened that year to make the auction so late. I know that the rains had stopped suddenly in the middle of January and a few weeks later I could see the crop was wilting.

It was the beginning of a time of strange faces around the farm. I was used to the itinerant workers who came to harvest the tobacco and work in the curing barns. Most of them were women from Macheke who walked the seven kilometres to the farm with babies strapped to their backs and perhaps a toddler or two trotting beside. It was for these *vawanana* that Miriam and I had started the crèche. But these new people were mostly men, demanding bread, money and firewood. At the end of April a group of five squatters beat up a teenage crop guard, Cloud Moredza, and stole some maize. James was furious.

"They call themselves 'war veterans'," he fumed, stamping into the kitchen. It was late and he had spent all afternoon at the clinic with Cloud. "War vets! I don't bloody think so."

"How is Cloud?" I took a beer out of the fridge to share with James but it looked like he was going to need one just for himself. I reached back in for another.

James shrugged. "You know how it is at that place. Made him wait for bloody hours, waiting room like Dante's Inferno. Finally got to see the so-called nurse. She actually seemed to be switched on. Not like that one who made such a mess of stitching my hand. Got Cloud stitched up in no time. But usual story. No muti, no plasters, not even a blerry aspirin."

"I called the police, like you said."

"And?"

"Well," I tried to phrase my answer in a way that wouldn't set off another tirade, "they said they haven't any petrol at the moment. But," I added, as James took a deep breath, "they said there's a possibility they might be able to make it out here tomorrow."

James made a grunting noise into his beer. Then he sat down at the kitchen table. I went over and rubbed his back.

We sat there, drinking and smoking. I remembered my first trip to the auction. It was just after Evan had been born and my parents had been visiting from Canada.

"Nico, take a picture of this!" We were standing at one end of the auction floor. In front of us, stretched out in long aisles, were sacks and sacks — huge sacks, thousands of sacks — of tobacco bales. I posed in front of one of the burlap sacks, Miguel in front of me, the baby in my arms while my mother directed the photo shoot.

"Careful, Connie!" James pulled us back between the bales, just as another man whipped by us, wheeling more bales. He pointed up to a sign behind me — CAUTION! BARROWS! -grinning and shaking his head. Then he moved away from us, through the crowds of buyers and sellers, down towards the other end of the warehouse.

The smell of tobacco was strong here, but not as strong as in our own curing barns at home. I had helped sort the leaves that year, one of many women doing this work with a baby strapped to her back.

The auction was like a dance. White men in suits and ties, formed a sort of conga line, pausing to pick up a slips of paper from the top of the open bales, muttering and jotting something down on the slips, raising their arms together like a Greek wedding and then pirouetted on to their next partner. The bales would be closed and put onto a barrow, whizzing off the stage, even as new bales emerged from the wings.

Except for Amai Kazana's funeral, I hardly saw James over the next month. He was in the tobacco barn most of the time, as well as building a boma to try to stop livestock from being poached. One afternoon I walked over to the barn.

There was a dirt track that slid down the hill and crossed the valley to the barn. At the bottom of the hill the path branched off and curved along the hill to the village, a collection of pole and dagga rondavels surrounded by maize patches. This is where the farm workers lived with their families. It was also where Miriam lived, in the small cement house with a tin roof.

I walked down the hill, past the stone barn we called the Python Barn, where after good harvests the women from the village would be singing and gossiping as they winnowed, past the small brick building which served as a crèche, empty now for the weekend. The grass was long and almost white in the heat. In the evening it would turn gold and in the early morning the dew and spiders webs would make it sparkle but now the grass, the hills, the sky were an over-exposed photograph. The sun pressed down on my head, the cicadas vibrated all around.

The barn was dark, and noisy. The women sorting the tobacco gossiped and laughed. The men in dark overalls and gumboots took the sorted tobacco and were pressing it into bales. I spotted James in his dirty white terry-cloth hat. He was helping fill the boxes for the bale press. Bunches of leaves were placed with the butts out and the tips overlapping. The rusty leaves were small and brittle. It would take a lot to fill one bale.

"How's it going?" I had to shout over the noise.

He looked at me blankly for a moment. He took his hat off, wiped his face with it and put it back on.

"I reckon we'll be finished in a couple of days." He picked up a leaf and showed me how easily it crumbled like dust in his hands.

I went outside, hoping for a breeze, but the air was still. There was only the sound of the cicadas. I lit a cigarette and watched the children playing in the yard. A small boy and girl were scratching in the dirt with sticks. Baby Nyarai was sitting near them, banging a rock on the ground. She tottered over to me and I picked her up.

My mind drifted to a time Moses, Miriam and I and Mushana and Miguel had taken some water and biltong and walked a long way up into the hills behind the mission and sat on a kopje overlooking the mission and beyond it the valley and the thornbush. Above, kites wheeled on wind we longed to feel. The cicadas buzzed. I remembered the boys had discovered a rock overhang with bushman paintings of a giraffe and an elephant.

At Amai Kazana's funeral the Zimbabweans around me picked up handfuls of dirt and threw them onto the coffin. I picked up a clod and looked at it, there in my hand. The red earth of Zimbabwe. When I opened my hand it was already crumbing into dust. I let it drop back to the ground

Baby Nyari had fallen asleep on her auntie's back, her little fists curled up beside her head. She was still too little to have her hair in braids, but on her feet were red plastic sandals.

14

April 1983

Mutamba Mission

Mutamba Secondary School had only four staff meetings a year —
one was held in January on the day before school opened for the
year, the other three were held on the last day of each term, after the
last of the students had left. The entire teaching staff sat in a semi-
circle around the edges of the staff room facing the Headmaster, Mr.
Mhanda, the Deputy Headmaster, Mr. Murerwa and the Assistant
Headmaster, Mr. Kazemi. Constance was not sure of the hierarchy in
the roles of the Deputy and Assistant, but she was pretty sure that
Mr. Murerwa trumped Mr. Kazemi, because the Deputy was
Zimbabwean and Mr. Kazemi was from Malawi. There was no
agenda circulated. Mercy Dube took copious notes, but Constance
never saw any minutes. She amused herself by composing
transcripts of the staff meetings in her head:

Welcome:

Mr. Mhanda asked for a volunteer to give the Blessing. There
being no volunteer, he called on Mrs. Machirori from the Religious
Education Department to give the Blessing.

Old Business: Cambridge Results:

Mr. Mhanda was surprised and disappointed by the poor results
in English Language and Literature on the Cambridge exams. He
asked why the results in these two subjects were once again far
below the standard expected at Mutamba School. Mrs. Karambira
stated that her department was short by at least two teachers and so

some of the Form Ones were not getting enough classes. This had a detrimental effect on the children's learning and caused them to lose ground. Mr. Sekeramyi said there was a shortage of Maths teachers but the Maths results were much better than the English ones. Mrs. Karambira said that only students who were good in Maths went into Maths, but everyone, no matter how stupid, was required to write English.

Miss Julia said that the students only spoke English in class. Outside of class they spoke Shona. She didn't want to mention any names, but it was well known that certain people in the Maths department weren't teaching in English, but were using Shona as the language of instruction. Mr. Sekeramyi denied teaching in the vernacular, but admitted that there might have been one or two times when he had used Shona to explain a particularly difficult maths problem. Mr. Shaw said that the Form Four results had been below expectations in all subjects, not just English. The students in that year had been admitted into the school before their Standard Seven results were known, so many of them were duds. After explaining what a "dud" was, Mr. Shaw went on to say that you couldn't make chicken salad with chicken shit. Mr. Mhanda thanked everyone for their useful and worthy comments. He urged the members of the English Department to pull up their socks, so that next year's exam results would reflect the high standards that Mutamba Secondary School was known for.

Barking Dogs:

Mr. Mhanda reported that he was still receiving complaints about dogs barking at night. He asked why this was still a problem. Mrs. Karambira said that some people kept too many dogs. Only one dog was necessary to keep away thieves. Mr. Sekeramyi said that it was better to have at least two dogs, since thieves did not usually work alone. Mr. Situmba said that he needed three dogs for hunting. It was not possible to bring down a bushbuck with only one dog.

Mrs. Dube asked him when was the last time he had killed a bushbuck. Mr. Situmba said he needed three dogs to guard against leopards when he was out hunting in the bush. Mrs. Dube asked him when was the last time he had seen a leopard. Mr. Mhanda thanked everyone for their useful and worthwhile comments. He urged all teachers with dogs to keep them …

Like everyone else, Constance moaned about these discussions and rolled her eyes whenever Sydney Sekeramyi spoke. But really, she didn't mind staff meetings, partly because they never lead to any action or change. Nothing was required of her or anyone else. There was something refreshing about the way the teachers directed unprofessional and personal comments at each other, under the benign eyes of the Headmaster.

New Business: Visit to Mutamba Mission of a Very Important Person.

Mr. Mhanda said he had some fantastic news to tell. Someone very important was coming to the Mission in October to attend the "Old Boys" reunion; namely the Prime Minister, Robert Gabriel Mugabe. There was a lot that had to be done in order to make the school shipshape for such a visit. He asked the teachers what they could do to make such a visit a success. Miss. Takawira said the Home Economics Department would provide the tea. She said the girls would make chocolate and cream cakes, ham sandwiches and sadza with relish. Mr. Shaw asked if the Home Economics Department could also make bacon buns. He had tasted Miss. Takawira's delicious bacon buns and he was sure the Prime Minister and all the other Old Boys would like them too. Miss Julia asked if the tea was going to be a private affair, or could staff members attend the party? Mr. Tirivavi said that he was an Old Boy so he expected he would be invited, but he wasn't entirely sure if any other member of staff …

Constance listened as one person after another volunteered to "make the school shipshape". Benjamin Mwira offered to have the Woodworking Department design a covered awning to be erected on the stage of the outdoor assembly area so the Prime Minister could be properly shaded from the October sun. The Art Department would paint a mural in the dining hall. The Form One Education for Production classes would cut all the grass around the school and plant new trees and flowers. Which reminded everyone that unless the fences around the school were mended, livestock from the village would eat any new foliage. Then Mr. Murerwa suggested that committees should be struck, so the work could be better organized. There was a rush to organize and name people to committees. When everyone, even Alex had put their name forward, Constance saw the writing on the wall and she offered to work on the "Beautification Committee."

"I can paint a banner "Pamberi ne Robert Mugabe" and drape it across the new mission gate that the Brothers are going to build," she told Julia, as they made their way back to her house for a drink after the meeting. She was feeling rather smug. Julia had been roped into the Fund-Raising Committee.

"Painting a banner? I rather think that's goes under the auspices of the Welcoming Committee." Julia stopped to pick a rock out of her sandal. "You don't want to step on any toes, my girl. No, I think you're going to have to tar the roads or whitewash all the classrooms."

"Ha."

Julia looked over at Constance and said, "Didn't you find it just a tiny bit creepy the way people were falling all over themselves to do some work? A bit out of the ordinary, don't you agree? Look at me, even. I'll have to sell raffle tickets or something. First prize: a *mombe*"

"Well, it's not every day the Prime Minister visits the Mission."

"Yes, but even people like Mercy Dube signed up. She can't be a fan of this government.

Constance made a non-committed noise in my throat. Julia didn't take the hint.

"There was one person who didn't sign up for anything. Did you notice?"

"Who? You mean Mr. Mhanda? His job is to supervise and thank us for all our hard work."

"No, there was someone else." Julia paused. "Mr. Okense."

I thought for a moment. "Are you sure? I hardly know the guy, but he seems pretty hard-working and accommodating to me.

"Exactly. That's why I found his shirking so out of character. If it had been Friend or one of The Bachelors I would have been a bit ticked off but not surprised."

"Well, he is from Uganda. Maybe it's a cultural thing." This was a stock explanation, used by both blacks and whites, whenever anyone behaved eccentrically.

Julia shrugged, which was the stock response.

August 1976

Nyadzonia Camp, Mozambique

At dawn on August 9th a combined force of the Rhodesian Army, known as 'The Flying Column' crossed the Pungwe River into Mozambique and moved toward the ZIPA camp, which had been established at Nyadzonia. The force traveled in ten Unimogs and four other armoured cars painted to resemble FRELIMO vehicles. They were equipped with several types of weapons, including machine guns and aircraft canons. The seventy-two soldiers were disguised in FRELIMO uniforms. The white soldiers had painted their hands and faces black. They entered Nyadzonia singing FRELIMO songs and completely fooled the guards at the camp.

The months leading up to "Operation Eland' had not been good ones for the Rhodesian security forces. ZANLA and ZIPRA had combined forces, albeit reluctantly, and the liberation war had resumed on three fronts along the eastern border with Mozambique. A growing number of white civilians, mainly farmers, were being killed. In March, Samora Machel had closed the border, cutting off one of Rhodesia's main supply routes. Prime Minister Smith and the Minister of Defence, P.K. van der Byl, came under increased pressure 'to do something.'

The soldiers had learned from captured guerillas that the camp contained an armoury, hospital, school and living quarters. They knew that at 0800 hours a general muster took place, which meant that virtually everyone in the camp, with the exception of the cooks, patients and hospital staff, would be in the parade grounds at that hour. It was later said by members of the Rhodesian Forces that this was the "largest single concentration of terrorists mustered throughout the entire war." It was estimated that there were over 4000 people in the parade ground that morning surrounded by the Rhodesian soldiers in their tanks.

A soldier in one of the tanks began shouting slogans in Shona through the loudspeakers. "Zimbabwe tatona" — we have taken Zimbabwe — and the crowd began to run towards the vehicle singing and cheering. The soldiers began firing, using rifles and machine guns. People were unable to escape because two armoured tanks were blocking the escape route. Many people who tried to get across the river were drowned. The firing continued until all movement in 'the kill zone' had stopped.

The Rhodesians withdrew from the camp, destroying the Pungwe River Bridge. They entered a village that had about 100 FRELIMO soldiers in it. The lead vehicle took the wrong turn and the convoy drove into a football field with no other way out. A FRELIMO officer went up to the lead tank to offer directions. The column began to turn around and leave the field, but two of the vehicles stalled. The FRELIMO officer noticed that some of the soldiers were actually white. FRELIMO began firing at the convoy. The convoy was able to escape with the help of Hawker Hunter jets.

It was now the time for the spin doctors (though that phrase was not used at that time) to spring into action. Both ZANLA and ZIPRA claimed that Nyadzonia had been a refugee camp. They claimed that the Rhodesian forces had shot indiscriminately into a crowd of unarmed children, women and men, wounding or killing over 1,000. A Dutch TV crew entered the camp on August 14 and reported that at least 1,000 people had been killed and over 1,500 wounded. In May of that year, the United Nations High Commission for Refugees (UNHCR) had visited the camp and given it refugee status. On August 25th, the Aga Khan, the head of UNHCR in Geneva confirmed this in a statement, "I have no doubt that a settlement of Zimbabwean refugees which has been receiving United Nations' assistance was attacked and that hundreds of refugees were killed and wounded."

This evidence was 'balanced' by claims put forward by Salisbury that Nyadzonia was an insurgent camp. P.K. van der Byl insisted it was a guerilla camp and produced 'documents' which showed that male Zimbabweans were taking military training at Nyadzonia. The Rhodesian government argued that the 'terrorists' always knew when the UN officials were coming to inspect the camps and so they removed the fighters, but left their families there.

What are 'families' doing in a military training camp? But this begs the question — did the Rhodesian government give a toss anyway? On July 2, 1975 van der Byl had stood up in Parliament and stated, "any village found harbouring guerillas will be bombed and destroyed in any manner." There were now at least 2,000 'political prisoners' in Rhodesian jails. To try to keep the fish from the sea, the regime was herding people at gunpoint into 'protected villages' also known as PVs or 'keeps'. The best estimates say that by the middle of 1976 around 800,000 people were living in PVs. It now seems that Nyadzonia was both a refugee camp and a guerrilla camp. The military trainees had been unwilling to leave their women and children behind, so they had taken them across the border with them into Mozambique. The results were disastrous.

But not completely disastrous. The Rhodies were now heavily dependent upon the largesse of the South Africans, who were paying half of Rhodesia's defence budget. The South African government saw the Nyadzonia massacre as a dangerous escalation of the war, threatening to 'destabilize' the whole region. Or maybe it was a handy excuse. In any case, on August 26th they turned off the tap. The Americans were also preparing to write off Rhodesia and at a meeting on September 18th in Pretoria, with Vorster and Kissinger, Ian Smith felt the screws tightening. He was forced to accept a '5-point plan' that called for a conference in Geneva with black nationalist leaders to bring about majority rule — within two years!

And not completely disastrous for ZANU and its new Secretary-General, Robert Mugabe. In the wake of the massacre, Samora Machel had summoned the nationalist leaders to Maputo so that he could express his sympathy to the Zimbabwean people. It was at this meeting that Mugabe identified himself as the Secretary-General of ZANU. He and Ndabaningi Sithole each claimed to be the true leader of ZANU and each claimed to have the support of the guerillas in the camps. Nkomo was still the big man in ZAPU, and he had the support of Bishop Abel Muzorewa but everyone knew that the ZIPA united front wasn't working all that well and that there were animosities and rivalries between Nkomo's ZIPRA fighters and the ZANLA guerillas. Samora Machel had risen to the leadership of FRELIMO from the ranks of the guerillas. It has been supposed that both he and Nyerere were hoping that history would repeat itself and that a new nationalist leader would emerge who could unify the various factions in the Zimbabwean liberation struggle. This, of course, was not to be. In the end, Nkomo ditched both Sithole and Bishop Abel Muzorewa and cobbled together an agreement with Mugabe to create the Patriotic Front in time to attend the Geneva conference.

15

The days were a little cooler now. The sun rose later and sometimes there was a pale, watery mist hanging over the mission, quickly lifting as the sun gathered force. On weekend mornings, Constance would sit up in bed, the blankets wrapped around, marking history essays, until the broad swathe of light pushed its way across the floor and up onto her bed. The emerald dove would begin its soft cooing. Then she knew it was warm enough to get up and make coffee, and have her first cigarette out on the little veranda, waiting for Miguel to get up, if he wasn't sleeping over at Mushana's, or for Alex, if he was around. If she was lucky, she could tune the BBC World Service in on the radio and hear the news.

On this particular morning the air was still so cool that she wore an old wool sweater over her pajamas and socks under her sandals. The air carried the smell of woodsmoke, dust, flowers and insects. She watched as Cheemo cautiously came out of the vines hanging down from the side of the veranda and began moving carefully across the ledge, hunting for bugs.

Two students came to the gate and quietly greeted her.

"*Mangwanani*," she answered.

"*Taswera?*"

"*Taswera zvedu.*"

They were carrying buckets and wanted to collect water from her tap, the water in the dormitories must already have run out, but when they saw the chameleon they gasped and froze.

"It's okay, boys. I'll stick him back into the vine. See, you can't even see him now."

The boys literally shuddered as she picked up the chameleon.

"No, madam. We can't come there," one of them said. They were sure about this. They would go next door to the Karambira's. They left, speaking to each other, loudly now and gesturing back towards her. Some other students, also in search of water, stopped and joined the discussion. Constance decided now might be a good time to go back inside for more coffee.

"What's that all about?"

Constance turned from her door and smiled.

"What's Shona for 'Don't go near that crazy witch, she keeps an evil creature in her house'?"

"You should thank me for giving Miguel that chameleon. A *tsotsi* will think twice about robbing this place."

He came up the stairs and took the cup out of her hand and put it on the ledge. He pulled her into him and began kissing her slowly. She felt him start to pull her towards the door.

"We can't," she murmured reluctantly. "Miguel is still sleeping inside."

The kept kissing and nuzzling each other, then she remembered the students. Their relationship was an open secret, but she was still trying to be discreet. Alex moved back and casually picked up her coffee and took a large gulp.

"What are your plans for the day?" She was always careful not to question him about where he had been the night before. Most likely out drinking with The Bachelors.

"I thought I'd head over to the bottle store a little later. Pick up some beer for tonight."

"Do you want me to drive you?" There was a rough road, cattle track really, that wound its way through the bush to the Sunset Butchery and Bottle Store.

"No, it's okay. My faithful African guide says he knows a shortcut."

"But how will you carry the beer home? Knowing you two, you're not just going for one or two each."

"Don't you know? Friend is my faithful African guide slash porter."

"Slash physics teacher. Ha."

"Ha. Yes, well, I might end up having to carry him back, plus the beer." He put down the coffee and fished into his pocket for a cigarette. "I know. Why don't you come with us? Bring your binos and we'll do some birding."

"Okay. But what about Friend? Will he want me along?"

Alex shrugged. "He won't mind." He took a reflective puff. "Might even be glad, come to think of it. You're a woman, so he'll think I've brought you along to lug the goods home."

She sorted through a pile of almost-clean clothes to find something to wear. Probably best not to wear shorts to the bottle store. It was warm in the sun and it would be even warmer trudging through the bush, she could wear this old cotton dress, and wrap a sweater around her waist, in case they came back late and it got cold on the way home. She made a mental note to ask Hannah in her next letter to send her some tights, since the female teachers weren't allowed to wear trousers to school. They'd be good to wear to bed as well, though they might out a damper on her sex life, such as it was.

Such as it was. What was it, exactly? Wonderful, warm and loving, but this far and no farther. There was a definite wall there, well, maybe not a wall, but a window. A high window. Constance could see herself jumping up and down in front of a door, trying to catch a glimpse of Alex through a small square window near the top. She couldn't get a good look, though she had a feeling he might be with someone else. But she refused to get a chair and stand on it so she could peer through.

Grow up, she scolded herself. If you want to know something just ask him. You're 25 years old, for Christ's sake.

She pulled on her dress and ran a brush through her hair, deciding not to pin it up, for once. She went out to the small lounge where Miguel was. He was lying on the floor, concentrating on driving his small metal cars into neat lines, according to some system of his own. With him was Nyasha, a Form Two student. Her father was Boniface, the school driver and jack-of-all-trades. Constance had known him to replace a window in Julia's house, fix Mary Karambira's cooker, drive to town to pick up supplies, and coolly shoot, with a shotgun, a green mamba that was spotted climbing up the rainpipe of the boys' dormitory, all on one Saturday. Nyasha had her father's fine bones and easy laugh and like him, she exuded an air of quiet confidence. Unlike him, she had all her teeth. Lately she had taken to dropping around on Saturdays. She listened to the radio, did her prep or read to Miguel. In return for supper she did the dishes.

"I'm walking with Alex and Friend to the bottle store," said Constance, as she bent to kiss the top of Miguel's head. "We're going to be doing some bird-watching. Are you hanging around, Nyasha?"

"Yes, I will be revising for my science test on Monday."

"Great. I was hoping you could keep an eye on things until I get back."

Constance gave Miguel another kiss and went out into the now-warm sunshine. She was halfway down the road when she heard running footsteps behind her. She turned.

"You have forgotten these, Amai." She smiled as she slung the binoculars around her neck. Miguel's accent and inflection were perfectly Zimbabwean.

Friend and Alex were already waiting for her out in their yard. Alex was sitting on the steps. He had on shorts and takkies, a yellow terry-cloth hat. He came over and kissed her, then went back to organizing his backpack — white plastic water bottle, camera, binos, Swiss army knife, collecting jars. Friend was sitting under the mango tree, chair tipped back, face hidden beneath a large, battered straw hat. He was wearing loose brown trousers, a bright yellow and red chitenge shirt and rubber sandals. Constance touched his shoulder.

He jerked his head up, then smiled and stretched. He stood and greeted her, shaking her hand.

They walked down the road to where it turned and ran parallel to the sagging barbed-wire fence that surrounded the school. Alex and Nice were able to cross it easily by holding it down for each other, then Alex reached and lifted Constance over. They began following a track into the bush.

The sky was cloudless and the sun warmed the air. There were still some signs of the last rains — some of the trees showed green leaves and there was still green grass pushing up in scraggy patches. A herd of goats moved placidly in the distance, their bells made a gentle song. Alex stooped and pointed.

"Are those monkey orange trees?"

"The fruits should be ripe now." They scrambled after Friend to the base of a small kopje. "Let us see if the baboons have left us some."

He gave Constance a round, smooth yellow ball. She looked at it.

"That's the fruit. The Shona call it mutamba. Here, let's slice it open."

"Like the Mission? Is that what it means?"

They showed her how to suck the slightly tart pulp from around the seeds.

Alex put some in his pack for Miguel and Mushana.

To Constance's eye, there seemed to be dozens of tracks, aimlessly splitting off and re-joining. They followed one that wound its way past a low hill. They could hear the baboons shrieking in the msasa trees as they walked by. Constance could smell the sun heating up the rocks and earth.

The walked in companionable silence for about half an hour, intent on waving flies away from their faces, skirting the thorn scrub. Constance was aware that there was certain tension between Alex and her because they had not made love that morning. He often reached out to touch her shoulder or take her hand. She leaned into him while she took a thorn out of her sandal. The sun was almost directly overhead now, bleaching the earth and sky of colour.

"Let us continue," said Friend. "It is not too much further to our destination."

"Hang on a sec." Alex held out his arm to stop Constance from moving and pointed with the other.

A small brown bird with black and white wings was hopping around on the ground, its long, thin bill probing for insects. Seeing them, it raised its crest and began crying 'hoop-hoop, hoop-hoop-hoop' excitedly, but made no move to fly off. Constance was delighted.

"I know that bird. I love it."

"You do?"

"Yes, a hoopoe."

"It's so comical. Look at her strutting around there."

"That is the male," said Friend. He seemed amused by her enthusiasm.

"I know. The female is not as colourful." She lifted up her binoculars and the bird, startled, flew off, its black and white wings undulating up and down like a butterfly. She watched until she could no longer see it against the white sky. Alex lifted her hair from her neck and blew gently, cooling her.

"Thanks guys, that made my day. Now that's something to write in my journal. If I bothered to keep one."

They started walking again.

"I'm going to miss this," said Alex abruptly.

"What?"

"This. The light. The smells. The bush."

Constance waited, her heart beating hard, for him to elaborate. Nothing. She moved ahead of him, her arm scraping against a bush.

"Constance."

She didn't turn around. Her feelings were pressing against the back of her throat, stopping her words.

"Constance. You know that my contract ends in six months. None of us is here forever."

Friend, up ahead, gave a significant cough. Alex laughed. "Sorry, Friend. You know what I mean."

Friend, without looking back, gave a forgiving wave.

Constance wheeled around. "I don't want to talk about this in front of Friend," she hissed, through her gritted teeth.

"Okay, okay." He reached out for her shoulder, but she shrugged him off. She turned to follow Friend.

They made good time the rest of the way. When they got to the bottle store, a low cement building, whitewashed with a strip of black paint running around the bottom, Constance had a splitting headache, which she knew from experience had a good chance of becoming a migraine. If she had any sense at all, she would have ordered a coke and sat in the shade with her eyes closed. However, the only shade in the compound was reserved for the ghetto blaster, which sat like royalty on a battered chair, asking 'Is this love?' Instead she bought a luke-cold beer and sat on the low cement wall in front of the shebeen, amidst the other patrons, all men in various stages of inebriation, smoking a cigarette and chewing at her cuticles.

Friend and Alex were on the veranda, drinking and laughing. They seemed not be bothered at all by her outburst and subsequent sulking. The sun was casting long shadows and everything was infused with a warm, golden light. She watched as a falcon lit off from a gum tree with shallow, rapid wing-beats. High in the sky, it began to glide in wide, lazy circles. She took another long swig of her beer and felt some of the tension drain away. Bob Marley stopped singing and someone shuffled over to change the cassette.

"Here, try this." Alex held out a piece of biltong "King makes it himself."

Constance gestured that she wanted to say something, but it would be awhile. She was chewing on a mouthful of very dry, very peppery biltong. Alex waited for her to swallow.

"Who's King?"

Alex pointed to the black, hand-painted sign above the entrance to the store.

Sunset Bottlestore & Butchery
Est. 1964
Mr. K. D J. Musami, Prop.

"Oh, so that's what the K stands for."

"No, it's really Kenneth, but he likes to be called King."

"I don't blame him."   Alex reached for the biltong, but Constance drew back her hand, smiling. "This is very good biltong." She took another bite and handed it back to Alex. They masticated in comfortable silence. Long notes from a harmonica drifted towards them from the ghetto blaster and then a screen door slammed and Mary's dress waved.

Constance swallowed and drank some beer. "Sorry I was such a bitch," she said in a rush.

Alex looked wary. "That's okay."

She moved over and made room for him to sit. He put his arm around her and they sat like that, drinking and chewing, watching the falcon gliding in circles, willing Mary to make that long walk from her front porch.

Macheke

October 1976

Back in Rhodesia, the war had intensified. The area between Macheke over to Mayo, then south to Headlands and Rusape became known over the next few years as the 'terror triangle'. The district was dotted with abandoned farms as their owners fled to the safety of Salisbury. Those that remained lived behind 'security' fences, armed to the teeth with rifles and shotguns and always within reach of the 'Agric-Alert' radio alarm.

A Macheke farmer, Scotty Fielding, drove out of his security fence on the morning of October 10 in his Land Rover. A farm labourer he knew waved him down. The man gave him a letter, which read, "Don't be afraid. We're not going to kill you, you are known to be a good employer." He was surrounded by seven men carrying the ubiquitous AK 47's, weapon of choice of every 'freedom fighter' in that era. Scotty politely offered the leader a cigarette. After a quick smoke, he was ordered to put two of the 'guerillas' into his vehicle and take them to his farmhouse. As they came near the house, Scotty thought to himself "Bloody hell!" and, putting the Land-Rover into second gear, drove it right into a tree, jumping out just before it hit. The vehicle flipped, trapping the two 'terrorists' inside. Reports in the Herald said he 'dashed heroically across the thirty metres into the house'; he himself told me later that he 'staggered' and it was only about ten metres, but anyway, he made it into the house, where he grabbed his rifle and shot it towards the men. The fighters managed to crawl out of the vehicle and escape.

That year, 1976, marked the beginning of the end of Rhodesia. This was the first year that white farmers came under attacks that, while never overwhelming to the white population as a whole, since the majority lived in the safety of the cities, were sustained and often deadly. Indeed, it was the very randomness of the attacks that made them so psychologically unnerving. You literally didn't know who or where the next target was. Up to then, while not unheard of — in April 1975 for example, two white land surveyors were ambushed and murdered in the Mtoko area — killings were rare. In this year, 1976, more than thirty white farmers or their wives and kids were killed, a figure that would climb steadily over the next few years. The attacks rapidly spread from the north-east so that by 1976 they covered the whole country. The 'settlers' began traveling by escorted convoys, armed with heavy machine guns, but these soon became targets of ambushes by the guerrillas. Later, even travel by air became risky, when Nkomo's ZIPRA forces shot down two planes on their way to Salisbury from Kariba in 1978.

So, Scotty counted himself lucky. He was called up to serve in the Police Anti-Terrorist Unit, nicknamed the 'Dad's Army', he later called them a lot of idiots bashing about in the bush. He soon came to realize that the munts were a lot more switched on than he had been led to believe. They always seemed to know where the unit was. But he reckoned he was only shot at four or five times. "Probably thought killing us was a waste of good ammo". When the ceasefire was declared in 1979 he was glad to get back to his farm in Macheke, keep his head down, and get on with the life he had always known.

16

Muraro Farm

June 2000

Tatenda came into the kitchen, baby Nyarai on her hip. "Goodwill is here to see you."

James and I exchanged looks. Goodwill Shoko, the foreman, stepped into the room, wearing the uniform of every male African farm worker:blue coveralls, gumboots and a floppy hat.

"I have something important to report, sir."

I sighed and went into the lounge to get my books. Goodwill had worked for us for many years. His 'something important to report' was always bad news — crop damage from hail or locusts, cattle rustlings, a brawl in the workers compound that meant James would have to drive someone over to the clinic for stitches.

"Gunpowder is here."

Samora followed me, looking for his bookcase. I shushed him. What was James doing bringing gunpowder onto the farm?

"How many are with him?" James sounded wary.

With him? James must be asking about other weapons.

"About forty. They are demanding to peg out the farm for their own plots. They are warning that no one must touch the pegs. They will be punished if they do."

"But this farm isn't one of the ones which has been gazetted for resettlement. I checked the list myself last week and it was in The Herald on Friday."

"Yes, sir. I told him that. But he is saying that he will decide which land is for settling."

I sat down in the old brown armchair.

"Well," said James calmly, "we'd better go speak with this chap."

"That is not all, sir. He is demanding that the farm provide him with some transports to take everyone to the ZANU-PF rally in Marondera on Sunday."

"Anything else?"

"Yes, baas, he says you must be leaving this place."

I went back into the kitchen. Evan and Kazana were still at the table, looking shocked. Samora sidled close to me and I automatically combed my hand through his thick mop. Goodwill was looking very uncomfortable, twisting his hat in his hands.

"Well," James repeated. "I think we must rather go and speak with this chap. How's his English?"

"I don't know. We were talking in Shona."

"You'd best come along then. This could be delicate and my Shona might not be up to the task. Don't want to accidentally call the guy an asshole or anything."

"What about us, Baba? What should we do?"

James looked at Evan, hesitating.

"I think we should go to school as we always do. Let's just act normal. I'll drive everyone today, otherwise we'll all be late."

James nodded slowly. "Okay." He reached for his hat. Goodwill said something to him in Shona. "Right." He turned back to me. "Connie, if you meet a roadblock, turn around and come straight back. Some of these men are armed."

By the time I had gathered the boys, their bookcases, Samora's lost cardigan and my car keys, James and Goodwill had already left in the bakkie for the compound. We piled into the old VW Beetle, which faithfully roared to life, and took off down the road. Before reaching the main road, I turned off to drop Samora off at the crèche.

Even before I got out of the car to check, I knew something was wrong. The yard should have been full of children at that time of the morning. "Stay here," I said to Samora. I ran up the steps to the veranda and tried the front door. It was locked. Looking in the window, I could see the tables and chairs, the shelves of toys and books. No children. No Amai Mushana.

"Get back in the car, my boy," I said.

"What's wrong, Amai? Where is everyone?"

"Nothing's wrong."

"There must be a holiday we've forgotten about," said Evan cheerfully from the backseat. "We might as well turn around and go home, Mom. No school for us today."

"Don't be silly, Evan. I'm a teacher, remember? They'd have told me if school was cancelled."

I fiddled with my keys, then made a decision. "Listen, we're all going to be late for school anyway. I think I'll just drive over to Amai Mushana's and check up on her, then drop you big boys off at school." I leaned forward and started the car.

"Can I stay with Amai Mushana today?" Samora yelled over the engine.

"We'll see, otherwise you'll have to come to my school with me."

Samora groaned and looked sulky. "And you'll behave yourself, my boy. No trying to flush your takkies down the teachers' toilet."

The memory of his last day spent with me at school cheered Samora up. He looked out the window and began whistling.

We were coming close to the workers compound. I slowed down. There seemed to be a lot of people milling around on the road. Then I saw the barrier. A tree branch was resting on piles of rocks set up on each side of the road. Four men were manning the roadblock. I stopped the car and rolled down my window. Just on the other side of the barrier I could see the bakkie, parked in the middle of the road. James and Goodwill were standing with a group of five or six men of various shapes and sizes, all with rifles slung across their chests. Goodwill was speaking to the only one not dressed in army fatigues. I assumed he was the ring-leader called 'Gunpowder'. He was a heavy man, wearing a cheap-looking purple polyester shirt with long sleeves and jeans held up with a belt sporting the largest buckle outside of Texas. Though it was not a warm day, he kept wiping the sweat from his face.

One of the 'ex-combatants' strolled over. He was wearing camouflage trousers, a ZANU-PF shirt, sunglasses, takkies and a beret. Also carrying an AK-47.

"Mangwanani," I spoke pleasantly, extending my hand.

"Maswera?" he asked, looking into the back seat.

"Taswera," I lied. "Maswera wo?"

Pleasantries over, he cocked a thumb towards the compound. "No one is permitted. You must turn back."

"I am just here to see an old friend. This is her grandchild. We want to know if she is well."

"No one is permitted in or out of this place today. We are going to take these houses to stay in."

"But, can't we just go —"

"No. You must go back."

"Okay, okay.

"It is time for you to kick the road." He banged the hood of the car with his hand. At that moment, I saw the leader of the invaders whack Goodwill hard across the face. His head shot back and his hat went flying. He would have fallen if James had not reached out and caught him. I watched as one of the other thugs jabbed Goodwill in the stomach with the butt of his Ak-47. He staggered back again, holding himself.

"You must be leaving now," insisted my buddy with the beret. He was banging hard on the hood of the car. Both Evan and Samora were yelling at me to help Goodwill. The other men at the roadblock stood up and were pointing their rifles. My hands were shaking as I tried to get the car in reverse. After what seemed like minutes, I finally managed it and stepped on the gas wildly, careening back towards the side of the track. I was able to steer back towards the centre and turned around, grinding the gears in my haste. This seemed to amuse the 'vets' no end. We could hear them laughing and hollering after us.

I drove straight home, my hands rigid on the steering wheel, staring straight ahead. The boys had fallen into a shocked silence. When we got back to the house I told them to go inside and stay there. Then I walked back to the big security fence. I had just swung the gates shut and was trying to find the right key on my chain, when I heard the bakkie roaring up the road, a rolling cloud of dust. Shading my eyes, I could see figures in the back, but I couldn't tell who was driving. The truck's horn blared insistently as it got closer. I could see James now, and Goodwill beside him. I pulled the gate back towards me and the bakkie came barreling through. I pulled my cardigan up over my face to block the dust.

"Shut the gate, shut the gate."

I did as I was told, but I couldn't lock it. "I don't have my key!"

James ran over and grabbed my keys out of my hand. He found the right key and snapped the bolt shut, locking it. Behind me, I could hear people getting down from the truck, talking excitedly. James stood there for a moment, breathing heavily, looking down the road. I touched his back, but he shrugged me off.

"What the hell were you doing at the compound? I thought you said you were going straight to school?"

"I was, but then the crèche was closed so I thought I'd better check on Miriam so —"

"So you thought you'd just take a wee jaunt over to the workers compound, where you knew a bunch of fucking munts were hanging out with their guns? And you thought you'd bring the children along; make it a nice family outing? Are you out of your fucking mind? I just couldn't believe it when I saw you there, I saw that nig-nog pointing his gun at you and I thought, I thought—"

He breathed in sharply and wiped his eyes on his shirt. I reached out and this time he let me take him in my arms. "I'm sorry, I'm so sorry." He nuzzled into me, breathing deeply.

"Ach, its okay. I knew when I married you that you'd be trouble."

It came to me that Goodwill was still in the truck.

"I saw Goodwill. Is he okay? Do you think we should telephone for the police?"

"We may as well do, but I doubt they'll come. Goodwill is going to be fine, but he's plenty shook up, I can tell you."

We moved apart. James went over to the bakkie and helped Goodwill climb down. He said something to him in Shona. I went over to him and touched his shoulder. Blood was running down the side of his face.

"I'm so sorry, Goodwill." He smiled wanly at me. "Lets get you inside. Tatenda can patch you up." We each took an arm and began steering Goodwill toward the house.

"I reckon by tomorrow things will be back to normal."

"How's that?"

"I talked with Gunpowder. He's what passes for brains behind this invasion. Told me the whole farm was going to be pegged for plots. Said we'd have to leave. He threatened me, said I'd be killed if I or any of my workers touched the pegs."

"Is that when he started roughing-up Goodwill?"

"No, that came later. I told him, okay, he can peg the farm, but I said 'Look, over three hundred kids pass through the farm every morning on their way to school.' I told him it would be his responsibility to tell three hundred kids not to touch the pegs and he would have to punish them if they knock the pegs over. That seemed to make him consider his options. He pow-wowed with his comrades and then he said he was leaving. Goodwill was just negotiating the price for removing the roadblock when you drove up. Well, you saw what happened."

"What an asshole!"

"Yeah, well, after that display of manhood, plus all the cash I had on me, he gave the order for the barrier to come down. We didn't stick around to say thanks, just hopped in the bakkie and drove back here like a bat out of hell."

"And that's it? They're gone?"

James shook his head. "For now, maybe." He turned toward the house. "I'll help you get your books out of the car. Christ, I need a beer!"

James stood, leaning against the counter. He looked much as he always looked after a hard day on the farm — the white farmer beer-belly rounding out his sweat-stained shirt, faded, dirty shorts, black oil stains on his legs, burrs sticking out on his socks. His beard had been completely white for a few years now, but his moustache was still red. He gulped his beer and with his free hand twirled one of his remaining grizzled curls around his finger.

"Do you think they'll come back?"

He seemed to be fascinated by Nyarai, who was calmly and methodically eating her bread and jam. "What?" He looked at me and said patiently, "Of course they'll be back."

"But you told me our farm hasn't been gazetted. It's not on the list. You said so yourself."

"Connie", he reached behind to put his empty beer on the counter, "it's not about lists. It's not organized that way."

"What are you talking about?"

"This is all about Mugabe keeping power. He's targeting MDC supporters, providing transport for these thugs, giving them weapons and sending them out to harass and terrorize. I don't know how many farms have been invaded, but I reckon it's over 500 by now. People are being beat up and thrown in jail, killed. It's mostly the Af's who suffer, of course. They get kicked off the farm along with the owner, but unlike him, they can't bugger off to Melbourne or Sussex."

Or Vancouver. "What about Loganfield?" Loganfield was Scotty's farm. It had been invaded in April, but Scotty had seemed to come to some kind of uneasy truce with the squatters, who had allowed work on the farm to continue with little interference, in exchange for Scotty turning a blind eye to some cattle rustling and the cutting of trees for huts and firewood.

James picked out a cloth from the sink and used it to wipe Nyarai's face. *"Nyarai, shamwari venyu vari kupi?"* The baby looked back at him solemnly and then reached up her arms to be lifted down. We watched her toddle of into the lounge. She sat down heavily by an old basket. She pulled the basket towards her, dumping wooden blocks onto her lap and around her legs. Lady opened her eyes, but did not lift her head.

"Do you want some tea?"

"Ta. Just a cuppa. I'll just have the rest of this bread and jam. Looks like our wee friend left me some."

I filled the kettle and put it on the electric cooker.

"So what about Loganfield?"

James shrugged. "With any luck, Scotty can plant and bring his crop in, but it's well known he's an MDC member. The farm's bound to be gazetted for resettlement in the next round."

"I should never have gone to that rally."

Another shrug. "Ach, we don't know. Maybe someone saw you there, maybe someone saw Miriam, maybe this is Situmba's doing?"

"Mr. Situmba? The one from the club?"

"Yeah, he's the local Zanu big man. Nothing happens here without his say so."

"Wow." I fished around in the cupboard for the tea canister. Jolly Mr. Situmba, owner of the Macheke hotel and the Macheke bottle store. Whenever we met him he had always had a lolly in his pocket for the boys. "He's one of the governors of the secondary school. I've been teaching there for fifteen years!"

"Maybe it's not him. This is organized chaos, this is."

The kettle began whistling. I poured the water into the chipped brown teapot. "Maybe things will be better after the elections."

"It's a gamble. But if we lose, we lose big."

I set the teapot on the table and found another mug. I sat back in my chair and lit a cigarette, then put my feet up into my husband's lap.

"I thought you were going to quit?"

"I am. But not today. Not today."

17

October 1983

Mutamba School

The entire mission was in a fever pitch. The main road into the mission had been paved, a new gatehouse built and the guard issued with a new uniform, though, as Julia pointed out, the perimeter fence had not been repaired. After much discussion, the menu for the Old Boys' Tea was set — cream cakes, bacon buns, sadza and relish, samosas, tea, Mazoe, Fanta and Coke. Then someone pointed out that the villagers, who would flock to see their leader, would have to be fed as well.

"But at a separate venue," said Sydney Sekeramyi. "When the povo find out about the food they will be here in large numbers."

Lovemore Sibanda made a weak joke about loves and fishes, which everyone pretended to find amusing, then they began arguing about where and what to feed the masses.

Finally it was decided to build a couple of fires by the Form One block. The school cook, her assistants and some students would man the sadza pots and dish out sadza and relish to all and sundry.

The music master, Mr. Kavaneti, had the choir practicing every day before supper and had told Constance that they had chosen 'an eclectic program of hymns and secular songs'. The students had been informed in no uncertain terms at morning assembly that those who were not going home for the long weekend were to be in full uniform on the big day and any 'miscreant' would be given a thorough beating.

Benjamin Mwira, the carpentry teacher, was in charge of painting the dining hall, venue for The Tea. Somehow Constance had ended up as his helper. After arguing half-heartedly for cream-coloured paint, she had bowed to the inevitable and was now up on a rickety ladder, painting the walls a lurid green.

"We're not doing the ceiling, are we?" she called down to Mr. Mwira. "Because if we do, we'll need to send someone to town for another paint roller. Are those blinds teak?"

Benjamin Mwira was on the other side of the dining hall, near the windows. He had taken down the venetian blinds and spread them on the canvas cloth covering the floor. Like many things at the school, they had seen better days. Covered in a thick layer of dust, many of the slats hung crookedly and some were cracked.

Mr. Mwira said "Mahogany," casually. He ran his hand along one of the still intact slats, then wiped his hand on his trousers. "These are easily repaired. But first they must be cleaned." He rose to his feet and walked over to the doorway. Shading his eyes from the brilliant October light, he looked up and down the road. Then he saw what he wanted and began calling out to someone in Shona.

A couple of high, sweet voices answered and a moment later two girls appeared, each carrying a bucket. Constance recognized Nyasha Msika and Gracious. They were dressed in typical weekend clothes — loose cotton skirts, t-shirts and flip-flops. Gracious had a scarf wrapped round her head, Nyasha's hair was in her signature intricate braids. They had been on a water collecting expedition and had probably been intercepted on their way back to their dormitory to do their laundry.

Mr. Mwira left to get his tape measure. The girls got to work cheerfully. After greeting Constance, they went into the storeroom and came out with cleaning supplies. Chatting and laughing, they liberally splashed water over the four sets of blinds. Constance wondered if this would damage the wood, but decided to keep her mouth shut.

She carefully climbed up another couple of rungs, hoping the can of paint wouldn't fall. She could have sworn the air was even hotter up here and she felt as if the ceiling was pressing down on her. Flies swirled desultorily around the room or buzzed tonelessly against the windows. As she lifted the brush, Constance could feel something running down between her shoulder blades. It was either sweat or her hair falling down. Only one more wall and she would be finished.

"Amai Miguel, please borrow us that ladder."

She looked down on the long, lean figure of the boarding master, Mr. Maredza. From this angle she could see he had a bald spot on the crown of his head. He was holding a screwdriver and a light bulb. "I have been sent to change the light."

The round light fixture covering the only bulb in the dining hall was full of dust and insects. As she climbed down, Constance said, "If you like, I can clean that covering. Otherwise, we won't be able to see the light anyway."

Mr. Maredza nodded, then turned and barked something at the two girls. It seemed they were being assigned another task. Nyasha got up from cleaning the blinds and pulled the ladder into the middle of the floor. She steadied it for the boarding master as he climbed to the top and began to unscrew the bolt above his head.

Constance went out onto the verandah, squinting against the brilliant light. She rolled her aching shoulders. The air felt almost as oppressive outside. There was not a cloud in the sky and no breeze. She wanted a cigarette, but was too tired to go back inside to get one out of her bag. Instead, she sat down on the steps. There were still students moving up and down the road, collecting water or heading over to the tuck shop. She greeted a group of about a dozen kids heading to the tennis courts. They had three racquets and one ball between them. On the patch of grass between the road and the second form classroom block a goat was methodically munching its way through a hibiscus bush. She turned her head toward the rumble of a familiar engine coming from the direction of the teachers' houses.

Julia came roaring up to the dining hall. It looked as if she had half of the school's bachelors crammed in with her. Constance recognized her banker, Mr. Simango in the coveted front seat.

Julia leaned out the window and said something.

"Pardon?" Constance yelled. She shrugged to show she couldn't hear.

Julia turned off the engine. "I said I hope you don't mind. I'm heading into Marondera to see if I can flog some more of these damn raffle tickets."

"What are you going to do, hawk them on the street corner ?"

Julia laughed. "No, I'm going to drop these guys off at The Hotel and then head over to the Country Club. Maybe I can chat up the white farmers and get rid of the whole lot."

"If anyone can do it, you can."

"Anyway, we'll be back before it gets dark. Do you need anything in town?"

"Can you stop at the bookshop and see if they have The Guardian?"

"Sure thing. Will I see you at Alex's braai later?"

Constance felt her face grow red. "No, I think I'll be feeling bagged after all this painting. Probably hit the sack early. You can bring the car back tomorrow."

October 1976

Geneva

Whatever might be happening on the ground in Rhodesia — an ever-growing influx of fighters, increased attacks on white farmers which were answered by raids on camps, such as Nyadzonia in Mozambique, the rounding up of civilians into "Protected Villages" — at the Geneva Conference it was clear that the comrades had won the fashion war.

Picture this: The Smith faction stays at the stuffy, traditional Hotel du Rhone. They wear new suits, but alas, Rhodesian tailors are working from 1950's patterns. The old white men look as though what is left of their hair has been cut by their wives at the farm kitchen table. Making matters worse, they use copious amounts of hair oil and strategic combing. They all seem to wear the same black-framed reading glasses. They look like old men, stiff and uncomfortable. Smith and his foreign minister, P.K. van der Byl, use cricket metaphors in their press conferences, coming across as unintelligible to the readers of the New York Times and worse, as 'toffs' to the readers of the Sunday Telegraph.

The Patriotic Front faction, led by Mugabe, Tongogara and Rex Nhongo, are staying at the new, hip Intercontinental Hotel. While no one could accuse Mugabe of being a slave to fashion (he is, after all, a known Marxist) his serviceable safari suits and large rectangular glasses give him the air of a no-nonsense policy wonk. He uses boxing metaphors, which everyone can understand. Rex Nhongo , the ZIPA commander, who is at the conference under duress, having been sent by Samora Machel, makes his appearances in fighting trim, his camouflage cap sitting jauntily on his head. "I have come just with the clothes on my back," he tells one reporter. Apparently, Machel was so angry with him for his lukewarm support of the conference, that when he ordered him to Geneva, he didn't let Nhongo go to Chimoio first to pack a change of clothes.

But it is Josiah Tongogara who wins the battle for best dressed guerrilla. Tall, dark and handsome, he wears denim suits, with no tie. He smiles warmly. He is relaxed. He jokes around. He has charisma.

"Christ!" the reporter from the Rhodesia Herald says to the photographer in the bar of the Intercon. He has just finished filing his report of a news conference with 'PK' at which the foreign minister has actually used the cliché 'sticky wicket'. "If this is the best we can do, we might as well pull the plug now."

In fact, the conference dragged on for another six weeks. In fact, the only thing both sides agreed on was that the conference was, in the words of Tongogara's aide, Moses Masekesa, "a load of crap." In fact, everyone knew that Nkomo and Mugabe had been forced into announcing the creation of the Patriotic Front. And Rex Nhongo's reluctant appearance at the conference, far from signifying unity, led Smith to believe that Mugabe had little control over the ZIPA guerillas in Mozambique. On its side, the Patriotic Front had nothing to lose by sticking to its demand for majority rule.

When the conference was finally adjourned in November, the Rhodesians flew home, determined to keep up the fight. Little did they know that only a couple of months later, Samora Machel would arrest the ZIPA 'radicals'. Mugabe would emerge firmly in control of ZANU. The new guerilla army, ZANLA, would be under the control of General Josiah Tongogara.

18

October 1983

Mutamba Mission

Constance was late for the Prime Minister's speech. Miguel had reluctantly agreed to have a bath, but he drew the line at wearing his school uniform. "But its Saturday" he kept repeating.

"You want to look nice for the Prime Minister, don't you?"

Miguel shrugged. "I guess. Why is he coming?"

"He used to be a student here."

Miguel looked interested. "Will he be wearing his school uniform?"

"No, but I'm sure he'll be nicely dressed. It's a way of showing respect, Miguel. You don't want Mr. Mugabe to see you in those tatty shorts. And you must wear shoes. And not those filthy takkies, either," she added.

A steady stream of people had been passing along the road in front of their house all morning, all dressed up like Christmas trees, all carrying gifts for their leader — a pumpkin, a bag of oranges, a live chicken. Constance wondered what Mugabe did with all that food. Did he take it home and actually eat it himself, or did he give it away to the poor people? She hadn't thought about giving him anything, but now she felt a bit anxious. Would she be committing a huge faux pas if she showed up without a cake or a basket of mangoes? Never mind, it was too late now. But then as she was ushering Miguel out through the kitchen, something caught her eye. Someone from back home had sent her a calendar of iconic Canadian

155

scenes — Lake Louise, Quebec City, Peggy's Cove. There were only two and half months left in the year, but she had never written on it and she doubted the Prime Minister would actually use it to keep track of his appointments. Maybe he would like the pictures.

The crowd spilled beyond the hard-packed earth in front of the assembly hall onto the tough brown grass in the quadrangle between the blocks of classrooms. A haze of dust rose up to their knees as people shifted and shuffled. Hot and a bit out of breath, Constance stood at the back. She could hear someone speaking, but she couldn't see over the heads of the people in front of her."

"Amai, I can't see," Miguel complained.

"Well, that's what we get for being late. Shush now, people are trying to hear the Prime Minister."

An elderly man in front of her turned and surveyed Miguel and her. He murmured something to the person in front of him. A large woman with a baby on her back turned and then moved aside. The old man gestured with his knobkerrie for them to go through the gap they had made. Constance hesitated, then the old man nodded vigorously and the woman pulled Miguel forward.

In this way they wended their way until they were at the foot of the stairs of the veranda. Robert Mugabe was standing, delivering his speech. He was wearing a dark suit. He spoke animatedly, in English for the most part, without notes. The light glinted on his large, thick glasses every time he moved his large head.

Every so often he would say something in Shona and the crowd would laugh. He himself would break into a wide smile, his white teeth against his dark skin transforming his face completely from acerbic Marxist to jovial man-of-the- people.

Behind him sat a select row of dignitaries and staff. Brother Julius and Brother Joseph had old Brother Cecil propped up between them. On the other side sat the board of governors and Mr. Mhanda and Mr. Murerwa in their university graduate robes. She wondered if Mr. Mwira had a place on the dais because he had painted the dining hall. He was also wearing robes. Mercy Dube and Miss Takawira were wearing high heels and cocktail dresses. There were some other well-dressed men of various ages. Constance wondered if they were other Old Boys or just part of Mugabe's entourage. She wasn't surprised to see that Julia had managed to wrangle a place for herself front and centre. She was wearing an elegant linen dress that showed her curves to full advantage. Constance admired her hair, which was piled up on top of her head, adorned with a hibiscus blossom. How did she get it to stay up there like that?

"Amai, I want to go over there." Miguel said, pointing "Friend and Alex are there. Look."

Constance followed his arm to a place just below the veranda and off to the side. The Bachelors were standing there together. There were all dressed to the nines. Even Friend had ditched his Nyerere shirt for a suit and tie.

At that moment Alex looked around and saw her. He nodded and looked as if he was about to come over, but instead Constance bent down towards Miguel. She gave him a little push. "Okay, but behave yourself."

Mugabe seemed to be winding down. He was thanking the Brothers and the Headmaster and said he was looking forward to speaking with some of his old teachers at the reception after. "As some of you may be aware, I could be quite naughty when I was a schoolboy. It will be a nice change to have Brother Cecil offering me tea and cakes instead of a good caning."

The crowd laughed and began applauding. Many women in the crowd showed their approval by ululating. Some of the men raised their knobkerries or fists in salute and shouted "Pamberi!" Constance, looking back over the crowd, noticed two white men standing at the edge.

Up on stage Julia leaned towards the tall man sitting beside her, giving The Bachelors a generous view of her cleavage. The man leaned toward Julia, to catch what she was saying. He leaned his head back and laughed, a laugh Constance could hear over the crowd. A laugh she recognized.

The school choir had taken the stage. Mr. Kavaneti, wearing white gloves, a back choir gown and platform shoes, began directing his singers. She tried not to stare at Moses Masekesa. She was sure he hadn't seen her. Was it just her imagination, or had Julia inched her chair closer to his?

Beautiful, beautiful Africa
Beautiful, beautiful Africa
We will always remember
Beautiful Africa

Stop being an idiot, she told herself. She concentrated on the Prime Minister. It was impossible to tell if he was enjoying the song. She had once seen a news clip on television of Bishop Desmond Tutu on a platform, dancing and singing along with a choir, thoroughly having fun. Obviously Mugabe was made of different stuff.

Long live Comrade Mugabe
Long live Comrade Mugabe
We will always remember
Long live Comrade Mugabe

The people down below began swaying and singing. There was more ululating. The song ended and the Headmaster thanked the choir for a job well done. Everyone on the stage began getting up and the crowd down below began milling around. Many of the villagers were leaving, no doubt in a hurry to get to the sadza.

"Let us go up to the platform." Constance turned and found Miriam and Mushana at her side.

"Are we allowed?"

"Oh, yes." Miriam inclined her head in the direction of the verandah steps. "You see, all the staff are going up." And indeed, a small queue of teachers was snaking up to meet Mugabe.

They joined the line behind The Bachelors. Alex, ahead with Miguel, stopped and made some space, but she pretended not to see and continued chatting with Munorwe Simango and Miriam.

Mugabe had remained sitting. On one side stood the headmaster, on the other sat Moses. Constance watched as Mr. Mhanda introduced Julia. She had to bend over as Mugabe greeted her, shaking her hand vigorously. Constance wondered if he was enjoying the view. Julia straightened and sidled gracefully in front of Moses, who was now standing as part of the reception line. They said something to each other, and, when Julia was made to move on by the pressure of the queue, she reached up and touched his shoulder.

Constance had been so mesmerized by this that she didn't notice that Alex and Miguel were waiting for her beside Mr. Mhanda. "Ah," said the Headmaster as she came close. "Prime Minister, this Alex Shaw, a teacher from Canada."

The Prime Minister reached up and shook Alex's hand. "How long have you been here in Zimbabwe?"

"Almost three years, Sir."

"Well, thank you for your service to our country."

Alex nodded and moved over slightly.

"And this is another Canadian teacher, Amai Miguel and her son." Constance shook Mugabe's hand.

Miguel handed Mugabe the calendar and said something in Shona in his piping voice.

Everyone laughed. "Did she, indeed?" said Mugabe, turning to Miguel. He leaned forward and took both of Miguel's hands between his. "How old are you, Miguel? Do you go to school?"

"Yes, but I don't like it very much." More laughter. "I like football and herding cattle."

"You are a real son of the soil," declared Mugabe, smiling. "But you must work hard at your studies so you can grow up to take care of your mother and father." He nodded to Constance and Alex, then turned to Miriam and Mushana.

"Hello, my friend," said Moses, taking Miguel's hands between his. "I'm Moses. Do you remember me?"

"Yes, yes!" Miguel nodded vigorously. "The hoopoe man."

Alex was looking over Miguel's head, his eyebrows raised. Constance wanting to make a point, leaned toward Moses as she reached out her hand. Unfortunately, the point was lost as she felt her ankles wobbling. To regain her balance, she steadied herself on Miguel's head.

"Ouch, Amai!"

"It's lovely to see you again, Madam," said Moses smoothly. His handshake was brief, his eyes already looking past her down the line.

§

159

"Here, I got you something." Alex thrust a large glass into her hand. She took a sip and looked up, surprised. Alex put his fingers to his lips.

"Shh. Courtesy of Friend." He had to yell to be heard.

"I'll have to make sure I thank him. Later. When I can move from this spot. How did you even find me in all this?"

"The advantage of height. I can actually see over the heads of everyone here."

Constance took another swig. "I don't suppose you've seen Miguel?"

"I have. He and Mushana are over by the grub, stuffing their faces."

"Oh God. I told him the food was for the adults."

"Don't worry about it. The crush in here is so bad, no one can even see the food, let alone get to it."

"Speak for yourself." Julia nudged Alex with her elbow, grinning. She had a large glass in one hand and a sausage roll in the other. "Ah, I see you've both been to Friend's private cellar." She offered them each a bite, then finished the sausage roll off herself, licking her fingers. Then she drained her glass.

"What did you think of the speech?"

"I was late. He seemed to have the crowd in the palm of his hand."

"I liked the announcement that the days of schools like Peterhouse remaining exclusive are over."

"Of course that plays well here," said Alex.

"You don't think he's sincere?"

He snorted. "How many children of the government attend Mutamba?"

Julia shrugged.

"So where are they going to school?"

"Peterhouse, Churchill School, Founders High School, St. George's College, Falcon College."

"You're awfully cynical."

"I thought I was stating the obvious."

"Well, off to find more sustenance."

"Alex says Miguel is over by the food. Can you tell him I've left? I have to get out of here."

"My pleasure. He's with that gorgeous hunk who sat next to me during the speech." She grinned and was soon lost in the mass.

"I have to get out of here." Constance was too tired to yell, but Alex must have heard her. He began shouldering people, clearing a path for her. Constance tottered after him.

"Sorry, sorry."

They finally made it onto the stoep. There were fewer people out here and it was marginally cooler. Constance bent over to take off her shoes. Alex reached down to steady her. She shook him off.

"What's your problem?"

She straightened, juggling her shoes and glass. Beer spilled down the front of her dress.

"My problem? What's my problem?"

"Yeah, you'll hardly talk to me these days." He looked warily at her.

"Hardly talk to you? Hardly talk to you?" She pushed her bangs back from her forehead.

"You didn't think I was going to stay here forever, did you?"

"Well, why not?" Her voice was high-pitched and strained with the effort not to cry. "I mean, not forever, obviously, but at least until," she hesitated, then went on in a rush "until I finish my contract."

"That's almost two years from now!"

"So? What's to stop you from staying here with us? You love it here. I know you do. Why can't you stay?"

"I wish I could." He put his hand under her chin and looked appealing at her. "I have to go back to my job in Saskatoon, my leave of absence runs out at the end of December. I have to go back."

"Saskatoon!," she wailed, batting his hand away. "No one ever has to go back to Saskatoon." She was crying now. "If you really loved me, if you really cared about Miguel, you'd stay."

Alex shrugged helplessly. Everyone near the dining hall was looking at them. Some part of Constance knew that she was going

161

to be horribly embarrassed later, but like a drunk at a party who can't refuse that third martini, she pressed on.

"The truth is, you don't really care all that much about me. Do you? You have another girlfriend back home, don't you? Don't you?"

"Of course I care about you. Look," he said urgently, dropping his voice, "we need to talk. Can I come over to your house tonight?"

"You're kidding, right?"

"No, I —"

"Because we're finished. The Zambezi River will dry up before I sleep with you again. Ouww!" She forgot she had taken her shoes off and she brought her foot down hard on a thorn. Yelling in pain and anger, she began hopping backward toward the dining hall. "I'd gouge my eyes out with this thorn before I slept with you again!"

Her audience hadn't had such fun since Benjamin Mwira and his wife had had a knock-down, drag-out fight out in the road after he had been discovered philandering with their maid. Somehow, the fight had ended with both Mrs. Mwira and the maid wrestling him to the ground, screaming at the top of their lungs. The poor guy finally shook them off and made a dash for the safety of his car. He had to suffer the indignity of sitting locked inside his beloved Peugeot sedan as his wife and mistress pelted curses and old maize cobs at him, while the crowd hooted and roared their approval. Now, seeing the blood spurting through her hands holding her foot, they rushed forward to offer their assistance and advice. She felt a hand on her elbow, and then someone picked her up and began carrying her towards the dining hall. Looking around through her tears and the tangle of her hair, she glimpsed a white arm. She began squirming.

"Put me down. I mean it!"

"Glad to, miss." Constance felt herself being lowered onto the steps. She sat up. It was one of the men she had seen at the speech, the shorter one.

He pulled a handkerchief out of his pocket. "Here, give me your foot, please." Then he turned to the crowd and said something in

Shona. "It's alright, I've just asked someone to go and get you some bandages and some muti."

"I knew I'd seen you somewhere before. You're that Rhodie farmer I met in Marondera last year!"

He smiled. "I didn't think I'd made much of an impression."

"What are you doing here?"

"My farm's not too far from here. Gave the staff the day off to come and see the big chief. Thought I'd come and join in the fun, since there's not much doing on the farm today anyway."

A large shadow fell over them. It was Amai Tendai, the matron. "Amai Miguel, what have you done to yourself? Here, let me have a look."

She pulled the blood-smeared cloth away and began dabbing professionally at Constance's foot with Dettol. She looked at the farmer. "Are you the one who sent for help?"

"Yes. Name's James Fielding." He and Amai Tendai shook hands.

"Ah, yes. I knew your mother." She turned back to Constance and began wrapping her wound. She said something to James in Shona and he laughed.

"What are you two saying about me?"

"I said you are just like these small boys. Running around here without shoes on."

"I only took them off a few minutes ago because they were killing my feet."

Alex joined them on the steps, her shoes dangling in hand. "Do you want these back or should I get rid of them?"

Constance hesitated. She never wanted to wear them again, but they were very expensive shoes and they were red. "Why don't you take them, Amai Tendai?"

The matron had a pin in her mouth, but she managed to smile and held out a foot encased in a very large white takkie. It had to be at least a size nine. She finished with Constance's foot and patted her knee. "Leave them outside your gate tonight. By the morning they will be gone. But you can't walk home shoeless. I will send someone to fetch Miguel. He must go and fetch you some other shoes." She turned to James. "Help me up, please."

"Tatenda," said Constance. "Thank you so much."

The matron held out her empty palm and shook it, the African sign for nothing. "Hazeku ndaba."

Just then Constance felt a small body hurtling against her back and two arms wrapping around her neck. "Hey!"

"Sorry, Amai. Are you okay? Baba Cloud told me you have a cut foot."

"Yes, I'm fine." She pulled Miguel into her lap. "Listen, I need you to go to our house and fetch me some shoes. My sandals, okay? You know where they are, eh? Right by the front door?"

Alex, James and Amai Tendai were all looking at someone behind her. She twisted awkwardly and shaded her eyes.

"I came to see if you needed any assistance." It was Moses.

"Moses used to be a doctor," said Miguel excitedly.

"No, no," he said, "not a doctor. I was a medic during the war."

"She has already been treated, Comrade," said Amai Tendai. "I applied Dettol and a bandage."

Constance held out her foot. Alex moved over so that Moses could sit down beside her. "You can see Matron has done a very professional job."

"This looks fine. What happened?"

Alex and Constance's eyes slid together for a moment. "I took off my shoes because they hurt my feet and then I stepped on a thorn."

"Amai, your feet are not puncture-proof like mine," said Miguel.

"So you must go and fetch the shoes from your house." Moses leaned back on his elbows.

"I'll go with you," said Alex. "I know where they are."

Constance shot him a furious look, which was intercepted by Moses. He raised his eyebrows.

"He's not my boyfriend," she hissed.

"Not anymore," said James, laconically.

"Yes, there's a great deal of water in the Zambezi River," said Moses. He reached across to James. "My name is Moses Masekesa."

"James Fielding." They shook hands.

All three were silent for a moment, watching Miguel and Alex walking away, hand in hand.

"So you're a Mutamba Old Boy," said Constance.

"Actually, no. I'm a member of the government. Deputy Minister of Health."

"Wow. I'm impressed."

"You should be. I took time out of my schedule to accompany the Prime Minister here."

"Why?"

"You once told me this was your school. I wanted to see you again."

Constance felt her face growing hot.

On her other side, James gave a little cough. "Great minds think alike. While we're baring every aspect of our private lives."

Constance heard light, clicking sounds behind and turned. Julia was coming across the verandah, looking poised and graceful in her high heels. She was with Munorwe Simango, the manager of Barclays Bank.

"Constance! There you are. Someone inside said you had severed your foot and had to be taken to the hospital."

Once again Constance held out her foot. Julia sat down between her and Moses. She held her glass up to Mr. Simango.

"Munorwe, be a doll and fetch me another drink." She looked around enquiringly. "Anyone else?"

James was the first to speak. "Thanks, no. I think it's time for me to push off home." He rose. "I'll go and round up my brother."

Moses also got to his feet. "I too must be getting back to my duties."

James spoke to Constance. "Take care of that foot, Miss." He touched his cap and nodded in Julia's direction.

"Yes, as Deputy Minister of Health, I order you to remain off it for the next few days."

Constance looked up at Moses, shading her eyes. "Miguel will be sad he didn't get to say goodbye to you."

"Tell him I will see him again soon." He nodded to Julia and reached down and touched Constance lightly on the head.

Julia could scarcely wait until both men were out of earshot. "How did you do it?"

"What?" said Constance, defensively.

"You, looking so pretty and helpless, with your foot practically in that gorgeous man's lap, while that Rhodie farmer looked on longingly.

"Don't be silly. Not everyone is as man-crazy as you are."

But she could still feel the warm touch of Moses' hand on her head.

December 26, 1979

Mozambique

The 'official' story about the death of General Josiah Tongogara is sketchy, taking up only a paragraph or two in any of the 'definitive' accounts of the struggle for Zimbabwe. The facts are stated baldly. After a deal for a ceasefire and one man, one vote elections was signed at Lancaster House on December 19th, Tongogara left London and flew to Maputo. He was traveling to Chimoio on Christmas Day to brief ZANLA commanders on the ceasefire. His vehicle tried to pass a FRELIMO lorry and slammed into it. Tongogara, sitting in the front passenger seat, was killed instantly. Or so the official story goes.

Another story. Tongogara had grown up working on a farm owned by Ian Smith's family. Charming and genial, he disarmed Ian Smith at Lancaster House by speaking fondly of Smith's mother. "Say hello, ask her about the sweets she used to give me and if she has still got some for me." In this way, it was said, Tongogara had helped broker the agreement. Lord Carrington, chair of the conference, called Tongogara a 'moderating' influence, someone who could soothe Mugabe's temper and work both sides of the room. In any case, a deal was worked out. It gave the white farmers a guarantee that their land would not be taken from them for at least ten years.

Another story. Tongogara supposedly met secretly with Joshua Nkomo, the leader of ZAPU. They could only have been discussing unity between the two nationalist movements. Some say that Nkomo and Tongogara had already cooked up a deal, going back to Tongogara's release from jail in Zambia, back in October 1976. Nkomo put pressure on Kaunda to get Tongogara released. Tongogara would support Nkomo for prime minister of Zimbabwe and in return he would be given command of the army. Whether this was true or not, it is well known that Mugabe was adamantly opposed to any unity deals with ZAPU.

On December 25th, Tongogara was on his way to give the guerrillas at Chimoio details about the ceasefire, details that would have angered many of them. They believed they were on the verge of military victory and they would have viewed the ceasefire and the conditions laid out in the Lancaster House Agreement with deep suspicion. The guerillas were expected to come in from the bush and lay down their arms at assembly points, most of the arable land would remain in white hands. Some say that in his hurry to reach the camp, Tongogara pushed his driver too hard, so that the driver fell asleep at the wheel, crossing the road and hitting an oncoming truck. Or he pushed his driver too hard, so that the driver tried to pass when it wasn't safe, slamming into the back of a FRELIMO lorry.

Or Tongogara was dead before he ever got into the car. He was shot in the stomach and bludgeoned with an axe while he slept. His body was cut open so the bullets could be removed and the whole thing would look like a car accident.

Like all conspiracy theories, this one depends largely on magnifying details, zeroing in on coincidences and endlessly scrutinizing inconsistencies. Mountains are made out of molehills, tenuous connections become bridges of steel. There was the old story that Tongogara might have been involved in the murder of Herbert Chitepo. Did Samora Machel still harbour suspicions? The vehicle which killed him was, after all, a FRELIMO lorry. In their last meeting, Tongogara is supposed to have told Machel, "I know nothing about the death of Chitepo." Why would he be protesting his innocence?

Or did Mugabe do him in?

At first it was reported that Tongogara was died on Christmas Day. A few days later, the date was changed to the 26th. This is surely suspicious, even though we are talking about a time before cell phones and a country with an eratic telephone system. It was two days before his body got to a morgue. A white undertaker from Salisbury was asked by ZANU to determine the cause of death. He looked the body over and declared the death a result of an automobile accident. But no photographs or autopsy report have ever been made public.

But there are other photographs. Tongogara, tall, handsome, jovial at the Geneva and Lancaster House conferences. Tongogara, the commander, in camouflage fatigues, sitting at a table, with a kerosene lantern, shortwave radio and map, pen in one hand, and A-K 47 propped up against the table, the decisive leader, commander of a guerrilla army. Tongogara in a "smart casual" suit, urbane and relaxed, the charismatic diplomat who could help broker a deal with the enemy. Tongogara, holding secret talks with Nkomo, advocating unity with ZAPU. He must surely have been a thorn in Mugabe's side.

"Almost no one in Lusaka accepts Mugabe's assurance that Tongogara died accidentally", a CIA agent wrote at the time.

I don't know about Zambia, but certainly almost everyone in Zimbabwe felt Mugabe had Tongogara's blood on his hands. Even in the first heady post-war years, when children could still be heard singing sweet songs in praise of the Prime Minister as they herded cattle or carried water, everyone I asked told me quite openly that Tongogara had been assassinated on Mugabe's orders.

Everyone except the one who could tell the story in the first person. The eyewitness. The one who was sitting in the back seat of the car. "I survived because I was wearing a seatbelt. Tongogara never wore a seatbelt, but I'm a medic. I'd seen too many bodies mangled from car wrecks."

Almost everyone associated with the death of Tongogara has by now either followed him to the grave or has one foot in it. His four bodyguards have all died, murdered some say, because of what they knew. Samora Machel died in 1986 when his plane (so they say) was shot down by the South African army. Joshua Nkomo died in Parirenyatawa Hospital of prostate cancer in 1999. Ian Smith died in

South Africa. But Mugabe lives on, a vampire who survives by sucking the blood from his countrymen, dining with the ghost of Tongogara.

19

November 2000

Macheke Secondary School

"Fifty dollars tea money." Mr. Chaminuka smiled apologetically at me as he shook a biscuit tin under my nose. "I'm sorry, Amai, but we are almost out of funds."

I reached for my purse, slung over the back of my chair, and groped for my wallet. "I hate to date myself, Mr. Chaminuka, but I can remember when fees for the social fund were two dollars a month".

I found the right bills and put them in the tin. Mr. Chaminuka nodded his thanks, but didn't move away.

"Ah," I said. "You'll be needing more. Who are you collecting for today?"

"Mrs. Mogwe." Another apologetic smile.

"Mrs. Mogwe?" I was surprised. Mrs. Mogwe was a new member of staff. Young and pretty, she taught Home Economics. "Is this for someone in her family, or —" I paused, but Mr. Chaminuka waited, smiling sadly behind his thick glasses. "Is she ill herself?"

"I believe she is very ill. The Headmaster has said she will not be returning to work."

I pulled a wad of bills from the bottom of my purse and began unwinding the elastic that held them together. "Where has she gone? Does she have any family to help her out?" This was my grocery moncy, but it couldn't be helped.

Mr. Chaminuka shrugged. "Her sister has come from Mrewa to ask for assistance. We shall send the funds we raise back with her."

"What about her husband?"

Mr. Chaminuka shrugged. "I don't know him."

All morning I kept thinking of Mrs. Mogwe. I didn't really know her, but I liked to see her, gracefully moving up and down the verandas between classes in a bright apron, or at tea break, laughing and arguing good-naturedly with some of the younger teachers. After the bell was rung for the end of the day, I rushed out of class, not bothering to pack up my books.

"Ah, there you are, Knowledge." He was still in his classroom, seated at his desk, but I had to crane my neck around to see him.

"Oh, hello, Edson. I'm sorry to interrupt, but I need to speak with Mr. Rutanhire."

Knowledge said something to Edson. I waited while he gathered up his books. He spoke softly as he brushed by me in the doorway. "Goodbye, Sir. See you tomorrow, Madame."

"What is the problem?"

"Did you hear about Mrs. Mogwe?"

"Yes, I was made aware of the situation yesterday. Her sister came to see the Headmaster yesterday to ask if the school could help."

"Does she have Aids?"

Knowledge shrugged. "Perhaps. I don't have that information."

I had been in this country for almost twenty years. I had come to the realization some time ago that even though I lived and worked alongside Zimbabweans and could function in this society, get along with people and accept and, in most cases, even embrace and enjoy Zimbabwean culture, there were still times when I would feel myself clenching my hands in frustration, biting my tongue lest I begin some kind of diatribe, probably starting with the dreaded phrase 'You people …

I took a deep breath. "Listen, you know my son is in Canada. He's studying medicine. He's told me that there are very effective drugs which can help people who have AIDS. No, listen, these treatments can save people, at least for a long time and they can work and look after their families and everything. They're called antiretrolls or something."

"Antiretrovirals."

"Ehe. Of course, you're a science teacher. You must know more about this than I do."

"Perhaps not. We have been told these drugs are dangerous, that those governments in the west want to use Africans as guinea pigs to test these drugs. We have been told these drugs don't work. Those people with AIDS had better eat garlic and sweet potatoes."

"Knowledge! You don't believe that, do you?"

"I said that is what we have been told. But Constance, you must know that this is not a simple problem, with a simple answer. Even if this muti works, it is going to be very expensive. Look around you. People have no money to buy food. How can they hope to pay for this medicine?"

"The government of Botswana is providing every person who is HIV-positive with treatment."

"Botswana is a rich country. Zimbabwe is —" he searched for the right word.

"—poor and crippled by a corrupt and evil government!"

For a moment I thought Knowledge might take offence, but his face remained bland.

"I'm sorry, Knowledge. That was impolite."

"Madam, there is nothing you can tell me about my country that I don't already know."

"And much you could tell me that I don't."

We stood there for a moment, nodding sagely at each other. Then I burst out again.

"We should do something! Don't laugh!"

"I wouldn't dream of it, Amai. Yes, we should do something. I think I may have an idea."

"What? A demonstration? A protest rally?" I toyi-toyied across the front of the classroom, my fist in the air.

This time Knowledge laughed. "Possibly. Though that kind of action will surely incur the wrath of the government. But there are other tactics."

"Such as?"

173

"We must ally ourselves with other like-minded souls. The secretary general of the PTUZ is a former classmate of mine."

"And PTUZ is -?" It seemed an unfortunate acronism.

"The Progressive Teachers Union of Zimbabwe."

"Well, well," I said. "Still waters run deep. Isn't PTUZ," I lowered my voice and looked over my shoulder in mock fear "a radical, subversive organization?"

"Madam, it is only sensible in these times to be circumspect about one's political leanings. Not all of us have a foreign passport."

"Point well taken." Everyone knew that it was dangerous to be seen to be leaning 'the other way'. MDC supporters were beaten, jailed and in some cases, killed. People without ZANU cards were denied jobs or not allowed to buy grain from the Grain Marketing Board. No joke in a country where many families went two days between meals, where malnutrition, Aids, unemployment, and inflation were endemic. What would happen to Knowledge and Praxedis and baby Tapera if Knowledge lost his job? They were already living close to the bone. Not to mention Knowledge's mother and god knows how many other relatives that depended on him for whatever he could spare. "So what do you think we should do?"

"There is a meeting of the union in Harare in the next few weeks. I propose that I go and ask the executive to support our call for the WHO to fund the cost of ARVs to all those Zimbabweans who need them. Our pupils are dying, our colleagues are dying. It is time to take a stand."

"Do you want me to go with you?"

"I think you can drive me to town, but it would not be wise for you to attend the meeting with me."

"Right," I said briskly. "Well, I would be honored to act as your driver."

"Zvakwana." We shook hands.

"Zvakwana, my friend."

I spent the next few weeks anxiously waiting for Knowledge to tell me our trip to Harare was on. I planned to tell James that I had to take Knowledge into town to deal with the death of a relative — a grimly plausible story in these times. I had already set the stage by casually mentioning Knowledge's sick auntie at lunch the day after we had made our pact. James would have hit the roof if he had known what Knowledge and I were up to. Then he would have tried to stop me from going, and I would have had to 'disobey' him, leading to angry words from both of us, hurt feelings and lingering resentment. Anyway, I wasn't being totally deceptive. He would know I was driving Knowledge to Harare, he just wouldn't know the real purpose.

Two weeks went by and then three. The boys and I were walking to school every day to save gas — I needed at least quarter of a tank to make the return trip to Harare and it was getting increasingly difficult to find petrol. When the station in Macheke had gas, the line-up was daunting, cars snaking down the road, past the country club and into the main street. I rationalized that all that walking must be canceling out the cigarettes. I hadn't been able to cut down on my smoking at all. Just the opposite.

Then exams were over and school let out for the summer break.

But then, after so many days, it seemed Knowledge might miss the meeting.

"We have three hours to get to Harare," he told me. He was standing at the front door, holding his briefcase. "I just received word. My uncle is not expected to last the night."

"Not your uncle, your aunt," I hissed.

"Sorry, sorry. Yes, my aunt. My grief is unhinging my mind."

"Not to worry." I had to admit he looked suitably solemn. "Let me just grab my purse. James!"

James came out past the dining table into the lounge. "Mangwanani, Knowledge," he said casually, though he must have been surprised to see him standing at our door in a suit and tie on a Saturday morning. "I'd offer you a beer, but I suppose you don't have time. I'm sorry to hear about your aunt."

"Thank you, sir. I've just had word from Harare. It's good of you to allow Amai Miguel to give me a lift."

"No matata," he said dryly. "All for a good cause, yah." He turned to me. "Do you need any dosh?"

"No. I'll just drop Knowledge at his family and come straight back."

James nodded. "Good. I don't like the idea of you driving in the dark. Too many mombes on the road." He gave me a kiss and shook hands with Knowledge. I looked around for my purse.

"Take care of yourself, Knowledge," James was saying. "Harare is full of crocodiles and hyenas these days."

"Hold on a second," he said to me. "Better take your cardigan. And don't worry about petrol. I filled your tank with some from the bakkie, so you're set."

There was a time when I drove, or was driven, into town every couple of months or so. In the early years of our marriage James and I would sometimes leave the boys with the nanny and spend the weekend at the Jameson Hotel. The road was a good one, eucalyptus tress on each side, snaking up across the Mashonaland plateau, past Macheke and Marondera and Goromonzi, past tobacco and maize fields, clusters of huts set picturesquely in front of red kopjes, the occasional farm gate with a curving dirt road lined with jacaranda trees leading to the kind of house I lived in, ugly, skinny village dogs, black people waiting by the side of the road, waving their hands up and down for a lift, smiling children waving and calling to us from the side of the road.

I always waved back.

"They're shouting 'Look at the ugly white man and his stupid wife', " said James. He slowed down and leaned out the window, yelling something back. The children laughed and began chasing the car.

"Very mature of you, dear. Now I know where the boys learned it."

Get off my road, you bloody baboons!

These days the road was potholed, but the gum trees still stood sentinel. The fields were still full of tobacco and maize, the farm gates were still there and I assumed most of them were still owned by white farmers, though I knew some had been 'liberated' and given to 'war veterans' or, more likely, given to Mugabe and his cronies. Many others, like Scotty's, were on the chopping block, but so far, no action had been taken. It was like the 'phony war' in 1914. Scotty had planted tobacco and maize, just as he had every year since he had taken the farm from the old man. Even though he might not be allowed to harvest.

People still waited by the side of the road, as many as ever, but they seemed more listless, sullen even. Some children still smiled and waved, but I was afraid to take my hands off the wheel. Everyone looked thinner, shabbier.

The road became busier as we came to the outskirts of Harare. Buses, packed to the gills with passengers, lorries with people perched precariously on top of the loads of maize or cement bags, people riding black Chinese bicycles, people walking, people crammed into sagging cars or 'pirate' taxis. The smell of diesel, heat and flame tree blossoms. We passed the drive-in theatre and the municipal campsite.

I turned off Samora Machel Avenue onto Simon Mazorodze Road, heading south. I slowed down and drove carefully. This was a part of town I had not been in for many years.

"Turn left here," said Knowledge, indicating with his hand. "You will drop me just up ahead, at Highfield School."

"Is that where the meeting is?"

"It's better you don't know. But I'm meeting some colleagues here.

"Yes, just here."

I pulled to the side of the road. Knowledge got out, then extracted his briefcase. We shook hands.

"Are you sure you don't want me to meet you somewhere to give you a lift home?"

"It's better you go straight back. I may be quite some time, even overnight."

I hesitated. "Well, then. Good luck. Watch your back, eh?"

Knowledge raised his eyebrows.

"I mean take care of yourself."

§

I meant to drive straight back to Samora Machel and out of town. This was a part of town I had never thought to revisit — a part of town I never thought about much anymore, one way or another. But some how I found myself driving up Derry Road.

I stopped across the street from the house. I shaded my eyes from the glare of the noonday sun. It looked almost the same. Probably better. It was no longer painted a hideous green, and the garden looked neat and tidy. The proteas Moses had planted for me along the brick path to the house were beautiful in their red December blooms.

I sat, looking, but not seeing what I was looking for. Knowing what I wanted to see, but knowing the past was closed to me. I could see in my mind's eye a young woman, smiling to herself. I could see her clearly -the long dark hair held back with a silver clip, the blue dress showing her collarbones and arms and legs, feet in black sandals. She is sitting on the stoep, drinking a glass of bad red wine, watching a flock of waxbills thrashing and bobbing as they drink at the garbage can lid used as a bird bath. I could see all this. I even knew the dress was new — part of a Christmas parcel from the girl's mother — and I knew that the girl was happily waiting for someone.

Oh, Moses. Where are you?

I felt a desire, so strong it made my hands on the steering wheel tremble. I wanted to get out of the car. I wanted to walk across the road, open the gate and walk by the proteas. If I sat on the stoep and waited, surely he would come. If only I could sit with him one more time, playing with the four bronze wire bracelets on his wrist.

A door slammed and a young woman came out onto the veranda. She was wearing jeans and t-shirt. She walked around to the side of the house and I lost sight of her for a moment. Then she came back, holding a gushing hosepipe in front of her. She walked over to the proteas and started watering them.

I started the car and drove away.

20

December 1984

Harare

"And please help yourself to a drink at the bar." The high commissioner's wife pointed down the stone steps, bordered by red bricks set at angles into the earth, to the lawn and pool. Constance had arrived late, having taken a taxi from her hotel. She looked around, trying to get her bearings. People were clustered all over the place. There was a particularly large group hanging around a thatched bhundu hut by the pool. That had to be the bar.

Constance got a gin and tonic and surveyed the crowd. Mostly young, mostly white. A few of the older men, both African and white, were in safari suits. The younger men wore shorts, or khaki trousers or jeans. The white girls who worked for the NGOs wore cotton skirts with t-shirts, the smattering of black women shimmered in their satin and ruffles.

"Constance! Over here!"

Sheena, hugely pregnant, was expertly brandishing a cigarette and drink in one hand and waving with the other. She and Ron were standing under the syringa tree near the edge of the yard where a cluster of Fallers was seeking shelter from the sun.

Margaret, wearing a chitenge, introduced her Zimbabwean boyfriend, a fellow teacher. Constance was startled when Jean-Pierre stepped forward and gave her a hug. She moved away and turned to Sheena.

"Sheena! Look at you! I heard your news, but I didn't know you were so — so —"

"Gargantuan? It's a great look isn't it? Sheena As Chesterfield."

"—so far along. When are you due? You must be so excited."

"Any day now. I can't wait. That's why we're hanging around Harare. Where's Miguel? We were looking forward to seeing him!"

"He's gone to spend a few days with his friend Mushana in the village. You should see him, he's a big boy now. Much more excited to be herding cattle somewhere out on the lands, than spending New Years with me in Harare. How are you, Ron?"

"Oh, I'm hanging around Harare, too." He was also holding a cigarette and drink in one hand. The other brushed his hair out of his eyes. "Wishing I was with Miguel, out on the veldt, herding cattle."

"Listen to him! Don't be such a wanker, Ron! The truth is, he's promised to stay with me through the birth and hold my hand."

"Ah, come clean, Sheena," said Ted. He had come up behind Sheena, carrying a wicker lounge chair. "You don't want Ron there to hold your hand. You need someone to keep your smokes lit and your drink topped up."

"He may as well make himself useful. He's terrified, you know. If I don't keep him busy he'll go and faint on me."

"It's her condition," said Ron, patronizingly. "She doesn't know what's she saying. Look, darling. Ted's brought you this lovely chair to sit in. Why don't you see if you can stuff yourself into it?"

"Do you think it's appropriate to make a joke about a pregnant woman drinking and smoking?" Margaret said earnestly.

"Of course not, but go ahead," cackled Ron. "Let's hear it."

"I'm serious. I don't know if I've told you this before, but I used to teach in northern Saskatchewan on a native reserve —"

"— I think you maybe mentioned it briefly one time," murmured Sheena

"and many of the children suffered greatly from FAS. The intellectual and social problems this caused for them and for their community was devastating."

She paused. Constance pretended to be looking up into the syringa tree. She was damned if she was going to ask what FAS was.

"Did I hear you correctly?" It was the Zimbabwean boyfriend. "Did you say native reserves?"

Something passed over Margaret's face. Annoyance? Embarrassment?

"That's what the land set aside for the aboriginals is called in Canada. I can understand why you find it offensive, Jackson." She turned to her audience. "Given the historical parallels. With the TTLs."

Constance stopped faking disinterest. "Aren't you making the same point those Afrikaner politicians tried to make when they visited Canada a couple of years ago? Saying apartheid was no different than the Department of Indian Affairs."

Two bright spots of pink appeared on Margaret's face. She opened her mouth but Jackson spoke first.

"I didn't say I found your words offensive. I just didn't know if I had heard you correctly," he said mildly.

"Yes, but —"

"I would like to continue this discussion at a later time, but right now I would like another beer." He looked around and smiled genially. "Does anyone else want anything at the bar? Sheena? Ron? Miss -?"

"Constance. No, I'm still working on this one, thanks."

"Just one beer for me then, Margaret."

"I'll go with you," said Constance quickly. Margaret looked a bit stunned. "Ditto," said Sheena. "I have to pee every five minutes now. And, of course it's worse with all the booze I drink. Ron, help me up, you sot."

The braai had been lit and a cook was tending it, helped by a huge white man in a Tilley hat and wire-rimmed sunglasses.

"That's the High Commissioner," said Margaret. She seemed to have recovered. "I had a meeting with him last week. To discuss my project."

"What project?" Constance said dutifully. "Do you mean your work with Mozambican refugees?"

Margaret looked blank for a moment. "No, no. I'm doing something really interesting. I'm looking at studying how land is being redistributed to peasant farmers here in Zimbabwe."

"That does sound interesting," Constance said.

"Oh, it is. Very little land has been allocated to black farmers. I believe much of the work I'm doing is quite groundbreaking."

"No pun intended" said Sheena, sotto voice.

"Tell us about your boyfriend," said Constance. "You said he's a teacher?"

"Yes, we're colleagues. Actually, his aunt is my landlady. You know, don't you, that I live in a hut in the village?"

"Ah, yes," said Sheena. "The famous hut."

"I felt it was important to experience real living conditions."

"Unlike someone who lives in teacher housing, side by side with her local colleagues. Working hard at the job she was sent here to do. Having a baby in Parirenyatwa Hospital. Oh wait! That would be me."

"Let's find you a toilet," said Constance. Margaret had a stubborn, resentful look, like a dog who was afraid of losing her bone. "It's too nice a day to argue, girls."

They were able to edge away from Margaret in the crush at the bar. "That woman just sets my teeth on edge. Only two minutes of conversation and I want to throttle her."

"You're not alone," said Constance, reassuringly. "I used to think she was the way she was because she wasn't getting any sex, but I guess we can discard that little theory."

A tall blonde girl turned, a beer bottle in each hand.

"Is that self-righteous prig here? I thought she'd be off negotiating an end to the civil war in Angola or something?"

"Julia!" they both squealed.

"You got here! I was wondering if you would make it." Constance turned to Sheena. "Julia was in Zvishavane visiting with a friend."

"Yes, Constance was nice enough to lend us her car. We just got in this afternoon.

"You said 'us'. I guess that means Munorwe is with you?"

Julia giggled and cocked her head back over her shoulder. Munorwe Simango, nattily dressed as always, moved forward through the crowd.

There was a pause after they shook hands. "And this is our friend, Sheena. Did you have a good visit with your family?"

"Very good, thanks."

"Listen girls, you haven't lived until you've spent Christmas in Zvishavane. The beer hall alone is worth the trip. Guess who we saw there?"

"Ian Smith?" hazarded Sheena. They all laughed.

"No! Thomas Mapfumo. He was incredible. And he had his brother with him. And his brother is a fire-eater. It was incredible!"

'What do you mean, fire-eater? Like in the circus?"

"Kind of. Show them, Munorwe."

Munorwe did a credible mime of lighting a torch and swallowing the flames.

"Wow," said Sheena. "Impressive."

"Well, you had to be there, I guess."

"And The Blacks Unlimited were playing in the background," added Munorwe. "It adds a certain panache."

"Anyone else we know here?"

"Dear old Ted. We're hoping to persuade him to get out his guitar later so we can belt out a chorus of 'Kumbiya'. I think I saw Dodie but I haven't had a chance to say hello yet. Oh, Jean-Pierre is here, being awfully friendly, but I haven't see Gina." She smiled apologetically at Munorwe. "Sorry, this must be boring for you."

He shrugged. Julia patted him on the shoulder.

"That's because Gina's not here."

"Oh?"

"Yeah. Rumour has it that she's dumped him for an Aussie." Julia leaned forward conspiratorially. "Turns out they grow more than just sheep in Australia. I hear he's a fine looking man."

The party wound its way lazily into the night, as most parties in Africa do. The guests stuck mostly to the shade, lolling on the well-watered grass, talking and laughing. They ventured out now and again to get another drink or greet a friend. There were occasional bursts of energy. Some of the livelier volunteers challenged each other to croquet but the red clay tennis court remained empty. A few people were splashing around in the pool; others sat on the edge, dangling their feet in the water. A marimba band played for awhile, marking the official start and end to the cocktail hour. The sun's rays softened from harsh white to golden. Guests wandered to and fro from the braai, plates piled with steak, chicken, boerwoers, salad and sadza. The High Commissioner and his wife strolled from group to group, making pleasant chitchat.

Constance lay on her back under the syringa tree, her arm covering her face.

"This is one of the things I like about Zimbabwe." Ted's voice.

"What? The food?" Sheena's voice.

"No. The slow pace of life. Though this steak is pretty good."

"Well, it's fine if you're a carnivore, but I'm a vegetarian and I'm getting a little sick of spinach and beans." Constance lowered her arm and squinted through the sun's last rays. It was Lois, one of The Complainers.

"Well, it doesn't look as if you're exactly wasting away."

Silence. Lois was on the chubby side. Constance put her arm back over her face and pretended she hadn't heard.

"Don't mind her, Lois. It's her condition. She doesn't know what she's saying. Listen darling, why don't you I get you another steak? I don't think you've quite eaten the whole cow yet."

"Sorry, Lois. That was a bit rude of me, wasn't it? My point was—"

"Does anyone else want anything while I'm over there?"

"—we've all gained a little weight. Well, all of us except Constance. This isn't exactly a hardship posting."

"Oh, there's always something to bitch about," said Julia, slapping at a mosquito. "We're all going to be eaten alive in a few minutes."

"The enormous cockroaches," said Dodie. "I learned long ago in Malawi to keep a can of Doom ready at all times. Otherwise the suckers get completely out of control.

"The bad wine," said Ted. "Good beer, though," he added.

"No hockey," said Ron. The women groaned.

"The heat," said Sheena.

"The broken water pumps," said Lois. "Honestly, we were without water for six days at our school."

Silence. Constance thought of adding the slow queues in the post office and bank, but the moment passed.

"Great climate," said Ron. "I wonder what the temperature is today in Edmonton?"

"Great people," said Dodie.

"Wonderful students," said Sheena. "They can melt the heart of even a hardened veteran like me. *'Madam, let me carry your books'.*"

"No hockey." Laughter from the women.

"The samosas from the dhukka in Plumtree."

"Thomas Mapfumo."

"When someone smiles it's like lifting the lid on a piano."

"The birds. The doves and the louries and the sunbirds."

"The scent of the gum trees. The earth after the rains begin."

"The red earth."

When Constance woke up, her right arm was stiff and painful from angling over her eyes. She raised herself up awkwardly. She was alone under the tree. The sun was gone, replaced by a thin new moon and a ceiling of stars. As Julia had predicted, the mosquitoes were out in droves, whining incessantly, brushing intimately against bare skin.

The group had moved from the syringa tree over to the fire pit at the bottom of the yard. The High Commissioner, with the help of Dodie's husband Albert, was pulling a log into the fire. Julia was sitting with Munorwe on one of the stone benches. He had his arm around her. Sheena had moved her lounge chair; or most likely Ted had moved it for her. Ron sat beside her, his face lit by a cigarette. Margaret and her boyfriend were sitting side by side, not touching. Lois was next to Jean-Pierre and they *were* touching.

Then Albert launched into a sea shanty in a surprising baritone. Most of the Canadian men joined loudly and drunkenly in on the refrain

Constance leaned over to Julia. "Do we have to stay to see in the New Year, or can I sneak out without offending anyone?"

"Munorwe and I are heading over to the nightclub in Highfield for a bit of dancing. The Bhundu Boys are playing. Want to join us?"

"I guess I'll have to, won't I? You still have the keys to my car."

I was told we'd cruise the seas for American gold

Fire no guns! Shed no tears!

Julia patted her skirt pocket. "Why, so I do."

"Shall we wait for the end of the song then and express our thanks?"

"Gosh, no. This song goes on forever. Wave and smile. We can phone over tomorrow."

21

January 2000

Macheke Township

At morning assembly a student handed me a note. *Let us meet at the clinic at 5 o'clock today.* Knowledge. I looked around and smiled my agreement. Knowledge gave an almost imperceptible nod, then pointedly looked back down to his hymn book.

I missed seeing him at tea break, though whether this was incidental or deliberate wasn't clear to me. I ate my peanut butter sandwich with the school librarian, Susie Magaya.

"Thank heavens the rains have come."

"Ehe. But they are quite weak. We must hope it will soon be raining dogs and cats."

The headmaster, Mr. Muzenda, got heavily to his feet from the battered chesterfield across from us. He slurped his tea down, then banged his spoon against the cup. The room became quiet.

"I am sorry to have to tell you that our colleague, Mrs. Mogwe, is late."

There was a collective sigh. Several murmurs of "Shame". Mr. Chingonzo crossed himself.

"I have just spoken with the brother. He is saying the funeral will be on Saturday in Mrewa." Mr. Muzenda cleared his throat. "I will now give the floor to Mr. Chaminuka of the Social Committee."

Mr. Chaminuka was standing by the window ledge, where the teapots and plates of sandwiches and biscuits sat. He finished chewing.

"The family of our late sister will need assistance with the funeral costs. We ask you to donate generously. Also, we are arranging transport for those people who will be attending the funeral."

"I now call upon Mrs. Tangwenda to say a prayer for our dear late sister."

Everyone bowed their heads.

"Dear Lord. We are praying to you on behalf of our colleague, our sister, Amai Dambudzo."

I opened my eyes and looked up. I did not know that Mrs. Mogwe had a son. I wondered if there were other children.

"We ask you to take care our dear friend's soul. We ask you, Lord, to help her children —" Mrs. Tangwenda's normally clear, strong voice faltered. She swallowed and continued in Shona, which I could only follow through the tears in her voice.

I glanced sideways at Susie. Her hands were covering her face, but I could see the tears seeping out. I looked surreptitiously around. The women were all crying, some beginning to rock back and forth, crumpled tissues pressed to their eyes. The men were all quiet, stony, sombre, their heads bowed. All except Knowledge. He was standing in the doorway and the eyes that met mine were clear and dry.

Unlike many of my fellow whites, I had never had any problem with so-called 'African time'. My roots were in the Kootenays, where no one worried too much about punctuality, and if I managed to arrive somewhere on time it was pure dumb luck. And, as I pointed out to James many times, the Rhodies were no better. Hadn't they coined the phrase 'just now', which meant some vague time in the next four or five hours?

So while I didn't deliberately leave for the clinic a half hour late, neither did I use the chimes of Big Ben on the BBC world service news as a signal to get my body in gear and out the door. Instead I poured another cup of tea and helped myself to another biscuit. After all, the meeting might go on for some time and I was bound to be late for supper. Also it had rained earlier, our first hard rain of the season, and I wanted the ground to dry out a little more before I made the trek into the village. Also, Evan and Kazana came running in, breathlessly telling me that Evan's chameleon, which had been missing for several days and presumed lost forever, had turned up on the verandah. I had to come and see for myself.

So I didn't get to the clinic until around six o'clock. The summer sun was still casting long shadows, the clouds completely gone from the high darkening sky, the air sharp and sweet with the red, wet earth. Already the ishwa were rising in swirls from holes in the earth. I jumped over a oozing rut which was just outside the clinic door and scraped my shoes across some bricks lying near the door, adding slabs of laterite to others already drying there.

Living on a farm and raising three boys, I had often been to the clinic. Miguel had once broken his wrist, jumping off the wall of the squash court at The Club. Samora had had impetigo and scabies. And Evan had needed stitches more that once. James had once badly cut his hand opening a sack of fertilizer. And many, many times I had driven sick or bleeding workers here. So I knew the clinic well. I knew the grass 'courtyard' where the patients sat and waited, more and more of them in recent years, the flaking green paint and inadequate single light bulb, the smell of Cobra wax rising from the meticulously polished cement floor mixed with the smell of bleach and medicines, and of course I knew the nurse, Amai Power.

I was later than I'd meant to be. The meeting was in full swing, with Knowledge at the head of the table, chairing. Susie Magaya was sitting beside him, taking notes. In the eight years I had known her, I had never heard her utter a single political, much less controversial remark, yet there she was. I pulled a chair up to the table and found a space next to Mr. and Mrs. Chingonzo. Mr. Chaminuka was there, and Cyprian Dhiliwayo, the geography teacher. Father Bernard, the priest from Monte Casino, the Catholic mission, was there. Amai Power was there, in her starched white uniform, complete with cap and the badges Zimbabwean nurses wore indicating their rank. The only other white person there was a heavy set man, who I knew vaguely as being connected to the African Reformed Church.

Amai Power's assistant, a skinny young man, the latest in a series of incompetents, came in from the kitchen rondavel at the back, carrying a large pot of tea.

The meeting paused to greet me. I got up to make myself useful. I helped Tendai fetch cups, and serve the biscuits. Mr. Chaminuka and I stood outside in the 'courtyard' having a cigarette. Even in Zimbabwe it was no longer okay to smoke inside a health clinic.

When the meeting resumed, Knowledge had Susie read back from her minutes, "to inform those of us who were unavoidably delayed." It seemed the group had spent its time so far discussing what to call themselves.

"Many of us are members of the Macheke Health Committee," explained Amai Power."

"But not all of us, Sister," said Knowledge. "And I think some members of the Health Committee are not here." I made a mental note to ask him later who was missing and why.

"Which is why, after some debate, we have elected to call our committee the Anti-Retroviral Action Group," said Brother Bernard.

"Now," said Knowledge, "we need to decide on our course of action."

"It seems obvious to me," said the white man. He had a large, veined nose and the red, blotchy skin that marked him as long-time resident. "We need to pressure the government to provide medicine to Aids patients."

There was an uneasy shifting around the table. I agreed with the white man, but it was politically incorrect for me to say so.

"But how to pressure, that is the question," said Cyprian, after a moment. "We know this is not an easy thing."

Now I could jump in. "I agree. We need to think of a way to do this without making the government angry."

"Yes, that is the key point," said Susie Magaya.

"Well, think about it," I fingered my copper bracelets. "How does this government respond to any challenge or criticism?"

"Beatings, harassment, jailings, assassinations," said Red Jowls. Susie put down her pen.

"Apart from that."

More silence, then Knowledge slapped the table. "Ah, yes. We must blame foreign governments, especially the British."

"Exactly," said Mr. Chingonzo. "We must present ourselves as patriotic Zimbabweans, calling upon the international community to assist us."

"No, we must demand that the running dogs of colonialism make amends for their exploitation of us Africans by giving us the medicine which we are entitled to."

"Yes, yes," said Mr. Chaminuka, eagerly. "That should go over very well with the government. Very well."

"But how are we going to get our message out?" I asked. "Let's face it. Most people in Zimbabwe don't even know where Macheke is, let alone people in the rest of the world."

"And people here are apathetic," said Amai Power. "Apathetic and very ignorant."

Brother Bernard spoke in his reedy voice. "We need to give people hope and we need to educate them."

I guessed now was not the time to mention the Bishop's latest diatribe against condoms.

"We need a strategy," said Knowledge. "A strategy that will bring many people in Macheke on board the bandwagon."

"I know you're speaking figuratively," I said. "But do you mean that we'll have some sort of demonstration or rally?"

We all looked at Knowledge. He nodded.

"Yes, after we have marshaled our forces."

"What do you mean by 'forces'?" asked Cyprian.

"Anybody, Everybody. Teachers, students, farm workers, the ones who own the farms, the businessmen, people from the mission, people from the township." Knowledge made a sweeping gesture that took in everyone around the table. "Look at us here. We all have some different organizations and societies we can mobilize. Amai Power, you must work with the Health Committee. Those of us who are teachers can do some agitating at the school."

"I will speak to my flock about this," declared Red Jowls. "But I must tell you that I will not be using words of hate. I will be speaking about compassion and hope."

"And justice," added Father Bernard.

191

22

January, 1984

Harare

In Africa, dancing is not a spectator sport. Everyone at the Mushandira Pamwe Nightclub was there to gyrate, leap, spin, stomp, shake. The beer flowed freely and by midnight everyone was pretty much blasted. Men and women eyed each other for opportunities, hoping to get lucky. And there was the odd pickpocket in the crowd, or prostitute, sidling up to one of the better-dressed men waiting at the bar for drinks.

But really, these were secondary pursuits. Everyone, drunk or sober, man or woman, thief, whore or government employee, was there to dance.

Just before midnight, The Bhundu Boys took a break. Constance and Julia pushed their way through the crowd towards the bar, hoping to find Munorwe. Now that the band had stopped, they could just about hear each other over the crowd. And just about see each other through the cigarette smoke. The room was stifling.

Maybe because they were the only white women in the place, the line at the bar, several men deep, made way for them. They each got a beer and pushed back to the side of the dance floor, near the wall.

Constance held her sweating bottle up to her temple. She could feel the sweat dribbling down between her breasts and under her arms. Her face was probably red and sweaty, not that anyone would see in the dark, with all the smoke. Julia still looked cool and collected, except that one of her bra straps was showing.

Constance reached up and pulled her hair out of a ponytail. "Can you hold my beer for a minute, Julia? I have to get this hair up."

"Perhaps I can be of some help."

She felt a rush of — what? Whatever it was, her heart was certainly thumping away madly. "Hey, Moses."

"Hello." He reached over and took her beer. "Good evening Miss Julia."

"Hello. Did you just arrive?" Julia raised an eyebrow and looked pointedly around.

"Yes, unfortunately just as the band stopped playing. But then I saw you across the room and I wanted to greet you and wish you a Happy New Year." He took a long drink.

"Did you bring a date?" Julia asked. Moses frowned slightly. "I mean, are you with anyone?"

Constance focused on twisting her hair up, but out of the corner of her eye she saw Moses shrug.

"I find myself on my own this evening."

"Look, there's The Bhundu Boys. They're going to start the countdown in a few minutes. Excuse me while I go and find that boyfriend of mine. I can't let him kiss just any old girl at midnight."

"I seem to have finished your beer," said Moses, after a moment. "Let me get you another one."

"Oh, no, that's okay."

"No, no, I insist."

There was drum roll and one of the musicians announced the beginning of the countdown to 1984.

Great, thought Constance. Another New Year's Eve without a man to kiss. At least last year she had been with her parents and Miguel. Looking around at the crowd happily shouting out numbers along with the band she felt lonely.

The crowd cheered and ululated, while the band broke into a *jit* version of Auld Lang Sang. Julia and Munorwe were against the wall, kissing. This normally would have raised a few eyebrows, but now everyone was too drunk to care.

She felt a hand on her shoulder. "Here." He raised his bottle to hers. "Happy New Year, Constance."

She smiled and took a swig. "Same to you, Moses."

After a few moments he said. "How is the food?"

She looked around. She couldn't see anyone eating. "I don't know. I've never eaten here."

"No, not the food. I said the foot. How is your foot?"

She was still confused. "My foot?"

Moses held up his thumb and forefinger, measuring something. "The thorn."

"I guess I'm not going to live down that little scene in a hurry, eh?"

"Don't worry. You must know by now that we Africans love a good drama. We like lots of shouting and screaming. And if there's some blood involved, so much the better."

"Now you're generalizing." She reached out and touched his arm. "I think everyone loves to see other people acting crazy." Oh, God, he's going to think I'm flirting with him.

"And Africans love to gossip."

"Well, so do white people."

Moses seemed to find this surprising. "Is that so? Well, I heard a very interesting rumour just today."

"You did?"

"Yes. I have it on good authority that a certain Canadian girl is now unattached."

"Who have you been talking to?" Oh, God, he's flirting with me. "Let me guess, her name begins with the letter J."

"My source is confidential." The band, after a few ragged notes, launched into a song, full throttle. "So, the foot is okay?"

"It's fine!" yelled Constance.

They were both dancing.

He took her beer and drained it, put the empty on the windowsill, kept dancing.

They were both dancing, but Constance wasn't sure if they were dancing together. For one thing, Moses took up a lot of space on the floor. He took wide, leaping steps from side to side, he crouched low and sprang back up, he turned full-circle. He was a wonderful dancer in a room full of wonderful dancers.

For another thing, he made no attempt to match her moves or to have Constance follow him. Sometimes he touched her arm or held her hand for a moment, then he moved off again.

Between songs, he would pull her close, both of them breathing hard.

As soon as they got into the house, he pulled her into his arms. Even while they were kissing, he was pulling her across the dark room. She felt as if she was melting away. She leaned into him and they stumbled. She felt her arm brush the wall, then she was pushed back against the wall. He was kissing her, his hands reaching under her dress, pulling her into him.

She felt herself being dragged out of sleep by a raging thirst and an urgent need to pee. She could usually ignore one or the other, but not both. Sunlight flowed into the room.

She sat up carefully, pushing her hair out of her eyes. For some reason the bed was pushed into a corner of the room, the window on one side and the wall behind. She crawled down to the foot of the bed and slid out onto the cool cement floor. She found her dress in the pile.

The bathroom was easy to find. There were only three other doors in the hallway. One set of French doors showed what looked like a dining table. One door was shut. The open door was the bathroom.

She peed. There was no glass, so she stuck her mouth under the faucet and drank greedily.

She turned the other tap to check on the hot water situation. After a few seconds the water ran hot. So the geyser above the tub was working.

There were a few thin towels on a shelf by the sink. One small mirror above the sink. A few extra bars of soap. Toothpaste and a couple of toothbrushes.

She pulled back the shower curtain. Another bar of soap and a bottle of shampoo. She picked it up. Crowning Glory. There was a picture of a smiling African woman, all gleaming white teeth and Afro. The kind of cheap shampoo they sold at OK Bazaar.

She looked into the mirror and touched her face. Her skin felt raw. Her eyes were surprisingly clear. Her hair was lank and she could feel every strand growing out of her scalp. She put a dab of toothpaste on her finger and rubbed it over her teeth, then ran her tongue across her teeth.

When she turned on the shower, the drumming water seemed too loud for this early in the morning. She quickly turned it off. But then she heard the doves begin their incessant coos, interrupted by a motorcycle roaring by. She turned the tap back on.

She stood for a long time, eyes closed, the lukewarm water gushing over her. She washed her hair with Crowning Glory, which smelled like red licorice.

She wrapped her head in one of the towels and quietly made her way down the hall. The dining room and lounge were one large room, separated by two steps that ran the width of the room. Windows, covered in inevitable burglar bars, ran along the front of the house. There was a fireplace on one wall, used often, judging by the scorch marks in the parquet floor. A beige area rug in the centre of the room. An ugly, heavy brown 'lounge set' — chesterfield and two matching armchairs — nondescript coffee table covered in books and newspapers. Rubbing her hair gently, Constance went over to the coffee table. Sections of The Guardian and The Weekly Mail from Johannesburg competed for space with a copy of a Shona novel lying open, pages down on the October issue of Moto magazine. Nadine Gordimer's latest novel. A mug half-full of cold tea sat loftily on a battered, soft-cover War and Peace. There were no pictures on the walls.

The kitchen was at the back of the house, through the dining room. She draped the towel around her shoulders and began opening cupboard doors, finding a box of Nyanga tea, the rest of the mugs, a box of matches. She filled the yellow Kango kettle and lit the gas burner. While she waited she read the bottom of the matchbox.

FRIENDS IN OUR COUNTRY

At the start of a new day, greet a Ndebele by saying 'good morning friend' in his own language.

There was a drawing of a bald African wrapped in some kind of traditional cloak. A speech bubble from his mouth said *"Lotshani Mkhozi".*

Moses stood in the doorway.

"You're up early."

He was wearing jeans and a t-shirt.

"Did I wake you? I tried to be quiet."

"No, it's fine. I'm just glad you haven't left. Are you making tea?"

"Yes. And learning Ndebele." She held up the matchbox.

He came closer, looked at the box and smiled. "Ah yes, matches from South Africa, land of racial harmony. No need to get rid of apartheid. Just learn a few tribal greetings."

He opened the cupboard next to the cooker and brought out a bowl of naartjies. They stood side by side with their backs to the kitchen counter, peeling their oranges.

"Have you lived here long?"

Moses looked up from his task. "About six months."

"It's nice. Do you like the neighbourhood?"

He raised a shoulder. "It's alright. In actual fact, I'm not here all that often."

"Your job must keep you pretty busy."

Another shrug. He broke off a section of orange and began eating. Constance turned her attention to her own naartjie. The kettle hummed on the cooker.

He finished eating and wiped his arm across his mouth. "In actual fact, I'm not in Harare much these days."

"I hardly every come here myself. The last time was about a year ago. I met my parents here. You remember. We ran into you at Victoria Falls."

"Of course. How are they?"

"Fine. They have some vague plans about coming next year. We'll see."

She kept talking while she made the tea. "I really only came this time because Julia wanted to go to the party at the High Commission. How many?" She held the spoon poised above the sugar bow.

"Just one. Do we have any milk?"

She thought this was an odd question. How would she know? She looked in the fridge and found some Lacto. "Here, you do the honours." She watched as he bit off a corner of the bag and squirted some sour milk into his cup. He cocked his head in the direction of her cup, eyebrows raised.

"No thanks." She covered her tea.

He shrugged and rummaged in the same drawer where she had found the matches, coming out with an elastic, which he used to close the bag.

"Happy New Year." He raised his mug.

"Same to you. Let's sit outside, eh? It's so beautiful this time of day."

There were no chairs out on the veranda, so they sat side by side on the stoep, where the morning sun was gentle on their bare feet and legs.

They were quiet with each other for a long while.

"There's something I've been wondering about for a while."

"Ah, what is that?"

"Do Zimbabweans look out the window in the morning and say 'Gosh, what a beautiful day'? Or do you just take it for granted?"

He shrugged. "I don't know about others. Myself, when I came home from overseas, I was so happy to be back in the sun. But now I know it will be here every day, so I don't think about it much."

"Where were you? England?"

"Ah, no. I was in China for my military training."

"And what was that like?"

Another shrug. "I was happy to come home." He swirled the last of his tea to capture the sugar. "Actually, I was also in London for a conference once. It rained every day. I hardly saw the sun."

"So the opposite of here."

"Perhaps. There people look for the sun and here we long for the rains."

"Why is it we never seem to have enough of what we need?"

"Because if we had enough, we would no longer feel the need."

Constance sat up, excited. "Yes, yes! That's it. I do believe you've hit on something, Moses."

He smiled, enjoying her enthusiasm. "A paradox of life. One of many, I think." He stretched, putting his cup down. "Shall we go back to bed?"

She allowed herself to be pulled to her feet. Then she followed him back into the house.

The sun was flooding through the window. They began taking off their clothes. Constance crawled onto the bed and over to the window. Through the torn screen and burglar bars she caught an impression of burnt grass, jacaranda trees, some bushes. She closed the curtains. They were too short, so a band of sun made a path over the sheets which where twisted at the foot of the bed. Then Moses' arm was around her waist. She closed her eyes and turned into him.

January, 1980

Mashonaland East District

Salisbury Airport was the place to be. On December 12, Lord Soames flew in, sent out from Britain to oversee the terms of the ceasefire and ensure an orderly transition to majority rule. A son-in-law of Winston Churchill, he was a colonial govenor straight from Central Casting. A former high commissioner to France, he went through the charade of "conferring" independence without the slightest hint of irony. He gravely inspected honour guards, attended official functions and gave interviews in which he doggedly stuck to platitudes and clichés like a hockey player caught outside the dressing room between periods. In all fairness, at a cursory glance, Rhodesia had all the trappings of a colony. Loads of dark-skinned people, exotic animals, heat, dust and flies, white men with blotchy red skin and knobby knees in charge of the place.

On Boxing Day, crowds of supporters, bussed in from Bulawayo, joyously greeted Damiso Dabengwa and Lookout Masuku, the ZIPRA commanders, as they flew in from Lusaka. No sooner had that lot cleared out of the airport than it became jammed again, this time with ZANLA supporters from the townships. Watched nervously by trigger-happy members of the Rhodesian army, they sang and toyi-toyied their hearts out, until the arrival at 7 pm of Rex Nhongo and forty-one ZANLA commanders. At this point, neither ZIPRA nor ZANLA command knew about the death of their leader, Tongogara.

Over the next few days whites from Borrowdale and Glen Lorne flocked to the airport to witness the arrival of the Cease Fire Monitoring Force. The young women, wearing blue eye shadow and lacquered hair, their skimpy dresses from Barbours hinting at the slackening and softening to come, pronounced the soldiers from Britain, Australia and New Zealand 'too supah' (they politely refrained from commenting on the Kenyan and Fijian men in the CFCM), while their menfolk sucked harder on their Madisons and wondered out loud how the bloody hell had it got to this?

The body of Josiah Tongogara came home, flown on a chartered Air Mozambique Viscount. Both ZANLA and ZIPRA commanders were there, as well as his widow, Angeline, his children and other family members. The mood was somber, respectful, but the leaders were obviously in a hurry to get back to the headquarters in a teacher training facility in Mount Pleasant.

In spite of two cracked ribs and a broken wrist, Moses Masekesa only spent two nights at the teacher training college dorms where the two guerrilla armies had set up their headquarters. Over the objections of Nhongo, who said he was needed to help co-ordinate Mugabe's imminent return, Masekesa left Salisbury and went out into the countryside, persuading local guerilla commanders to bring their fighters to the local rendezvous points (RVs) for transfer to various assembly points (APs) scattered around the periphery of the country, away from cities and white farms. This part of the ceasefire agreement *was always going to be difficult. Not only was the timeline extremely tight — the week between December 28 to January 4 — but there were concerns that many of the commanders in the field would refuse to accept the ceasefire, or, having accepted it, would balk at having to surrender their weapons and move into the AP's, where they were sitting ducks for the Rhodesian Army. And Tongogara was dead.*

While Rex Nhongo and Lookout Masuku went on the radio to appeal to the guerrillas to report to rendezvous points, Masekesa moved into the bush, meeting with regional and sectional commanders, often working side by side with members of the CFMF. Every time the old Land Rover jolted on the dirt tracks, the pain shot through his taped chest. He favoured his broken wrist, basically driving with one hand. Every so often the Land Rover would lurch across the road so that it was almost into the thornscrub and elephant grass. A few cows doggedly 'grazed' among the termite mounds and bushes. Women, carrying hoes on their heads, babies on their backs, walked down the middle of the road, calmly moving aside at the last moment.

The CFCM set up their camps near mission schools, in the tribal trust lands. They waited in the heat, dust and flies for the guerillas to walk in from the bush. Days passed and only a trickle of men appeared.

Down to the wire, on January 4, the intervention of the PF liaison officers began to bear fruit. At RF's and AP's around the country, guerillas began reporting in droves. They marched in smartly, brandishing their AK 47's, chanting 'Pamberi ne Zimbabwe'.

These photos, alongside ones of grinning 'terrs' shaking hands with grinning CFCM officers struck a combination of rage and fear into the hearts of many Rhodies. Truly, the world had turned upside down. And in case any of the whites were still living in denial, the rally at the Highfield football stadium, celebrating the home-coming of Robert Mugabe, drew such an enormous crowd that the photo of the event, taken from the air, took up almost the whole front page of the Herald. The unthinkable began to cross some people's minds. The icy Mugabe, the epitome of the ruthless Marxist, might actually become the Prime Minister. In desperation, many whites began to hope that Nkomo, who was jovial and, if his girth was anything to go by, liked a beer by the braai, would be the people's choice.

Masekesa was not at the stadium in Highfield on January 27 when Mugabe returned. He elected instead to stay out in the bush. According to Dabengwa and Nhongo, most of the guerillas by this time were in AP's, though the Rhodesians claimed thousands were still at large. It was Masekesa's job to try to keep the fighters inside the AP's during the election campaign. Not an easy task, given that the Rhodesian security forces had been given carte blanche to roar around the country, intimidating and harassing ZANU-PF supporters.

An election rally in Rusape near the end of February was a case in point. The powers-that-were-about-to-be-no-longer, in a last gasp, refused to let ZANU-PF use the town's football field, so the venue was hastily changed to the soccer pitch of the township school. Admittedly, this was only exchanging one rough, muddy patch of earth for another (the rains had finally come) but it meant that the ZANU-PF candidate was late for the meeting. By the time Jackson Mungwira, a lawyer who grew up near Headlands, and his 'election team' pulled up in a battered station wagon, a large crowd had already gathered. Many of them were wearing the white shirts with the ZANU-PF rooster. Under the watchful eyes of fifteen or so white police reservists backed up by armoured vehicles, machine guns and sullen expressions, the crowd was fairly reserved, but at the arrival of Mr. Mungwira, they begin toyi-toying and ululating. 'Pamberi ne Zimbabwe. Pamberi ne Mugabe!' The candidate opted to deliver his speech at the far end of the field, in between the goalposts. He was well-spoken, a former star keeper with the Warriors: the land belongs to the people who toil on it, the mines belong to the people who work them, this is what socialism means.

A football analogy "We will win even though the referee is for the other side. He is trying to give us a red card, but we will not be defeated. We will not be intimidated."

His speech was interrupted by a small plane flying over, buzzing the field, dropping leaflets before disappearing behind the msasa trees. They showed a peasant woman, crying as her two children were torn from her outstretched arms by two stern guerillas holding AK47's. The pamphlets were crudely drawn, but there was no mistaking the likeness of the two 'comrades' to Robert Mugabe — the dark-rimmed glasses were a dead giveaway. But just in case the point was missed: 'Communists will take your land and your children'. Proving Mr. Mungwira's point, the crowd seemed to find the leaflets funny. They began singing and chanting. 'Voterai Jongwe.'

The candidate moved among the electorate, glad-handing, dancing, giving the closed fist black power salute. He and his team got into their car and roared away, off to another rally farther into the TTL. Four kilometres up the rutted road they were stopped at a roadblock manned by Pfumo reVanhu (black Rhodesian Security Force auxiliaries), ordered out of their car at gunpoint, arrested and held for three nights at the Rusape jail.

All across the country variations of this theme played out, as the white regime maliciously and fearfully 'showed these munts who's boss'. Thousands of ZANU-PF supporters and candidates were harassed, threatened, beaten up, arrested. All under the benevolent eye of Lord Soames and his Election Supervisors.

Just outside Gokomere, Moses Masekesa was dragged from his vehicle by the police, handcuffed and taken to Chikurubi prison, where he was kicked in the head and genitals because he refused to sign an 'admission of guilt'. Ironically, it may have been Jackson Mungwira who secured his release. Just out of the clink himself, Mungwira filed a writ of habeas corpus in the High Court for a bus-load of his supporters who had been locked up in Chikurubi after they were arrested following one of his rallies. When the Attorney-General finally released them all, without charges, Masekesa was included in the bunch.

23

April, 1984

Nyanga

It was cooler there in the mountains, especially in the evenings. Walking through the lobby on her way back from getting her cardigan from the car, Constance stopped, her eye caught by a painting hanging near the fireplace. An idyllic landscape of misty mountains, trees and a waterfall, it matched the chintz curtains and floral-covered furniture. Only the ruby-throated sunbird flitting across one corner of the canvas acknowledged an African setting.

An elderly couple was sitting in the overstuffed armchairs next to the fire. She was knitting an afghan; he was drinking a cup of tea and looking out through the glass doors to the wide lawn, where a croquet game was in full swing.

Constance managed to find an empty table in the sun on the terrace. The lawn sloped down to the lake. The place was full of families. The kids sat sucking on orange Fantas, or lurid red or green Sparletta. The adults were into tea, Coca-cola, beer, gin and cigarettes.

"Mummy, please, please can I have a pony ride?" A chubby blonde girl with pale blue eyes whined at the next table. "Ouch! Mummy, Gavin's just kicked me under the table. Mummy!"

Gavin, a cute, impish type with short, sandy hair and freckles lifted his straw from the bottle and sprayed his sister with pop.

"Gavin! You horrid boy. You must stop teasing Helen." The mother, a hard-faced blonde with long red nails to match her voice, did not look up from her magazine.

Constance watched as Gavin reached over and yanked hard on one of Helen's frizzy braids. She tried to twist away. Her elbow hit her Fanta, knocking it over.

"Ow! Mummy! Make him stop!"

The mother lurched back as the orange syrup began running over the edge of the table onto her lap.

"Gavin, really! Andrew, make him stop."

The father put down his paper. "Stop it, both of you, or I'll knock your heads together." He picked up a box of cigarettes that was in the path of the Fanta. He looked around, pausing for a second on Constance.

"Waiter!" He snapped his fingers. "Clean this up now, please."

The family sat in their chairs pulled back from the dripping table. "Honestly," the mother whined. "I only get one holiday a year. One holiday a year. And this is how you children behave. Next time Daddy and I will leave you at home. I won't have you ruining my holiday."

"I'm going down to the lake," Gavin interrupted. He got up and scampered off. The mother put her magazine on her lap and began pushing back her cuticles with the nails on her other hand. Helen slumped into her chair looking sullen, her white belly sticking out between her t-shirt and terry cloth shorts. The father folded up his paper and lit a cigarette. He looked towards the lake and then lifted his paper.

A waiter appeared and began sopping up the mess on the table.

"Mummy, can I have another Fanta? Please, Mummy."

"No, you've just spilt one drink. I'm not getting you another."

"Please, Mummy. I want another Fanta. Please, Mummy!"

The father spoke from behind his paper. "Waiter, bring us another Fanta."

Helen scraped her chair back to the table, a grim, victorious look on her face. The mother shrugged and went back to her book.

Constance caught the waiter's eye as he turned. "Excuse me, please. Can I have some tea? And a glass of water?"

The father closed his paper. "So Ronald Reagan is off to visit the Chinese." He pointed to the headline.

"Yes, I guess so."

"Says here they gave him the big 21-gun salute. What part of America are you from?"

"Nowhere. I'm not American. I'm Canadian."

"Sorry about that."

"Not to worry."

A pause while his mind slid from the well-worn American stereotype and tried to focus on this new, blurrier image.

"Name's Andrew Lennox. The wife's Priscilla" — the mother put her book down and gave a thin smile, "and the piccanin here is Helen."

"And you have a little boy called Gavin."

"Ah, yes. He's a bit hard to miss."

"Well, I've a boy of my own. A very cheeky rascal."

"How long have you been in Zimbabwe?"

"It's coming up two years. I'm teaching at Mutamba Mission, south of Marondera."

"Super. That's a Catholic mission, isn't it?"

She nodded. She let the implication that she was some kind of missionary hang in the air.

"Well done! Bloody hard work, I should think."

"Andrew, language." Another thin smile from Priscilla.

"Sorry, Miss. Wife can't take me anywhere."

"Not to worry. Please call me Constance. When you say 'Miss' I feel like I'm back in the classroom."

"So how do you find Zimbabwe? Everyone treating you all right?"

"I love it. Everyone has been so kind and welcoming. It's been great."

"Place to live? Getting enough grub?"

"Fine. In fact, the food is wonderful. I've never eaten so much steak."

"Ach, you should have tasted it before the war. Cut like butter. Melted in your mouth. Right, Prill?"

Priscilla tapped one of her talons against a bottle. "And the Cokes were colder."

Constance let this pass. She had heard these kind of bizarre beliefs expressed before. It was as if these whites had joined a cult of nostalgic fundamentalists. Paradise Lost was Rhodesia 'before the war'.

"What about the locals?"

"Fine." She said this firmly.

"Good for you! Must be jolly tough work, though."

"Not at all. I love teaching. It's lots of fun."

Priscilla looked up from her nails. "Are they intelligent?"

"Pardon?"

"Are they intelligent? Do they learn anything?"

Constance looked at the people across from her. "Well, let me put it this way," the white couple leaned forward, smiling, expectant, "I completely understand why you people wanted to keep your own schools and keep the black kids out," more smiles and nods, "because you couldn't compete with them in a thousand years. Wouldn't be much fun would it, to see all the white kids at the bottom of the class?"

She bumped her knee on the metal table as she scraped back her chair. Priscilla and Andrew were staring at her. Helen had stopped slurping her Fanta, her eyes darting back and forth between the grown-ups.

Constance turned away, rubbing her knee. She bumped into someone.

"Is everything all right here?" Moses put his hand on her shoulder.

"Fine. Just bumped my knee." She began moving away. "Did you catch anything?"

"No fish. But Miguel has a frog in his pocket."

"Where is he?"

"He has been sidetracked down by the lake. He has met another kid and they are harassing the ducks."

"Oh, god. It's probably that little boy from the ghastly family I just had a run-in with."

"Ah yes, I thought you looked a bit red. What was that about white children being at the bottom of the class?"

"I let those stupid people push my buttons." She smiled as she saw Moses' eyes slide down the buttons on her cardigan. "It means I let them get to me."

Moses shifted the fishing rods so he could take her hand. "Unfortunately, some of our white citizens still cling to these old attitudes."

"You must get rude comments all the time. How do you stand it?"

He shrugged. "It will take some time for some people to adjust to the new reality. Some of them will never accept." He massaged her hand gently with his. "They are like those old Japanese soldiers lost on those islands in the Pacific Ocean. They are still fighting a lost war."

"They make my blood boil, sometimes. Honestly, if I never hear the words 'before the war' again, it'll be too soon."

Moses chuckled. "Amen. Anyway, you probably took a few years off their lives back there."

"How so?"

"By holding hands with a black man."

The Troutbek Inn was fully booked. It was the Easter long weekend, one of the two weekends every year that the servants were given time off to go back to their villages or the townships and so the white 'madams' packed up their families and headed for hotels and resorts across the country, where they could still be waited on hand and foot. The inn was also hosting the annual convention of the Zimbabwean Dental Association.

Charlotte noticed them at supper. "Those must be the dentists." It was mixed, well not mixed, layered really — mostly men, mostly white, but a few Indian males and several women. She decided that the white women were wives. They were all sitting together at one end of the long table, loudly getting sloshed. The two Indian women, one in a sari, might have been dentists, or wives. It was hard to tell. They talked quietly to each other. All the men ignored all the women.

"A herd of mombes. A pack of hyenas. A convention of dentists," mused Moses softly

"The weekend at the Troutbek was as dull as a convention of dentists."

He raised an eyebrow. "Not at all. I am finding this foray into one of the enclaves of settler society quite enlightening."

"Still, not quite the dirty weekend you had in mind when I invited you to come with us." She glanced over at Miguel, but he was engrossed in something across the room. Gavin, two straws stuck up his nose, was crossing his eyes and sticking his tongue out at his sister. Constance, trying not to smile, looked away quickly and caught Moses grinning broadly.

"It reminds me of all the good times we had negotiating with Smith in Geneva and at Lancaster House, during the war."

"I know you're deputy minister of health, I know you're a doctor—"

"Not a doctor. I was a medic during the war."

"Medic, then." She kept count with her fingers. "You're not married, no kids. But not much else."

"What else do you want to know?"

"I don't know enough about you to ask. Okay," she straightened a bit in her chair, "how did you end up working with Mugabe? You must have been more than just a medic in the war."

He reached across the table and took her hand. His thumb caressed her wrist. "You know how you said you never again wanted to hear the words 'before the war'? That is how I feel about 'during the war.' For me, it's not a nostalgic time."

She didn't press the point. Not for tactical reasons or because she wasn't curious. But she was young, this was the beginning and she had lots of time.

More important was his hand on hers. She didn't want him to take his hand away.

§

The next day they decided to get out and away from the hotel and hike to the Nyanga Falls.

"I find all these pine trees irritating," said Charlotte. They were walking along the road. On either side were neat rows of a pine tree plantation.

"Don't they remind you of Canada?"

"Maybe. A little." She thought of great stands of timber, swathing high mountains that plunged into the ocean. "Like you, I'm not nostalgic."

"But you must miss your family. Your mother."

"Oh, sometimes. I guess. But they'll be out again soon to visit."

"Ah, yes. I remember them well from the Victoria Falls Hotel."

"I bet you do. They're not exactly wallflowers, are they?"

"What do you mean?"

"My father SHOUTING AT EVERYONE V-E-R-Y S-L-O-W-L-Y and my mom desperately trying to set me up with any man who looks as if he can tie his own shoes." But she spoke fondly.

They turned off the road. The rough dirt track took them back to Africa. Hemmed in by elephant grass, they moved in single file. If her parents were here, Hannah would be demanding that Nico take a photo of Miguel, a brown boy skipping ahead in a blue floppy hat.

"She's thrilled, by the way, that we're together. She had her eye on you that time we met at Victoria Falls. Though maybe you didn't notice, she's so subtle."

"It's a mother's duty, to make sure her daughter is properly married."

"What about your mother? Is she worried that you're not married yet?"

"Certainly. She has the lobola ready."

"Really? Does she keep a couple of cows on hand just in case?"

He laughed. "All that is part of the negotiations. I will have to take you to meet her and your parents, too. They will decide how much you are worth. Of course, these days we also give cash and refrigerators and cookers."

She shaded her eyes and watched as Miguel picked up a stick and began using it to gouge a line in the path.

"I should go a bit cheaper, eh? Slightly used, with a kid?"

He grabbed her hand and pulled her around. He actually looked shocked. "No. No! That won't matter. Actually, you have already proven your fertility. That makes you more valuable in our culture."

"Well, it's a moot point anyway. My mother and I are both feminists. We couldn't allow your family to pay lobola for me. In fact, Hannah is getting so desperate to marry me off that if you play your cards right, she'll pay you."

"Possibly she isn't aware of all the men vying for you."

"Vying for me? You're kidding, right? My last boyfriend dumped me!"

"Ah, yes. It must have been difficult for you. Especially as you would rather step on a thorn than sleep with him ever again."

"I believe I said gouge my eye out with a thorn."

"So now your eyes are safe. But what about that other suitor?"

"Jean-Pierre? Get real. I wouldn't touch that creep with a barge pole."

"I'm starting to see that my competition is stiffer than I thought."

"Not in Jean-Pierre's case. The rumour is his wife left him because he was impotent." Constance giggled and Moses allowed himself to smile.

"No, I mean that white farmer from that day at the school."

"You mean that beefy Rhodie. He was there to see the Prime Minister."

"A likely story."

"Well, whatever his reason for being there, I have no interest in joining the settler community. You saw those ghastly people back at the hotel. Tell me they don't make you ask yourself who the hell left them in charge for so long? Plus I wouldn't look good in a bad perm and polyester frock." She panted this last bit. They had crested the track and stopped for minute while she caught her breath. Moses called to Miguel to wait for them.

Constance saw the hoopoe first. She touched Moses' arm and whispered, "Look, a hoopoe," proud of herself for remembering the name.

The watched for a moment as the hoopoe tapped around the ground, looking for insects. Then, sensing them, it stopped and cocked its head, its bright eyes looking inquisitively at them. Constance reached for Moses' hand. Perhaps the movement worried it. In any case, the bird flew up into a tree and began calling. "Hoop-hoop, hoop-hoop-hoop."

"No prizes for guessing how that bird got its name."

"In my language we call it 'tuvo'."

"I guess I'll have to learn Shona now."

"Ah, no. It's better that you don't." They watched as the bird flew off to another, farther tree. They could hear Miguel calling from around the bend. Moses yelled something back in Shona.

Constance laughed. "Ah, yes, I see."

The bush around was becoming greener and denser as the track fell toward the river. They could hear the water. And then they came around another bend. Below they could see the track widen to a wide, rock-strewn path leading to the edge of the river. The falls were just above, rapids really, falling over a series of granite steps. They could see Miguel too, next to the riverbank.

"Miguel! Don't go too close to the edge!"

He might have heard her because he looked up and smiled and waved. But he didn't step back.

Pushing past Moses, she ran the rest of the way down. She reached the place where the path widened and leveled. He was still there, squatting down, poking at something with his stick.

"Look Amai, these are the ants that really sting if they bite you."

She felt Moses beside her. "Sorry. I panicked. Just let me catch my breath."

He put his arm around her. She leaned into him. The river tumbled down the gorge. The listened to the rushing water and to the little boy humming to himself and the beating of their hearts.

They moved as quietly as they could towards each other. Their kisses, the way her arms tightened around his back, the way he brushed her hair from her face, their hands entwined, the way he lifted her hips towards him, this was their own language.

"I love you so much," she whispered, after.
"I love you." He kissed her. Said something.
"What?"
"Ndiri kuti ndino kuda. I love you."

April1980

Rufaro Stadium

Afterwards, no one could remember which two government officials had invited Bob Marley to play at the independence ceremonies. Though already popular with the black population, it would take his death, a year later, to make him into an icon, and when he and his entourage arrived at Salisbury Airport, just hours after Prince Charles had flown in, the dignitaries sent to meet him, including Joshua Nkomo in his capacity as Home Affairs Minister, seemed to have trouble telling one Rastafarian from another. No one seemed to know exactly what to do with Marley. All the hotels in town were fully booked, so he has forced to bunk in with several band members in a guesthouse outside the city. They were escorted to the Prime Minister's residence by some soldiers who had already begun celebrating. Marley was inveigled upon to sing 'No Woman No Cry' for Sally Mugabe; perhaps the presence of the drunken soldiers persuaded him.

The actual performance, held the next day at Rufaro Stadium, was described at the time by various witnesses as a 'bit of a bust', a 'debacle', 'complete anarchy' and 'disappointing'. The generator that was needed to run the twenty-foot high speakers that the Wailers used never materialized, so at the last moment, Dennis Thompson, Marley's sound technician, had to tap into the township grid, which blew out all the power in the village. Though Marley always maintained (at least publicly) that the concert was a 'great honour' he was apparently surprised to find out that he wouldn't be playing for the newly liberated masses — they were being kept corralled outside the stadium — but for an A-list audience that included the ZANU-PF hierarchy, the media, foreign dignitaries and world leaders such as Indira Ghandi. Nkomo complained that ZAPU hadn't been allocated enough seats. Ian Smith gave the event a miss.

Marley and the Wailers had been given to understand that they would be playing later in the evening, after the other events — Shangaan dancers, the choir from Mount Pleasant School, Thomas Mapfumo, the speeches, the lighting of the eternal flame. The opening acts, as it were. Consequently, when they were introduced right after the raising of the new flag, the band was not ready.

So, it wasn't until about half an hour after being announced, The Wailers launched into their first song. Hearing the music, the crowd outside the stadium began their own, less positive vibration. Shouting and banging against the gates, the crowd tried to force its way into the celebration. During 'I Shot The Sheriff" the police tried to restore order by shooting the mob with teargas, an irony not lost on some of the band. Aston 'Family Man' Barrett, bass player for the Wailers, said, "I feel my eyes and nose and think, from when I was born, I have to come all the way to Africa to experience teargas."

The spectators down on the pitch had already thrown themselves down as the clouds of teargas rolled over the grounds. The band sought shelter in a truck. Looking out, they could see people running in panic, women and children falling.

ZANLA soldiers managed to calm the stadium audience and the group went back on stage, minus the three female back-up singers who had hitched a ride back into town, thinking the show was over. The Wailers played a few more songs, ending with 'Zimbabwe'.

This story has been told to me many times over the years and there are several versions of it floating around. Details differ — the order of the songs on the playlist, for example, or whether Marley teased Judy Mowatt for leaving during the teargassing, saying "I guess we know who the real revolutionaries are" — but I am always struck by how consistently 'ironic' and prescient the themes of this story are. The way Africa sees itself as second-class, hence the need to bring in a big name like Marley to add credibility and luster. The lack of planning and general disorganization. The unseemly scramble by the new ruling class for the best seats. The utter contempt the ruling class has for the masses. The grinning, inebriated soldiers strutting with the AK-47's who might at any time turn belligerent. The use of those same soldiers to 'restore order' by tear-gassing and beating people.

I find that image — of Bob Marley singing "Africans a-liberate Zimbabwe" in front of a crowd of VIP's while the povo locked outside the gates weep from teargas, hard to get out of my head. It was as if the big boys in the ruling party thought 'we may as well start as we mean to go on'.

The next day, Marley performed for over an hour and half in front of over 10,000 'ordinary' Zimbabweans. I have heard that he was so depressed by the previous night's events that he didn't bother to do a sound check and gave an uncharacteristically perfunctory show. For some reason, I find this comforting.

24

Constance came into the staff room and pointed to her desk. The student, Ephraim, looked helplessly at the piles of notebooks already there. "Oh, just put them on the floor, Ephraim."

"Ehe Madam."

By piling several classes' worth of books on top of each other, she managed to clear enough space for marking. Now to find a red pen. She opened her desk drawer and found a couple of erasers, a box of matches *(You will make every Tswana very happy by saying 'good morning' in his own language.* Picture of a muscular, bare-chested man wearing a cloak and holding a walking stick, speech bubble *'Dumela Tsala')*, a bottle of dried out correction fluid, a wadded up tissue, a dead fly and a pen. Constance took the pen out and shook her head. This would never do. The pupils would be very upset if she corrected their essays using a blue pen. She knew this from bitter experience. They would sit, stone-faced in the classroom, and refuse to accept their books until she agreed to remark them using the right colour.

She sighed. Time to go and grovel at the feet of Mrs. Manyara, the bursar, who doled out two boxes of pens (one red, one blue) in January, along with a black marking book. These were supposed to last for the whole school year. After that, you had to go and beg for re-supplies. If you were sufficiently contrite you were given another pen, along with a stern warning not to lose it.

Constance turned to the only other person in the room, one of the new teachers from overseas. From Australia. Kyra, Kylie? Being new, she probably still had her box of pens and, more importantly, didn't know how hard it was to get more.

"Say, Kylie, do you by any chance have a pen I could borrow. A red one."

No answer. She must have the name wrong. She tried again, a bit louder this time.

"Er, Kyra? Can I borrow a red pen?" Still no answer. The stocky, dark-haired figure remained hunched over her desk.

"Kara!" Even louder. Christ, she sounded just like Nico, bellowing to be understood.

The girl at the desk finally turned. "It's Karen, actually."

"Sorry, I'm terrible with names. Look, are you okay?"

"Sure. I was just thinking about my boyfriend."

"Oh."

"Back in Australia."

"Ehe," said Constance, beginning to understand.

"Of course, we write to each other every couple of days and he promised to call me once a week, but the phones here are . . ."

"impossible. I know." She nodded again, more sympathetically. "What's his name?"

"Gareth. He's a mechanic. Has his own garage back in Brisbane."

"You must be missing him a lot. Do you feel it's making it hard for you to settle in here?"

"Yeah, I'd say so. He said he might come over during the long hols in December."

"Well, there you go, then," said Constance cheerfully. "That's not long now. You can take him somewhere romantic like Victoria Falls."

"I guess you've been to most places by now. Someone told me you've been here for two years, is that right?"

"Yes, but there's still lots I'd like to see. I haven't gone to Mana Pools yet. It's a wonderful place to camp on the Zambezi, but a bit remote and you can only get there in the dry season. I also have a dream about someday going into the Okavango."

"So are you on a three year contract? Is this you last year, then?"

"I'm not sure," said Constance, airily, as if this question was one she barely thought about. "I might renew my contract. We'll see."

"So you must like it here, then?"

"Very much. Except for the marking." She shrugged back towards the pile on her desk. "Listen, I'm looking for a red pen."

"So, she's feeling a bit low is she?" said Julia. She and Constance were cutting across the soccer pitch on their way home from school. "You should have told her to dump the guy."

"Julia!"

"Well, you know as well as I do that these long-distance romances never last."

"What about Winnie and Nelson Mandela? He's stuck on that island and she's under house arrest in Soweto or something."

Julia snorted. "That's different. She can't dump him – he's an icon! But just wait till he gets out. I give them six months."

"What about Alex and the girl we saw when we were snooping in his desk?"

"Not snooping. We were looking for matches. And you were his girlfriend, so he shouldn't have been hiding photos of his ex-lovers in his desk in the first place."

"But that's my point. She wasn't an ex."

"Ah, but we don't know that, do we. What if he just kept that picture so you'd think he had a girlfriend back home."

"You're so cynical."

"No, I'm realistic."

"That's what cynical people always say. Anyway, if he didn't have a girlfriend in Canada, why did he leave?"

"Because he wanted to. Listen, Constance, I liked Alex. He was a great guy and lots of fun, but he wasn't here for the long haul. You were lucky to get rid of him so easily. Dollars to doughnuts he has a picture of you stashed in his desk back home, where his latest girl can find it, draw her own conclusions and give him an excuse to be just ever-so-slightly detached. No," she continued firmly, "you're way better off with Moses." She broke off to kick a ball back towards some boys on the far side of the field. Even in sandals, her aim was strong and accurate.

"Ah, Moses." Just saying his name filled Constance with a rush of feeling.

"See! You're crazy about him and he's obviously madly in love with you."

Constance smiled apologetically. She thought this was true, but felt that it might be bad luck to say so.

"No, seriously. He's here every weekend, or else you're trekking into the Big Mango to see him. And he's taken you on holiday."

"Well, you and Munorwe go on holidays. You just got back from a trip to Kariba. Come in for a drink, would you?"

"Love to." They climbed the steps of the veranda. Julia sank back into the one chair with cushions and arms. Constance went into the kitchen and liberally splashed some Malawi gin into two glasses. She checked the fridge and found some tonic.

"Sorry, there's no lemon or ice.

Julia shrugged and leaned forward to accept her drink. "Cheers." She took a long slug and then sat back again. She made a pretty picture, one long leg dangling over the arm of the chair, hair twisted up in a neat bun. "What's Miguel up to?"

Constance was sitting in one of the hard-backed chairs 'student' chairs. She compensated by putting her feet up on another one. She waved her hand vaguely. "Not sure. He's probably with Mushana. Maybe herding cattle or out in the bush hunting birds. Moses made catapults for both of them last time he was here."

They sat and drank their gin and talked desultorily about this and that. Then they had another gin and shared a cigarette because they were both trying to cut down. The sun began to drop, the wind picked up slightly. Constance went inside to get some candles. She came back with a bottle of wine in her hand, some music following her.

They sat there, drinking and smoking, quiet now, as a woman from another time and place wished for a river to skate away on.

§

The regular Saturday afternoon students v staff football match always drew a boisterous crowd. Students, happy to have an excuse to avoid their prep or cleaning up in the dormitories, toyi-toyied along the sides of the pitch, drumming and singing their support for their fellow students. The teachers who could barely hobble together a full side and often had to rely on the services of 'ringers' like Munorwe Simango, or King Musani from the Sunset Butchery and Bottle Store, were also at a disadvantage when it came to their supporters. Not only were there never more than a dozen, a good five or six of these would be whites, barely able to muster a weak "Olay, Olay, Olay" on the rare occasions the teachers managed to score.

Constance had never before been to a match, even though Alex had often played. Of course, Miguel went faithfully to see his heroes, especially a boy in the fifth form who carried the moniker 'Concorde'.

"Man, he is so fast! He gets the ball and whoosh, he is just simply gone. Friend was left naked. Stripped!"

Though it was mildly satisfying to shake one's head or roll one's eyes on Monday as Godwin Mawuru, say, or Sydney Sekeramyi limped into the staff room.

"Ah, Amai, my shoulder is too painful. I was the victim of an illegal tackle."

"Illegal tackle!" snorted Julia. "I was at the game on Saturday. Every time the ball got anywhere near you, you fell over. I was sure I was going to have to sub in. Didn't you see me on the sidelines, warming up?"

"And Mr. Mawuru, I hear that next week the team is going to invite your wife to play instead of you," said Constance.

"Ah, no." Godwin Mawuru looked slightly pained, then he smiled, realizing he was being teased. "In actual fact, she did play football before we had our first born."

"But then you made her quit because she was better than you." More laughter. Constance was glad to see that Karen, from her desk on the other side of the room, was smiling.

But now here she was, cheering on the sidelines, heart thumping every time Moses trapped the ball, heart racing as he carried the ball down the field, moaning softly every time he lost the ball, exultantly screaming when, in the second half, he took a beautiful heading cross out of the air from Dominic Kanaventi, and volleyed the ball straight past the keeper. Mary Karambira began pounding her drum as Moses ran back to the centre of the pitch, arms raised, blowing kisses towards her and Miguel, into the arms of his teammates. The team began dancing and singing. Laughing, their supporters joined them.

Tshotsholosa, enzontaba stimela

Tshotsholosa, enzontaba stimela siphuma eZimbabwe

The student side and their supporters joined in. Anyway, they could afford to be generous, with a three goal lead. Then Sampson Karambira, who had temporarily abandoned his neutrality by strutting up and down the sidelines, to roars of approving laughter, finally blew his referee's whistle, and the game resumed. No matter that the teachers immediately let in an easy goal – Mr. Okense, the Ugandan teacher playing defence, tried to clear the ball in front of the net, but his pass was picked up before Friend could get to it and Tendai, the striker for the student team, deftly flicked it into the net – nothing could dampen their spirits.

Later, Constance stood out in the back of Friend's compound, holding an enamel plate piled high with sadza and stew ("you must have more, heh, heh, you are too little" said Boniface, who was in charge of the sadza ladle), talking with Nasir Nazooa, the new biology teacher from Mauritius, who was Friend's new housemate. The conversation was hard going. Though Nasir seemed a nice enough man, Constance found with the music blasting she could understand only every fourth or fifth word. It probably didn't help that she was trying to look around for, in no particular order, Miguel, Moses and her opened beer, while at the same time trying to look as though she was giving Nasir her full attention.

"I'm surprised you weren't out there today. Do you play football?" she asked loudly. Two years in Zimbabwe had taught her that this question would generate an enthusiastic reply, often lasting several minutes.

"No." Constance thought she heard the word "cricket". There was a pause while Nasir took a sip of Fanta. Then to her relief he launched into what sounded like an account of his glory days at university in India. Constance was able to glance surreptitiously around. Ah, there was Miguel, with Mushana and some other children, eating sadza out of a bowl.

"So, did you enjoy your time in India?"

Nasir nodded enthusiastically. "Very much, very much. Have you ever been?"

"No, but I'd love to." This wasn't strictly true. Right now she had no desire to be anywhere but where she was, but with the accent barrier it seemed too complicated to explain. Actually, she found she could now understand most of the funny story Nasir was telling about clearing customs in Bombay and even laugh in all the right places.

She felt Moses' arm around her waist, pulling her against him. He shook hands with Nasir, who complimented him on his goal.

"Ah, I was lucky, man." But Constance could tell he was pleased. And a little drunk. After the game he had given her a quick hug, run his hand through Miguel's hair, and then roared off with the rest of the team to the Sunset Butchery and Bottle Store.

"Our African men spend rather too much time in the shebeens," remarked Mary Karambira. She, Julia, Miriam and Constance were making their way back to the teachers' houses after the game. "You'll have to get accustomed to that," she added, looking sideways at Constance.

"It's not so bad," said Julia. "Sometimes those places can be a lot of fun."

"Ah," said Miriam. "But that is because you are a white woman. You can go to these places. If I was to go to a shebeen, all the people would be talking about me! No, its better I stay at home."

"Oh, yes!" agreed Mary. "Those women who hang around the bars and bottle stores are just looking for some money. They waggle their big bottoms and many men are too weak to resist. You young girls must be very careful. You must make sure that your husband is not spending too much money and time with those prostitutes."

"So are you saying there's an acceptable amount of time and money a man can spend on other women?" Constance meant it as a joke, but Mary and Miriam weren't laughing.

"This is all academic," said Julia briskly. "Only Mary here has a husband and I happen to know that Charles doesn't put sugar in his tea without asking her first how many spoonfuls. And," she added darkly, "if Munorwe even looks at another woman, I don't care how great her ass, that's the last look he'll ever get of mine."

Constance was thinking about this as she held her plate out to Moses. "Did you get something to eat?"

"Thanks." He scooped up some sadza and made it into a ball to dip into the sauce. "I'm so hungry I could eat a hyena." He took the plate. "Have some!" he said to Nazir.

Nazir dug in. Constance hesitated, then much less expertly, also began eating. The three of them stood happily gorging.

A tap on her shoulder. She looked around and saw King Musami. She moved to make room for him in the circle. She held out the plate to him and he took it. She, Nazir and Moses watched him silently as he cleaned the plate. When he was finished, he handed the plate back to Constance without looking at her.

"So, if you're not a doctor, what are you?" He spoke to Moses, picking up the thread of an earlier conversation.

"I work for the Ministry of Health."

"But in the war. What were you in the war?"

"A medic."

"A medic. A medic. What is that?"

Constance looked quickly between Moses and King.

"Someone who attempts to keep a person alive until they reach the doctor."

"Is that what you did? In the bush? During the fighting?"

"Sometimes." Moses smiled easily down at King. "Now I'm a bureaucrat in the ministry of health." Then he added something in Shona, passing his smile around the circle like a box of chocolates.

Mr. Musani said something in Shona. Constance felt increasingly uncomfortable. It was rude to exclude someone from a conversation by speaking another language. It rarely happened here at Mutamba, where most people had some level of English.

"You're just repeating old rumours." Moses was still smiling, but his voice was flat.

King became more agitated. Neighbouring clusters of people were looking at them. Constance thought she heard 'Tongogara'.

Moses raised his eyebrows.

"You speak about the truth. *Maiwe*, my friend, we both want to believe certain things, but the truth is getting in the way. Now I'm going to get another beer. Do you also need one?"

He held out his hand for King, and put his other arm around Constance. Cocking his head to include Nazir he said placidly, "And those of us who don't drink can dance. Mr. Nazooa, you can show us this sega dancing from your country."

25

Macheke Township

June 2000

It was a rare day in Zimbabwe. Normally in winter people could find some warmth by sitting out in their yards, their backs against the walls of their houses, or by huddling around a small fire, or even, if they were wealthy and had a vehicle, by sitting in their car or bakkie — a sort of solarium, I thought, and a practical one at that, since it was mobile and could be moved to follow the sun.

Today a pale gray haze hid the sun. Even after the morning mist finally lifted around noon, the sun refused to emerge. No birds sang, the children trotted along quietly to school, no singing from them either; there was no wind to rustle the trees. The land seemed empty and quiet and cheerless.

When I got home from school I was so cold I couldn't stop shivering. My teeth were chattering.

"Are you cold, Amai?" asked Kazana solicitously.

"I'll make a fire for you here in the lounge," said Evan, helpfully. "Samora, run and fetch some wood. And the matches. And how about a cup of tea, Mum? Samora, when you've finished with the fire, run and put on the kettle."

"Amai! Make Evan stop bossing me around. He's always bossing me around."

"Jesus, Samora! I'd have thought you'd want to help. As usual, I have to do EVERYTHING around here." Evan sighed. "Alright, I'll go and ask Tatenda to make the tea."

Speaking through clenched teeth, I ordered Kazana and Evan to fire up the donkey boiler. "Samora, come into the kitchen and help me make the tea."

I stood, huddling against myself, with my back to the wood stove, while Samora climbed up on a chair to fill the Kango kettle. I was tired, stiff with cold and hunger. After my tea and a hot bath, I wanted to climb into bed with a glass of wine and a hot water bottle and a book and read until I drifted off. No such luck tonight.

The Anti-Retroviral Action Group doggedly met once a month, doggedly 'apolitical', even as the evenings became more bitter, even as the political violence and intimidation became more bitter in the run-up to the parliamentary elections.

We never spoke, for example, about the results of the constitutional referendum. Just a few months previously Mugabe had received the shock of his life when the people of Zimbabwe said 'no thanks' to his generous offer to serve as their president-for-life. Though he managed to paste a smile on his face and pose on state television as an elder statesman, gracious in defeat, no one was fooled. It was only a matter of time before the axe would fall.

Literally. In Karoi, a farming district north-west of Harare, a mob of around 100 men, armed with axes, clubs and pangas, had broken into a farm house. They beat up the farmer and his wife and threatened to kill them both. Over the next few months, these kinds of 'invasions' became more frequent and violent. It was well known, though never mentioned at our meetings, that the government was supporting the 'squatters' with arms, money and transportation. By April the country was in the midst of a low-level war. It was not mentioned at our meeting in April when Tichaona Chiminya and Talent Mabika, two MDC activists, were murdered in a petrol bombing. It was not mentioned at our meeting in May when an opposition 'march for peace' held in downtown Harare was violently broken up by over 200 ZANU-PF 'comrades', who set upon the marchers with clubs and sticks. It was also not mentioned when David Stevens, a farmer from the Bulawayo area, was dragged from his house and murdered by a group of 'ex-combatants'.

We stubbornly stuck to our 'agenda', which remained largely the same from month to month. I was always a few minutes late. Father Bernard or Reverend Samuels would lead us in prayer. Knowledge chaired the meetings, with Susie at his side, taking minutes. At some time during the meeting, Tendai would bring in tea and biscuits. At some time during the meeting, usually during the tea break, Mr. Chaminuka and I would duck outside to smoke. Decisions would be made only after every single person around the table had their two cents worth, even if that meant restating, usually in a wordier version, points that had already been made, and then it was hard for me to figure out exactly what we had agreed to do. Our earlier attempts to bring others on board seemed to be going nowhere.

"I'll give you a drive over." James was leaning in the doorway between the kitchen and the lounge.

"Thanks." I couldn't help sounding pleased and surprised.

"Yeah, well, there's no moon tonight and it's a long walk over to the clinic. Too many odd sorts hanging around these days." This was a typical James understatement. We both knew that there had been work stoppages at Salama and Leyland Farms. The owner of Airlie Farm had been given a four-day 'eviction' notice. And the war veterans occupying Loganfield were now demanding that Scotty give them a share of the land.

"I wish you wouldn't go. A bloody waste of time if you ask me."

"I think so too, sometimes." But tonight the Swedish doctor from the clinic in Marondera was coming to talk to us about a program he was running that might work in the Macheke clinic. This was the first sign of action we had taken and I didn't want to miss it.

It turned out Dr. Jensen was Danish, not Swedish. Working out of the Marondera hospital, he was the only pediatrician in the triangle stretching from Chegutu in the south, Murewa to the north and Rusape to the east; an area of roughly 250 square kilometres and home to about one million people. He was also an AIDS researcher with the Global Fund to Fight Aids, Tuberculosis and Malaria. He had set up several programs in clinics. These programs were designed to prevent the transmission of HIV from mother to child during birth. All pregnant women who came to the clinics were tested. Those that were positive were given a single dose of nevirapine. There babies were also give a single dose. This dramatically lowered the transmission of the virus from mother to infant.

Celia Chigwida, the government official in charge of overseeing the program, told us all this. A big-boned, not unattractive woman with straightened hair, I watched her heavy gold hoops swing back and forth as she waggled her head while she spoke. Beside her, Dr. Jensen sipped his tea and brushed crumbs out of his beard. He seemed to be paying not much attention. I wondered how good his English was.

The government was willing to fund the training of health workers at the Macheke clinic to test for HIV and give the medicine.

There was a buzz of excitement around the table. This looked like progress. Celia Chigwida sat back in her chair, basking in our grateful smiles.

"We have not yet heard from our other guest. Perhaps Dr. Jensen would like to say a few words." Knowledge was following protocol.

The doctor shifted in his seat, put down his cup and stroked his beard. "I am looking forward to working with the Anti-Retroviral Action Group and the people of Macheke."

There was a pause, then we all clapped.

"Can we look at some timelines? When will the training start?" I knew that even if we talked about dates, they would probably get pushed back or ignored, but without something 'officially' recorded in the minutes, we didn't have a hope of moving forward.

Everyone looked expectantly at Mrs. Chigwida.

"The training will start within the next few weeks. In actual fact the training is quite straightforward. We don't see any problems with the training. Sister Priscilla," and here she stopped to squeeze out a smile for Amai Power, "will be trained by Dr. Jensen or one of the nurses from the hospital in Marondera. All of this will be fully funded by the government."

Dr. Jensen shifted in his seat. I thought he was going to say something, but instead he reached for another biscuit.

"And what about the medicines?" Knowledge kept his head down and seemed to be intent on the notes he was taking.

"That is where the difficulty lies," said Mrs. Chigwida. "In actual fact, the funds which are supposed to be coming to the government to pay for the drugs have been frozen."

"Frozen? For what reason?"

"Yes, and for how long?" added Cyprian Dhiliwayo.

"The conditions that have been set out require that all clinics and hospitals must have adequate AIDS counsellors, nurses and medical equipment."

"So, are you saying that our clinic here in Macheke won't qualify to receive Nevirapine?" Amai Power looked from Dr. Jensen to Mrs. Chigwida. Dr. Jensen, who was now swirling the last of his tea around in his cup, did not look up.

"As you know, we don't have the funds to upgrade every clinic and health centre in the country up to international standards. I suggest that you proceed with the training and then apply for the Nevirapine. By that time . . ." she shrugged.

By that time, the election will be over. If ZANU wins and the party thinks we've voted the right way, maybe we'll get our drugs.

There was a strangled noise from Dr. Jensen and for a moment I thought he was choking on his cookie. It turned out he was just preparing to speak.

"With all due respect, Madam, we will have difficulty sparing someone to train Sister Priscilla. You have heard of course about the raid on the hospital?"

Mrs. Chigwida stared back at him stolidly.

"Some ZANU-PF hooligans came into the hospital yesterday. They abducted six staff members. One of them was one of our student nurses, a young man named Thomas Phiri, who was dragged from the lecture room at the hospital, where he was taking part in the very training we are talking about tonight. One of our guards tried to stop them. He was beaten for that. The staff were thrown in a vehicle and taken to ZANU-PF headquarters. Thomas says a cloth was tied around his face and he was beaten with iron bars and sticks." So Dr. Jensen's English wasn't so bad after all.

"How do you know this? We are in the middle of an election. Most probably these are lies spread by our enemies."

"I know because I saw Thomas Phiri myself this morning. He is in the hospital with a broken leg and bruises and cuts all over his body."

There was silence around the table. I'm sure we were all thinking the same thing. It seemed to crass to ask when poor Mr. Phiri would be up and about and able to hot-foot it over to Macheke to help us out.

"Well then," I said brightly. "It seems we must discuss this matter further and see if there is some way we can make use of the government's generous offer." I shot Susie a look and cocked my head towards Knowledge. Years of sitting across from her at staff meetings paid off – she recognized the teachers' code and tapped Knowledge quietly on the shoulder. He looked up from his notes.

"If you leave us the application forms, Mrs. Chigwida, we will fill them out. Then when the hospital is able to provide us with the necessary training, we can submit them to your department."

Mrs. Chigwida nodded and began rifling in her briefcase.

Knowledge tapped his pen decisively on the table and sat up. "Perhaps we can begin a fundraising effort to raise the necessary funds to make the improvements to the clinic so that we can be eligible for the medication." Everyone, including Mrs. Chigwida knew that there was no way on earth the community was going to be able to raise any money. But no one, including Mrs. Chigwida, was going to raise that inconvenient truth.

"Madam, we want to thank you for coming all this way. Your presence at this meeting has been very helpful." She passed the forms over to Knowledge and he dropped them on the table without looking at them. "Will you be staying in the village tonight?"

"Yes, you are most welcome to stay at the guesthouse at the mission," said Father Bernard. "The Sisters made me promise to ask you. After all, it's a long drive back to Harare."

"It's alright. I'm going to stay the night at the hotel in Marondera." We all nodded approvingly. The Hotel had recently been remodeled; the old veranda on the front where we used to while away a Saturday afternoon after shopping in town had been torn off and a new, impressive entrance put on; the old dining room off the lobby with its scratched parquet floor and ceiling fans and French doors had been modernized with air-conditioning and wall-to-wall carpeting; the over-stuffed chintz wing-back chairs in the lobby had been replaced with leather sofas and ugly coffee tables; apparently there was now a wide-screened T.V. in the bar. I never went there anymore.

Reverend Samuels gave the blessing — the two men of the cloth alternated between the prayer and blessing that bookmarked our meetings — and then the meeting was officially adjourned. Underneath the scraping of chairs and the small gusts of conversation that broke out as we were let go, I turned to Dr. Jensen. "Listen, I've got an idea, but I'm not sure it'll go over very well with Mrs. Chigwida. Do you have a few more minutes?"

He looked startled, then nodded. Tendai gathered up the teapot and the empty biscuit plate. Susie drifted off after him. Knowledge and Amai Power were showing Mrs. Chigwida to the door.

"My mother is an RN and a public health nurse. She's due out next month for a visit. I'm pretty sure I could get her to do the training."

Dr. Jensen was nodding again, cautiously.

"But you'd have to sign off on it. To show the-powers-that-be that the clinic here was up to snuff."

"Up to snuff?"

"You know. Meeting the standards."

"Ah. Yes."

The rest of the committee, reluctant to go into the bitter night, was lingering around the table. Or perhaps they sensed something was up. Either way, their dalliance was rewarded when Tendai emerged from the kitchen with a fresh pot of tea. Susie followed with the biscuits. Knowledge and Amai Power shut the door on Mrs. Chigwida and turned to face us, both rubbing their arms against the cold. Knowledge looked around at everyone.

"I move that the Macheke Anti-retroviral Action Group reconvene to discuss how best the Macheke clinic can meet the requirements as set out by the Zimbabwe government and the Global Fund, so that we can start testing and treating mothers and babies as soon as possible."

Dr. Jensen reached for another cookie. "Father, it looks as if the Sisters will have a guest tonight after all."

26

December 1984

Mutamba Mission

Constance was the only person in the house awake. She quietly got up and cautiously untangled the sheet from the bottom of the bed, placing it across Moses, who was sleeping on his belly, one arm cushioning his head. Miguel was on a mattress on the floor. In the kitchen, she rinsed out a glass and filled it with water. She crept into the lounge, over more sleeping bodies. Sheena and Ron were on a large foamy, with baby Elsie tucked between them. She was surprised anyone could sleep. The door to Miguel's room was closed, but Nico's lusty snores penetrated the little house, drowning out even the roosters and the dawn chorus of the mission dogs.

She opened the door to the veranda. A bottle teetered but she caught it before it fell. She picked up an overflowing ashtray so she could sit down. Looking out across the thornbush, already alive with cicadas and grasshoppers, the soft jingle of a herd of goats, the soft greeting of the boy herding them, she thought, This is where I ought to be.

The peace lasted only as long as her cigarette. The baby started crying. Whispers and murmurs from Sheena and Ron. "Shit! Where are my glasses?" "Wait till I find mine, then I'll help you look for yours." "Anyway, it's your turn to get up with her."

"I will, just as soon as I find my glasses."

Constance went into the kitchen to make coffee and wash dishes. Her skin had the thin, delicate feel of a night of heavy drinking and

235

smoking. She picked up bottles, emptied ashtrays, swept the floors. Ron was making Elsie's porridge. Sheena sat out on the veranda, smoking. The baby cautiously hoisted herself up to the coffee table and began inching her way around it. Hannah appeared briefly, looking for a towel. No, she didn't need hot water. Nico could build a fire later if anyone wanted a bath — she looked significantly at the baby who was now gumming a rusk.

Moses called through the kitchen window "Can I make a cup of tea?"

"Please do," yelled back Sheena. "I was hoping my husband would offer, but I suppose I ought to know better."

"Listen, woman. I was going to get started just as soon as I finished feeding your daughter."

"It's alright, darling. I know filling the kettle with enough water for porridge and tea would take all your strength."

"See what I have to put up with? Moses, take my advice and stay single as long as you can, mate."

Miguel came onto the veranda, still in his pajamas. His feet were filthy. Another candidate for Hannah's bath. He was carefully carrying a bowl of porridge. "This is mine," he said to the baby. "Soon you will have yours."

Constance went back into the kitchen to start making toast. Moses was leaning against the counter, waiting on the kettle. They moved into each other's arms, kissing deeply.

After a moment, Constance moved away slightly and they pulled apart. Nico would be up soon, Ted would wander over from Julia's place, everyone would want toast and eggs, more coffee or tea.

"We should get going with that turkey." Hannah was in the doorway, on her way back from her ablutions. "Where is Nico? He can start peeling potatoes."

After they had bunged the turkey in the oven, the young people, as Hannah called them, went up to the court to play tennis. Hannah and Nico stayed behind to look after the baby and scrub vegetables.

Surprisingly, Sheena and Ron were both excellent players. Moses and Munorwe held their own, though neither of them had held a tennis racquet before this holiday. Constance would never be anything more than a barely adequate doubles player. Ted was fairly decent, but he drifted in and out of the game. Julia was almost as good as Sheena.

The court was ground termite mound, lumpy because the roller was broken. The net had a hole and sagged. There was no chalk to mark the lines. Yet, even years later, sitting on the dock of their summer cottage in the Muskokas, say, or shifting the old racquets to another spot in the garage, or driving by a neglected tennis court, all of them would remember those mornings on the tennis court of Mutamba Mission with great affection.

"Back to the fence, Moses!" Constance would yell, as she hit another of her soft serves. When Moses hit a quick volley at the net, Ted would whistle and shout "Poetry in motion!" Julia and Munorwe would both sprint wildly for the same ball, careening into each other as the ball sailed over. "Language, Ron!"

Time slowed in the afternoon.

It was time to clear the bridge players away from the table. Sun was setting in a mass of thick clouds – where had they come from?

Constance lit some candles. The sounds of the night pulsated beyond the light. She could hear frogs and birds, the rustle of lizards.

"Let Moses cut that up!" cried Julia, when Hannah brought out the turkey. "He was a surgeon in the war, you know."

"Not a surgeon. A medic," said Constance.

Except for the turkey, it was like all the other days so far. How could she know these innocuous activities – serving meals and drinks, playing tennis and bridge, the sound of a guitar, dancing, the baby laughing, would be moments she would try to recreate over and over again in her mind?

Last cigarette and brandy as Stan Roger's comforting baritone rolled out into the African night.

Moses put his arm around her waist and pulled her across the bed towards him. She felt the rhythm of his breath, or was it hers?

In the middle of the night Constance was awakened by rolls of thunder. She tiptoed out to the veranda and stood, watching the storm. The glorious wet earth, the rain splashing on red earth and stones, drumming on the tin roof and the trees.

27

August 2001

Macheke

Macheke Secondary School was nothing special. Four blocks of classrooms, plus another block for staff room, headmasters office and science lab, formed a quadrangle. White-washed stones made a path from each Form Block to the assembly area, where the flag was raised each morning as the children sang the national anthem.

Behind the Form Two classrooms were the soccer pitch, pit toilets and kitchen. There were at least fifty children in each class. The blackboards were pitted and scarred. There was constant battle between the teachers, who insisted on covering the boards with white chalk, and the blackboards, which had long ago decided to go on strike. The harder we ground the chalk into the boards, the more the boards resisted. But the teachers persisted. We had no choice. There were only a few tattered textbooks in each class, maybe a map, a bit of paper. It was exactly like hundreds of other secondary schools throughout Zimbabwe.

It was exactly like any other day. Just warm enough for the shade of the mango tree. Knowledge joined me. I reached into my bag and extracted a bottle. He hesitated for a moment, then let me pour a tot of whiskey into his cup.

"Cheers," I said, raising my cup.

"Cheers," he said. "What are we celebrating?"

"I've been married for fourteen years. I've been teaching in Macheke for fifteen years. I've been living in this country for eighteen years. Take your pick."

"How about – We've been friends for three years?"

"Two and a half," I corrected him. "You couldn't stand me for the first six months."

"No, I was ignorant. I didn't think we could have anything to talk about. But I watched you and I listened."

"And?"

"And I saw you were really just like us. You liked to gossip and make jokes. You liked the kids, but you complained about them all the time. You did not let Muzenda make you the head of the History department."

"Are you kidding? That was plain laziness on my part. I'd have to chair meetings and make decisions. Beside, Mr. Zongo is more qualified than I am."

"Here's to friendship, then."

"To friendship."

We drank. Silence. Then Knowledge lifted his cup. "And to the end of an era."

We drank. "Do you remember the time you drove me into Harare?"

"What? You mean way back in November. Last year?"

"Yes. Now it seems the teachers will be going on strike."

"Ha! It's about time! But I'll believe it when I see it."

"Oh, you will see it, Amai." He leaned forward. For a moment I thought he was going to grasp my hand in a gesture of solidarity, but he was only reaching for the whiskey bottle. "Look at this place!" He made a sweeping gesture with the bottle. He had decided to throw caution to the wind. "It used to be neat and tidy as a pin. Now look at it!"

He was right. The school had always been basic, but with an air of purposefulness. The paths were swept each morning, the classrooms whitewashed, the school sign on the main road proudly proclaiming it was only 5 km. to Beautiful Macheke Secondary School. These days, the classrooms were dirty, the children too hungry to sweep the grounds. How long had it been since I had heard the Form Ones singing as they carried water to their garden, or smelled a new coat of Cobra wax on the cement floor of the staff room? The water pump had been broken for over four months, and there was not enough money now to give the children their tea and bread at break time. As for the school sign, it had vanished last year, probably stolen for firewood.

"When will we be hitting the bricks?"

"No, Amai. This will be a non-violent strike. We will not be hitting anyone with bricks."

"No, I mean, when will be going on strike? Withdrawing our labour. Refusing to work."

Knowledge put down his cup and actually rubbed his hands together. "At the beginning of November."

I nodded. That made sense. This would disrupt the all-important Cambridge O-level and A-levels, not to mention the Standard Seven certificate exams.

"What are our demands?"

"We have a three-point manifesto. First: an end to political violence and intimidation. Second: the government must adequately fund schools. Third: a raise for the teachers. We will accept no less than the cost of living."

Given that the rate of inflation was now running at 55 percent, I didn't think much of our chances, but I also didn't think this was the time for cold, hard reality.

I reached for the bottle. "Workers of the world unite! We have nothing to lose".

28

February, 1985

Harare

Moses Masekesa stayed at Mutamba Mission well into January. Sheena and Ron left with the baby a week after New Year's. Ted followed a few days later. Nico and Hannah hung around a few weeks longer. On the weekend following the opening of school, Constance and Moses drove them into Harare, while Miguel stayed back at the mission with Amai Mushana. The four of them spent the night at the Bronte Hotel, then in the morning, Constance put her parents on the British Airways flight to London. After hugging and waving goodbye to them at the security gate, she and Moses drove to the green house in Highfield. They got home by about two o'clock in the afternoon.

Constance hardly noticed the car parked on the road beside the driveway. If Moses saw it, he didn't say anything. They went into the house, which felt cool and dark after the bright afternoon sun. Constance put on the kettle. She took her overnight bag into the bedroom and used the toilet.

Moses called from the kitchen.

"Pardon?"

"I'm just going out to the shops for some milk. Do you need anything?"

She came into the kitchen, zipping up her jeans. "Do we have gin?" She looked in the freezer and showed him an almost empty bottle. "And can you pick up some smokes?"

He kissed her. "I'll be back just now."

"I've heard about men like you. They pop out to the corner store for milk and cigarettes. The next time their wives hear from them is a postcard from Maputo."

He smiled and waved, not bothering to shut the door behind him.

She went into the lounge and sat with her feet up on the coffee table, smoking a cigarette. The kettle whistled. She filled the pot, smiling to herself, remembering the first time she had made tea in this house. Then she went back into the lounge and began fiddling with the dials on the radio, trying to find the BBC World Service. The neighbour's dog was barking.

Through the open door she thought she heard a car door slam. A lourie was crying — Go-Way, Go-Way! The bird kept screaming.

When she went out into the driveway she was relieved to see the Land Rover parked in its usual place. But there was a woman there, screaming. The Rhodesian Ridgeback ran up to her, barking.

Why was the shopping bag laying there, the carton of cigarettes falling out?

Then she saw Moses lying face down in the dirt.

29

September 2001

Loganfield Farm

Scotty Fielding had just poured himself the tot of whiskey he rationed himself to every Friday evening, when his foreman, Dambudzo, showed up at his door, saying that there had been a fight down at the workers' compound.

Scotty had held his breath for a while after the MDC rally in Marondera. He was pretty sure that he had been spotted at the rally by some of the local ZANU-PF henchmen. They had shown themselves to be a ruthless lot during the last election campaign. Breaking up opposition rallies was the mildest of their tactics. They beat suspected MDC supporters or set fire to their homes or had them sacked from their jobs.

A group of squatters had settled on the farm. They called themselves War Veterans. They built ramshackle rondavels and some of the women planted maize, spinach, tomatoes. Scotty knew they were taking cooking oil, sugar, candles and kerosene from the farm store, but he turned a blind eye. He also chose to ignore the occasional stolen cow or goat. He reckoned he was getting off easy.

This was another senseless war, another war the whites were never going to win, not in an thousand years. So he kept his head down and counted himself lucky. The months rolled on and he was able to harvest his tobacco crop and take it to market without too much trouble. He allowed himself to think that maybe the worst was over.

A Friday night dust-up in the workers' compound was not unheard of. Sometimes at the end of the month the men got into the home-brewed chibuku. Scotty tossed back his drink, and went to get the keys to the old brown Land Rover. He wasn't much for patching people up – truth be told the sight of blood had always made him feel a bit woozy – but if he drove down to the compound he would probably be able to calm the lads down.

They set off toward the river. It was a beautiful evening, not too warm yet, with the sky full of stars. They had only gone about two kilometers when Dambudzo made a sound and touched his arm. At the same moment Scotty saw the smoke, coming from the tobacco barn. He sped up, and took the next fork in the road.

They came up over a slight rise and saw a group of people milling around, watching the tobacco barn burn. Some of them turned as they heard the bakkie. They ran over to the road. A white station wagon was blocking it. Scotty had already slowed down. He stopped and waited for a moment. Some of the people had machetes and he could see at least one fellow with an axe. But then the sight of his tobacco barn going up in flames made him angry.

Scotty got out of the truck. The crowd did not move back to let him through. He felt himself being pressed back against the side of the vehicle. He was not a tall man and he could not see beyond the crush of people. Many of them were shouting, " Beat him. Beat him". Someone grabbed his arm and spun him around. His other arm was yanked back. It took a few seconds for him to realize that he had been handcuffed.

"You will come with us." A man spoke to him in Shona. Was it the same one who had handcuffed him? He was a big fellow, with remnants of muscle among the flab.

"Where to?" Scotty tried not to sound frightened.

He was punched in the gut. He bent forward. He could taste whiskey and he thought he might vomit. There were shouts of approval and some of the women ululated. Playing to the crowd, the big man hit him in the jaw, making his head jerk back and slam into the truck.

Scotty was lifted and thrown into the back of the bakkie. He heard more shouting, It sounded as if Dambudzo was being dragged from the truck. Scotty managed to get to his knees. Then he dragged himself to his feet. It was hard with his hands cuffed behind his back.

Below him, on the passenger side of the truck, the crowd was cheering and laughing as the big man beat Dambudzo with a shovel. Dambudzo was already on the ground, hemmed in by the crowd, unable to get away. He had his hands over his head. The big man brought the heavy metal blade of the shovel down on Dambudzo's hands and head, making a loud thud. Dambudzo's hands came down and he tried to roll away from the blows, but the crowd kicked him back toward the big man. The shovel came down on his head again. This time, without his hands to protect it, the blow must have shattered his skull or at least cracked it. He stopped moving, blood dripping from his head.

Scotty fell to his knees, lost his balance and fell onto his face. He could hear more shouting and ululating. He could hear car doors slamming and what must be the engine of the station wagon revving. Then someone started up the bakkie. He thought the station wagon drove past. Immediately the bakkie turned and followed.

When they came to the main farm road, he could tell that they were not going towards the workers' compound. If they stayed on this road, they would come to the road that led to the farmhouse. He hoped they might drive him there and dump him off, maybe steal the bakkie. Perhaps they would think that beating him up, handcuffing him and murdering his foreman would serve as warning enough.

He rolled over onto his shoulder. He tried to guess how far they would drive before the truck would slow and make the turn left, and climb the slight rise away from the river, toward his house. Several minutes went by. They had most likely passed the turn-off by now.

When they finally turned, it was in the wrong direction. Toward the river. They were leaving the farm and heading to the bridge. Sure enough, the driver shifted gears and the truck picked up speed on the paved road.

The bakkie was now being driven at breakneck speed. He thought he could hear shouting, then shots being fired. He tried to remember if he had left his shotgun in the truck and if it was loaded.

Suddenly the bakkie stopped and he fell over on his face again. There was more shouting, car doors slamming. He rolled over onto his side again. Twisting his head, he could just make out the roof of a building and a dark shape that might be a flagpole. Some government compound. It took him another minute or two to get to his knees, and then to his feet.

They were in the police camp in Macheke. It was strangely quiet now. He could see two policemen sitting on the veranda, under the only light. There were several vehicles in the circular driveway. The white estate car, of course, and in front of it, close to the steps of the police station, as if the driver had jammed on his brakes at the last minute, his brother James' white Toyota Hilux.

"Hey," he called out to the policemen. They looked around. Probably couldn't see him in the dark. "Hey. I'm here in this bakkie."

After a moment one of the men stood up and came over. He looked curiously at Scotty. He was very skinny, typical of the lower ranks. It was hard to be sure in the dark, but Scotty thought he had seen him before. He racked his brain to come up with a name.

"Manheru." They exchanged greetings. "Can you tell me what's going on?"

The man glanced over his shoulder.

The other policeman, afraid of missing something, strolled over. Or maybe he felt he should take over. He had maybe five pounds and two inches on the first chap. He nodded at Scotty. They exchanged greetings.

"Is my brother inside?"

"They are questioning him."

"Who. The police?"

"No. Those who brought him."

Shit. This was bad. "Can you help my brother?" Shit. He wished he could remember where he had seen the first man. He desperately hoped it was in pleasant circumstances.

They shook their heads, chuckling softly. "No, no. It's not possible."

"Do you know what will happen to us?"

They shrugged. "Maybe they will just give you a beating." They murmured something to each other, then turned away from him.

"I want to drink water." He thought this request would not be refused.

More murmurings. "I will go and fetch water," said the smaller man. He pointed to an outside garden tap. Just then the front door of the station was flung open. An African came out backwards, dragging James by the armpits. Three others followed them. One was the big man. He had exchanged his shovel for a shotgun. He impatiently motioned for one of his henchmen to help lug James down the steps of the veranda.

Almost at the same moment, the smaller policeman turned back to the bakkie and made a gesture that surely meant "Get down!"

Scotty dropped to his knees. Seconds later the tailgate dropped and James was thrown in. Scotty shuffled over to where his brother was lying. One side of his head appeared to be smashed in. Frantic, Scotty put his ear to his chest, trying to see if he was still alive. He was pushed back with the butt of the gun. The big man barked an order and one of the lesser thugs jumped into the back of the pickup. This one kicked Scotty in the head. He rolled away from James. As the big man lifted the tailgate, his shirt rose and Scotty saw something glinting in the light from the police station. It looked like an enormous belt buckle. Then he blacked out.

His head was pounding. His mouth was dry and he wanted to ask for water, but he was afraid to open his eyes. He knew moving either his lips or his eyelids would cause more shafts of pain to stab his brain. Just moving his eyeballs was excruciating.

It was quiet. Were they still at the Macheke police station? Where was his brother? He gingerly tried to open his eyes to suss out the situation. One eye seemed to be swollen shut, the other eye was blurry. Plus, he was lying on his side with his hands handcuffed behind him, so he couldn't exactly get a complete view of the place.

But he was pretty sure he had been moved. Either this was a different room at the station or a whole new venue. This was a bare room – cement walls and floor.

He closed his eye. He wondered how long he had been lying here. It seemed a long time ago that Dambudzo had called him for help. He wondered if he was even alive. He wondered what he should have done differently. Maybe he should have called for help himself, before he went charging out like some bloody idiot.

He heard a moan. He tried to turn to the sound, but he couldn't. Shit, he had thought he was alone in here.

"Scotty! Is it you, man?"

There was no answer. James could hear shallow, rasping breathing. He counted to ten slowly, then forced his body to turn over. Then he had to lie with his eyes closed, waiting for the pain to subside a little.

He opened his good eye. At least it was now the upper eye, so he had a bit better view of things. He could see his brother lying face down. His hands were cuffed behind his back.

James closed his eye again. This time he counted to twenty before he began to pull himself slowly across the floor. Each time he moved, shards of pain stabbed his skull. He had broken his collarbone years ago playing rugby at school. He thought maybe it was broken again.

"Hey man," he said to Scotty, nudging him in the back with his foot. It was then he noticed that there was no shoe on that foot. Now he remembered his shoe flying off as the ex-combatants dragged him from his bakkie at the police station. Scotty did not answer. He seemed to be unconscious, but he was breathing.

James wondered if anyone else knew they were here. Dambudzo had called from the radio in Scotty's truck, but was Dambudzo even alive now? He wondered what time it was. Connie would be worried sick, though she had an amazing inability to imagine the worst.

Behind him he could hear the door opening. A light was switched on. Men were shouting. He was kicked in the back and then the same foot pushed him onto his back. A shotgun pressed into his chest, then waved around to underline the main point.

"You will die. You will die. We will not let you destroy our country. We have had enough of you whites. Enough. You are going to die."

James lay with his eyes shut. He wished he could black out again. Whatever else you might want to say about them, these blokes had stamina. He remembered the all-night pungwes during the war. The speeches, the singing, the dancing, the drinking and carousing. They could go after him for the rest of the night.

Maybe he did drift off for a bit. One minute he was remembering the liberation war, the next he was being prodded to his feet. Then someone was waving the shotgun in his face. "It's time. We are going to take you to your graves. Hurry!" He tried to look over his shoulder to see what was happening to Scotty, but they were pushing him forward. Anyway, that was his bad eye.

It was the gray moment of dawn, before the sun has tipped the balance between day and night. James had never been here before. It was a small compound. Two white-washed buildings in an L-shape around a patch of dirt. The usual barbed-wire fence and sagging wire gate separated the compound from the surrounding bush. In the centre of the dirt yard a couple of women were cooking sadza over a fire.

James greeted the women in Shona. "Mangwanani, sisters." He wondered who they thought was standing before them, eye-swollen shut, wearing one shoe, beaten.

They muttered a greeting. Then James saw one of them look straight at him. He thought he saw something in her face besides indifference or contempt. Then her eyes flashed past him.

One of the thugs who had kidnapped him was dragging Scotty through the doorway. He called to the ones holding James to come and help him.

"No, no," said Gunpowder. He waved the shotgun. "Just leave him there. He's not going anywhere." He laughed at his joke. "Let us eat now."

One of the women ladled the sadza into a large metal bowl. She gave it to the circle of men squatting by the fire. Gunpowder put down the gun. He pushed James. "Let us eat now." He felt his heart lift a little. Surely they wouldn't bother feeding him just before killing him? But it turned out to be another one of Gunpowder's little jokes. With his hands cuffed behind him, James could only squat in the circle and watch as the others ate.

He knew he had to prepare himself now. It rare for an African to eat without offering food to another. They must already consider him dead.

Behind him the sun was rising. He closed his eyes and tried to stop time. The sun on his back, the smoke of the fire, the smell of sadza cooking, the smell of Africans eating beside him, Africans laughing and joking in Shona, the calm call of the doves. This had been his life for his whole life. "Ach," he thought. "I've had a good life." He said goodbye to his wife and boys, willing his thoughts to enter theirs, not believing that they would.

Then they were hauling him to his feet. They seemed calmer, now that they had eaten. "Come. It's time."

One of the women surprised James by speaking. "Let him go."

"What are you saying? We will decide what to do with our prisoners."

She pointed her sadza stick at Gunpowder. "Of course. But I know this man."

James squinted his good eye. He was sure he had never seen this person before in all his life.

"We know him too. He is an enemy of Zimbabwe. He is one of those who is living on stolen land! He is —"

She cut him off impatiently. "Yes, yes. But his wife is good. She is the one who teaches in the village. She taught my child. He loved her too much."

"Then he must be a fool."

"What are you saying? My child has got his O-levels. Let him go. His wife has helped many children."

Gunpowder thrust his belly out and shook his head stubbornly. "So, I am not shooting his wife." He jerked his head toward the man who had hauled James to his feet. "It's time. Let's go."

James was pushed forward. Two other men had managed to get Scotty to his feet but he did not seem to be with them. His head hung on his chest, his knees buckled. He would have fallen if not propped up.

They began dragging Scotty around to the side of the building. James felt the gun in his back. He began walking.

"Ishmael! Let him go! What would your father say if he saw you killing this man? He was in the bush, fighting with Tongogara and Masekesa, not shooting our children's teachers."

It took a few steps before James realized that the gun was no longer in his back. He stopped and tried to twist his arm out the grip of his captor. The pain shot across his collarbone. Floppy Hat said "Pamberi," but then he looked back and saw Gunpowder had stopped, the two men lugging Scotty waiting in the path behind him.

"Alright, this one can go. Take him away."

He was being pushed back toward the women and the fire. They had to step off the path to go around Scotty and the two men holding him. James tried to stop, to reach out his hand, to catch Scotty's eye, but he was jerked forward again.

This time he was thrown into the back of the Hilux. He wanted to hear everything, he desperately wanted to pass out, he wanted to go home, he wanted to get up and beat the shit out of these munts, he wanted it to be over.

Floppy Hat started the car. He backed up, revved the engine and spun out of the compound. James said desperately "Have they shot him?"

Floppy Hat either did not hear or did not know. Or, most likely, didn't care. Anyway, he didn't answer.

They dumped him somewhere along the Macheke River. There was some confusion when Floppy Hat demanded his shoes and James could only produce one.

"Where is the other veldskoen?"

He made James get up to make sure he was not sitting on it. He rummaged around in the back of the car, James offered his filthy socks to make up for the missing shoe, but Floppy Hat was not satisfied. James had nothing else to offer – his watch and wallet had already been taken.

Finally they drove off.

James sat. The river was low this time of year, waiting for the rains. It moved sluggishly along. He could see rocks poking up from the riverbed. When he was a boy, there had still been the rare crocodile in the Macheke. Many times he, Scotty and some of the farm workers' kids had hiked down to the river, to hunt. They knew that a giant crocodile had been speared in the river years ago. Chief Macheke had told them the story many times. Its heart was supposedly buried beneath the huge syringa tree in front of the hotel. That is why the tree grew so large. But they had never seen one, which was probably just as well, as they had only been armed with catapults, sticks and Scotty's pellet gun. Funny, he hadn't thought about that in years.

He wondered if his own boys knew the story.

He could feel the sun on his back, high in the sky. He must be on the north side of the river. He would have to cross over and begin the long walk home.

30

February 1985

Harare

The police report "detailing" the death of Moses Masekesa was one page long. It was typed on brown manila paper, with two carbon copies.

At 2:30 on Wednesday, April 10 the police got a call from Mrs. Carol Thorn that someone had been shot at 15 Derry Road in Highfield. When police arrived at the house they found the body of an adult African male lying face down. He had been shot two times. He was dead.

In her statement, Mrs. Thorn said she was in her front garden, with her dog. She saw the victim pull into the driveway in a Land Rover. She had seen him before and waved to him as he got out of his car. A red car drove up behind him. A black man got out of the car and called to the victim. The victim turned and the man shot him. As he turned and fell, the man shot him again. The man ran back to his car and drove away.

Mrs. Thorn was able to give the police a description of the car and the number plate.

Cde Emerson Munungagwa, Minster of State Security arrived. He positively identified the body in the mortuary van. It was the body of Moses Masekesa, age 37 years, born in the Bikita district under Chief Mazungunye. Cde Masekesa, a deputy-minister in the Ministry of

Health, was an ex-combatant in the Second Chimurenga. His mother, Francisca Masekesa, a nurse at Silveira Mission near Bikita, subsequently confirmed the identification.

A police car spotted the suspect's vehicle, a red Ford Fiesta, driving towards Mbare. They pulled him over and arrested the driver, Jackson Mungwira, without incident. In his car they found a Z88 pistol fitted with a silencer.

Mungwira is in the custody of CID. They have taken over the investigation.

Signed: Godfrey Muzonzini D/Cst

Constance was only allowed to read the report at the police station in Harare and then only after Moses' mother and Father Frederick, a priest from Silveira Mission, insisted. When she asked for a copy she was told that the report was not yet "legitimate" because it had not been stamped. Once the correct stamp was found a copy of the document would be sent to her.

She never received a copy of the police report. She was refused a copy of the autopsy report.

31

Macheke

At first James wanted Scotty to be buried in the family graveyard up beyond the homestead, but of course it was not possible for any of the family to set foot on Loganfield. So we buried Scotty quickly and quietly, in the cemetery in Macheke. There were only a few of us at the funeral. Sarah and Stephanous Potgeiter, Jake and Jackie Maddox, and a few other whites. Nico, Hannah and Miguel flew out from Vancouver. None of the Loganfield farm labourers came, except for a son of Dambudzo, named Phillip, and the old man, Reginald, who had cooked for Scotty for years. And my friend, Miriam. Father Bernard officiated and I read the eulogy James had written for his brother.

I bent to pick up some of the earth from the mound around the grave. It had not rained for a long time, and the soil was bone dry. It blew out of my hand.

"How is your mother?" I felt marginally better with one glass of gin already under my belt. I waved my glass in the direction of the dining room table. "Have more to eat, eh. There's loads there."

"Thank you. My mother wanted to come but in actual fact she is still mourning the death of my father. Everything is gone topsy-turvy. We really don't know what is going to happen now."

"She's not at Loganfield, is she?"

"No, she can't stay there. In actual fact, most of the farm workers are leaving that place."

I nodded " Where will you all go?"

Phillip shrugged. "Who can say? But you should know that the farm has been broken up into blocks. Everyone was told to put down their tools and no more working."

"And the farm will be given to the War Veterans." To Gunpowder. But I couldn't say this. My hand was shaking as I lifted my glass to my mouth. Miguel came over and put his arm over my shoulder.

"That is what some of the people are saying."

"Ah. And what are some other people saying?"

"They are saying that a man came out from Marondera in a big car. A ZANU-PF car. He is the one who is going to get the farm."

This was truly the tragedy. Not just that one white farmer and one black foreman had been murdered. But that over a hundred people were now jobless and homeless. Not that a dozen or so white farmers had been killed and a couple hundred kicked off their farms, but that thousands of farm workers had lost everything. I told myself this.

"Do you know who he is?"

He shook his head. "The people are saying he is a very rich man. He has some bottle stores and a butchery. Also he is the one who is owning the hotel in Marondera."

"You know him," said Miguel. Then I realized he was speaking to me. "We both know him. It's King Musami."

32

February, 1985

Heroes Acre, Harare

His mother did not want Moses buried at Heroes Acre. Set on a pretty, aloe-covered kopje overlooking Harare, it had been built by the North Koreans in what might be called 'late-Soviet' style, with massive granite tiers, a huge statue of the 'unknown soldier', the 'eternal flame' atop an obelisk and several friezes depicting battle scenes. All the 'comrades' had been carved with vaguely Asian features.

"Moses always liked the farm."

I smiled and nodded at Moses' mother. I waited for his brother, Kumbirai, to continue translating. "Maybe he can be buried there."

"I don't think that is possible." Kumbirai said something to his uncle. His mother looked mutinous, and said something to him Shona. "I don't think it is possible," he said again.

The uncle began a long-winded speech in Shona. I suspected from his pompous manner and the way Francisca kept looking as if she wanted to kill him, that he was in the Heroes Acre camp, but I couldn't be sure and I really didn't care.

My mind drifted to a time we had taken some water and biltong and walked a long way up into the hills behind the mission and sat on a kopje overlooking the mission and beyond it the valley and the thornbush. Above, kites wheeled on wind we longed to feel. The cicadas buzzed. I remembered a rock overhang with bushman paintings of a giraffe and an elephant. I wanted that day back.

I still remember that day and I remember the day they buried Moses. It surprises me now, how much I recall about that particular day. It was a very hot day. I wore a blue and white sleeveless flowered dress, ankle-length and black Mary-Jane shoes. I guess I thought they were the kind of shoes to wear to a funeral, but they were awful. Stones kept getting caught in them and I had to keep taking them off to shake them out. I remember Julia beside me — she was wearing a long dove-grey skirt and matching top. Ted played "Three Little Birds" because that was Moses' favourite song and the ZANU-PF choir belted out a few sonorous, mournful tunes. The prime minister made a short speech about someone I didn't know.

Another thing I remember. They were lowering his coffin into the grave. Everyone was still. Baby Elsie and all the other babies were quiet. Moses' mother and aunties stopped wailing. Suddenly, a dove burst out of the grave. It had probably been happy to find a cool, dark place to rest on such a hot day. A woman screamed and many people around me gasped. Kumbirai stumbled forward. For a moment we all thought he was going to let go of the coffin or fall head first into the hole. But he managed to recover and the coffin made it into the red earth of Africa without further incident.

It's funny what you remember.

33

Mutamba Mission

August 1985

We heard the flush of the toilet and the door opening. "Your turn," said Sheena.

"Thanks," I said. "We were just talking about Lois. She looks like a lost lamb out there."

"Well, rumour has it that little romance is over. Why do you think he was being so chummy with you?"

"You've got to be kidding!" I looked at Julia for support.

"Sheena's right. He sees you here without a man and being the insensitive dick he is, he moves in for the kill."

For some reason, I found this hugely funny. I began snorting with laughter. "Me and Jean-Pierre. Ha!" I tried to stop laughing, waving my hands in front of my face. "Margaret is more his type."

"Nah, he's probably right tired of those Mother Theresa types."

I was still laughing. "Listen, I have to pee really bad." As I closed the bathroom door, Sheena was still talking.

" — hasn't got a chance with Margaret. Not enough cachet. He's not even black."

I leaned against the sink. Heaving with laughter, the tears began streaming down my face. I screwed up my face to try to make them stop, but they poured out. I peed and flushed the toilet. I turned on the tap. I wiped my eyes. I found my hairbrush in my bag and took the clip out of my hair. Holding it in my mouth, I brushed my hair. I pulled my hair back into place. I wiped my eyes. I looked at myself in the mirror. A pretty, dark-haired girl with eyes that showed she had just been crying.

I snaked through the living room and out onto the veranda. I leaned against the wall and watched the people dancing in the yard.

Was that Nazir Nazooa and Karen dancing together? Miguel and Mushana were among a pack of small boys circling the dancers, chasing each other with sticks. Mary Karambira was dancing with her son, Emmanuel. Life was moving on. People would move together and move apart and move on.

"I was looking for you."

It was that beefy white farmer.

"I've been missing out all these years. Never knew they had parties like this out here."

I shrugged. "This is bigger than usual. It's Julia's last night."

"I know. She told me when she gave me the invite."

"Aha."

Ted was strumming absent-mindedly on his guitar, some old tune I thought I knew.

I sat down next to Mr. Okense. He nodded gravely at me. I smiled back.

"Can I top you up?" Julia proffered a bottle. She moved around the circle, pouring rye, humming softly. Mr. Okense lifted his cup. His thin wrist gleamed in the moonlight.

Think I'll go out to Alberta where there's good there in the fall

Moses had worn four wire bracelets on his good strong wrist.

For our good times are all gone and I'm bound for moving on

I felt tears forming again. I'm not crying again.

I'll look for you if I'm ever back this way.

The voices held onto the last note of the guitar. Then the African night reasserted itself. The rhythm of the crickets, a dog barking in the next compound, the cry of a bushbaby.

262

34

October 2001

Macheke

We toyi-toyied down the hill towards the line of police. We had only come about a kilometer, but already sweat was running down my face, out of my armpits and between my breasts. As we left the school, I had positioned myself near the back, just behind Mr. Mdzuri, the rather rotund Shona teacher, thinking I would probably be able to keep up with him. And so far I was, but just barely. We were jumping and stamping, in unison, with the open-handed MDC salute, chants of *Chinja*. It was all a bit much for a middle-aged white woman whose idea of strenuous exercise was to run in out of the rain. I was gasping for breath and concentrating hard on keeping Mr. Mduri's red and white t-shirt in front of me.

We turned at the hotel. The two people sitting on the veranda stared at us. We crossed the train tracks and went down into the field behind the primary school. I stopped, bent over, gasping, my hands on my knees.

"These primary teachers have too much energy," said Mr. Mdzuri, shaking his head, either in sympathy for me or in admiration of our colleagues. They did indeed put us secondary teachers to shame. Every one of them was wearing matching headbands and t-shirts. Their toyi-toyi, led by a large woman in a tight black skirt and white takkies, and blowing a whistle to help keep the time, looked effortless and joyous.

"Well, they didn't have to toyi-toyi all the way here," I pointed out. "but I hear what you're saying. Just look at those placards. Have you ever seen such lovely printing?"

Mr. Mdzuri nodded sadly and pointed to a sign held by Mr. Chaminuka, which had *Zvakwana* scrawled across it.

The primary teachers finished a rousing version of "Guns for the Army, Cardboard for the Teachers". Then Knowledge began speaking.

He thanked the primary teachers for their support and congratulated all of us on our bravery and solidarity. "I appeal to my fellow teachers. We must stand up for ourselves and for our students. We must honour our war veterans by holding this government to account. If we give in, we will be betraying everything they have fought for." (scattered applause) "I am so proud of you, my brothers and sisters. We will no longer accept these slave wages, but we must receive a pay increase that will allow us to live in dignity, to feed our families, to send our children to school. What kind of country is this, where even the children of the teachers are not going to be educated? (laughter and applause) What kind of country is this, where teachers are dying of Aids because there are no medicines and the hospitals are terrible and all the doctors and nurses have run away to work in Botswana? (laughter, but also cries of 'Shame!') What kind of country is this where schools have no books, no pencils, no chairs or tables, NO TEACHERS but the politicians can drive beautiful cars and live in posh houses? (louder cries of "Shame!') What kind of country is this where we have not seen an official from the Ministry of Education for over a year and our appeals and requests are met with a few creaking answers, as if we are talking to a tree (more laughter) or worse we are met with intimidation and violence."

Right on cue, a bakkie, with "ZANU-PF, Mashonaland East" emblazoned on its side roared up on the other side of the field. Behind it was an unmarked station wagon. We watched warily as both cars circled the rally. Young men leaned out of the windows, raising their clenched fists.

Knowledge turned back to us. He shrugged. "So, what shall we do?"

This was our cue now. I could only join in on the chorus.

Senzeni,

Tingadii,

What shall we do?

I could hear Scotty's voice in my head "Do you think those blokes drove out here just so you could serenade them? They've got guns, for Christ sake!" We were now singing another song about an old man.

Bvuma waunyana

You are worn out

More lorries pulled up, police vehicles, and other cars. "Those belong to the CIO, the secret police," Mr. Mdzuri informed me. "Of course, it's no secret what they will do to people that they take in for questioning."

"Yes, my family has had some experience with that."

Mr. Mdzuri nodded sympathetically. "Not just yours. I myself was taken in last month. They said all political meeting need the permission of the police. And I was just walking home from the shebeen with three friends. What kind of a political meeting is that? They kept me for two days. They beat me a bit and one of my friends had his ribs broken."

The thugs finished circling the soccer pitch and parked with the police vehicles among the gum trees. Some of them got out of their cars or climbed down from their trucks. Some of them had iron bars in their hands.

The teachers sang louder and whistled louder and danced harder.

"My husband has promised to come and bail me out at the police station," I yelled.

"Maiwe, that is a very brave thing." Everyone knew what had happened to James and his brother at the Macheke police station.

The thugs were now moving towards us. The police watched impassively. The singers did not falter or miss a beat.

And when I raised my arm, palm open, four bronze wire bracelets slid down from my wrist, glinting in the sun.

The End
Ouagadougou, Burkina Faso
May, 2008

Appendix

Lay Down Your Heart:
The Soundtrack

"Is This Love?" — Bob Marley

"Southern Cross" — Crosby, Stills and Nash

"Get Up Stand Up" — Bob Marley

"Turn Your Lights Down Low" — Bob Marley

"You Belong To Me" — Patti Page

"Zambezi-Zimbabwe" — Tony Bird

"Born In The Ghetto" — Oliver Mtukudzi

"Thunder Road" — Bruce Springsteen

"Barrett's Privateers" — Stan Rogers

"I Shot The Sherriff" — Bob Marley

"Zimbabwe" — Bob Marley

"River" — Joni Mitchell

"Three Little Birds" — Bob Marley

"Four Strong Winds" — Ian and Sylvia

"Todii" — Oliver Mtukudzi

www.ingramcontent.com/pod-product-compliance
Lightning Source LLC
Chambersburg PA
CBHW071851220626
47052CB00002B/73